Dr Thorndyke's Casebook

R Austin Freeman

HOUSE OF
STRATUS

This edition published in 2001 by House of Stratus, an imprint of
House of Stratus Ltd, Thirsk Industrial Park, York Road, Thirsk,
North Yorkshire, YO7 3BX, UK.

www.houseofstratus.com

Typeset by House of Stratus
Printed and bound in Great Britain by
Antony Rowe Ltd., Chippenham, Wiltshire.

A catalogue record for this book is available from the British Library
and the Library of Congress.

ISBN 0-7551-0352-1

Deemed 'the father of the scientific detective story', **Richard Austin Freeman** had a long and distinguished career, not least as a writer of detective fiction. He was born in London, the son of a tailor who went on to train as a pharmacist. After graduating as a surgeon at the Middlesex Hospital Medical College, Freeman taught for a while and joined the colonial service, offering his skills as an assistant surgeon along the Gold Coast of Africa. He became embroiled in a diplomatic mission when a British expeditionary party was sent to investigate the activities of the French. Through his tact and formidable intelligence, a massacre was narrowly avoided. His future was assured in the colonial service. However, after becoming ill with blackwater fever, Freeman was sent back to England to recover and, finding his finances precarious, embarked on a career as acting physician in Holloway Prison. In desperation, he turned to writing and went on to dominate the world of British detective fiction, taking pride in testing different criminal techniques. So keen were his powers as a writer that part of one of his best novels was written in a bomb shelter.

Contents

The Case of the White Footprints

"Well," said my friend Foxton, pursuing a familiar and apparently inexhaustible topic, "I'd sooner have your job than my own."

"I've no doubt you would," was my unsympathetic reply. "I never met a man who wouldn't. We all tend to consider other men's jobs in terms of their advantages and our own in terms of their drawbacks. It is human nature."

"Oh, it's all very well for you to be so beastly philosophical," retorted Foxton. "You wouldn't be if you were in my place. Here, in Margate, it's measles, chickenpox and scarlatina all the summer, and bronchitis, colds and rheumatism all the winter. A deadly monotony. Whereas you and Thorndyke sit there in your chambers and let your clients feed you up with the raw material of romance. Why, your life is a sort of everlasting Adelphi drama."

"You exaggerate, Foxton," said I. "We, like you, have our routine work, only it is never heard of outside the Law Courts; and you, like every other doctor, must run up against mystery and romance from time to time."

Foxton shook his head as he held out his hand for my cup. "I don't," said he. "My practice yields nothing but an endless round of dull routine."

And then, as if in commentary on this last statement, the housemaid burst into the room and, with hardly dissembled agitation, exclaimed:

1

"If you please, sir, the page from Beddingfield's Boarding House says that a lady has been found dead in her bed and would you go round there immediately."

"Very well, Jane," said Foxton, and as the maid retired, he deliberately helped himself to another fried egg and, looking across the table at me, exclaimed: "Isn't that always the way? Come immediately – now – this very instant, although the patient may have been considering for a day or two whether he'll send for you or not. But directly he decides, you must spring out of bed, or jump up from your breakfast, and run."

"That's quite true," I agreed; "but this really does seem to be an urgent case."

"What's the urgency?" demanded Foxton. "The woman is already dead. Anyone would think she was in imminent danger of coming to life again and that my instant arrival was the only thing that could prevent such a catastrophe."

"You've only a third-hand statement she is dead," said I. "It is just possible that she isn't; and even if she is, as you will have to give evidence at the inquest, you don't want the police to get there first and turn out the room before you've made your inspection."

"Gad!" exclaimed Foxton. "I hadn't thought of that. Yes. You're right. I'll hop round at once."

He swallowed the remainder of the egg at a single gulp and rose from the table. Then he paused and stood for a few moments looking down at me irresolutely.

"I wonder, Jervis," he said, "if you would mind coming round with me. You know all the medico-legal ropes, and I don't. What do you say?"

I agreed instantly, having, in fact, been restrained only by delicacy from making the suggestion myself; and when I had fetched from my room my pocket camera and telescopic tripod, we set forth together without further delay.

Beddingfield's Boarding House was but a few minutes' walk from Foxton's residence, being situated near the middle of Ethelred Road, Cliftonville, a quiet, suburban street which abounded in similar establishments, many of which, I noticed, were undergoing a spring-cleaning and renovation to prepare them for the approaching season.

"That's the house," said Foxton, "where that woman is standing at the front door. Look at the boarders, collected at the dining-room window. There's a rare commotion in that house, I'll warrant."

Here, arriving at the house, he ran up the steps and accosted in sympathetic tones the elderly woman who stood by the open street door.

"What a dreadful thing this is, Mrs Beddingfield! Terrible! Most distressing for you!"

"Ah, you're right, Dr Foxton," she replied. "It's an awful affair. Shocking. So bad for business, too. I do hope and trust there won't be any scandal."

"I'm sure I hope not," said Foxton. "There shan't be if I can help it. And as my friend, Dr Jervis, who is staying with me for a few days, is a lawyer as well as a doctor, we shall have the best advice. When was the affair discovered?"

"Just before I sent for you, Dr Foxton. The maid noticed that Mrs Toussaint – that is the poor creature's name – had not taken in her hot water, so she knocked at the door. As she couldn't get any answer, she tried the door and found it bolted on the inside, and then she came and told me. I went up and knocked loudly, and then, as I couldn't get any reply, I told our boy, James, to force the door open with a case-opener, which he did quite easily as the bolt was only a small one. Then I went in, all of a tremble, for I had a presentiment that there was something wrong; and there she was, lying stone dead, with a most 'orrible stare on her face and an empty bottle in her hand."

"A bottle, eh!" said Foxton.

"Yes. She'd made away with herself, poor thing; and all on account of some silly love affair – and it was hardly even that."

"Ah," said Foxton. "The usual thing. You must tell us about that later. Now we'd better go up and see the patient – at least the – er – perhaps you'll show us the room, Mrs Beddingfield."

The landlady turned and preceded us up the stairs to the first-floor back, where she paused, and softly opening a door, peered nervously into the room. As we stepped past her and entered, she seemed inclined to follow, but, at a significant glance from me, Foxton persuasively ejected her and closed the door. Then we stood silent for a while and looked about us.

In the aspect of the room there was something strangely incongruous with the tragedy that had been enacted within its walls; a mingling of the commonplace and the terrible that almost amounted to anticlimax. Through the wide-open window the bright spring sunshine streamed in on the garish wallpaper and cheap furniture; from the street below, the periodic shouts of a man, selling "sole and mack-ro!" broke into the brisk staccato of a barrel-organ and both sounds mingled with a raucous voice close at hand, cheerfully trolling a popular song, and accounted for by a linen-clad elbow that bobbed in front of the window and evidently appertained to a house painter on an adjacent ladder.

It was all very commonplace and familiar and discordantly out of character with the stark figure that lay on the bed like a waxen effigy symbolic of tragedy. Here was none of that gracious somnolence in which death often presents itself with a suggestion of eternal repose. This woman was dead; horribly, aggressively dead. The thin sallow face was rigid as stone, the dark eyes stared into infinite space with a horrid fixity that was quite disturbing to look on. And yet the posture of the corpse was not uneasy, being, in fact, rather curiously symmetrical, with both arms outside the bedclothes and both hands closed, the right grasping, as Mrs Beddingfield had said, an empty bottle.

"Well," said Foxton, as he stood looking down on the dead woman, "it seems a pretty clear case. She appears to have laid herself out and kept hold of the bottle so that there should be no mistake. How long do you suppose this woman has been dead, Jervis?"

I felt the rigid limbs and tested the temperature of the body surface.

"Not less than six hours," I replied. "Probably more. I should say that she died about two o'clock this morning."

"And that is about all we can say," said Foxton, "until the post-mortem has been made. Everything looks quite straightforward. No signs of a struggle or marks of violence. That blood on the mouth is probably due to her biting her lip when she drank from the bottle. Yes; here's a little cut on the inside of the lip, corresponding to the upper incisors. By the way, I wonder if there is anything left in the bottle."

As he spoke, he drew the small, unlabelled green glass phial from the closed hand – out of which it slipped quite easily – and held it up to the light.

"Yes," he exclaimed, "there's more than a drachm left; quite enough for an analysis. But I don't recognise the smell. Do you?"

I sniffed at the bottle and was aware of a faint unfamiliar vegetable odour.

"No," I answered. "It appears to be a watery solution of some kind, but I can't give it a name. Where is the cork?"

"I haven't seen it," he replied. "Probably it is on the floor somewhere."

We both stooped to look for the missing cork and presently found it in the shadow, under the little bedside table. But, in the course of that brief search, I found something else, which had indeed been lying in full view all the time – a wax match. Now a wax match is a perfectly innocent and very commonplace object, but yet the presence of this one gave me pause. In the first place, women do not, as a rule, use wax matches, though there was not much in that. What was more to the point was that the candlestick by the bedside contained a box of safety matches, and that, as the burned remains of one lay in the tray, it appeared to have been used to light the candle. Then why the wax match?

While I was turning over this problem Foxton had corked the bottle, wrapped it carefully in a piece of paper which he took from the dressing table, and bestowed it in his pocket.

"Well, Jervis," said he, "I think we've seen everything. The analysis and the post-mortem will complete the case. Shall we go down and hear what Mrs Beddingfield has to say?"

But that wax match, slight as was its significance, taken alone, had presented itself to me as the last of a succession of phenomena each of which was susceptible of a sinister interpretation, and the cumulative effect of these slight suggestions began to impress me somewhat strongly.

"One moment, Foxton," said I. "Don't let us take anything for granted. We are here to collect evidence, and we must go warily. There is such a thing as homicidal poisoning, you know."

"Yes, of course," he replied, "but there is nothing to suggest it in this case; at least, I see nothing. Do you?"

"Nothing very positive," said I; "but there are some facts that seem to call for consideration. Let us go over what we have seen. In the first place, there is a distinct discrepancy in the appearance of the body. The general easy, symmetrical posture, like that of a figure on a tomb, suggests the effect of a slow, painless poison. But look at the face. There is nothing reposeful about that. It is very strongly suggestive of pain or terror or both."

"Yes," said Foxton, "that is so. But you can't draw any satisfactory conclusions from the facial expression of dead bodies. Why men who have been hanged, or even stabbed, often look as peaceful as babes."

"Still," I urged, "it is a fact to be noted. Then there is that cut on the lip. It may have been produced in the way you suggest; but it may equally well be the result of pressure on the mouth."

Foxton made no comment on this beyond a slight shrug of the shoulders, and I continued:

"Then there is the state of the hand. It was closed, but it did not really grasp the object it contained. You drew the bottle out without any resistance. It simply lay in the closed hand. But that is not a normal state of affairs. As you know, when a person dies grasping any object, either the hand relaxes and lets it drop, or the muscular action passes into cadaveric spasm and grasps the object firmly. And lastly, there is this wax match. Where did it come from? The dead woman apparently lit her candle with a safety match from the box. It is a small matter, but it wants explaining."

Foxton raised his eyebrows protestingly. "You're like all specialists, Jervis," said he. "You see your speciality in everything. And while you are straining these flimsy suggestions to turn a simple suicide into murder, you ignore the really conclusive fact that the door was bolted and had to be broken open before anyone could get in."

"You are not forgetting, I suppose," said I, "that the window was wide open and that there were house painters about and possibly a ladder left standing against the house."

"As to the ladder," said Foxton, "that is a pure assumption; but we can easily settle the question by asking that fellow out there if it was or was not left standing last night."

Simultaneously we moved towards the window; but half-way we both stopped short. For the question of the ladder had in a moment become negligible. Staring up at us from the dull red linoleum which covered the floor were the impressions of a pair of bare feet, imprinted in white paint with the distinctness of a woodcut. There was no need to ask if they had been made by the dead woman: they were unmistakably the feet of a man, and large feet at that. Nor could there be any doubt as to whence those feet had come. Beginning with startling distinctness under the window, the tracks diminished rapidly in intensity until they reached the carpeted portion of the room, where they vanished abruptly; and only by the closest scrutiny was it possible to detect the faint traces of the retiring tracks.

Foxton and I stood for some moments gazing in silence at the sinister white shapes; then we looked at one another.

"You've saved me from a most horrible blunder, Jervis," said Foxton. "Ladder or no ladder, that fellow came in at the window;

and he came in last night, for I saw them painting these window-sills yesterday afternoon. Which side did he come from, I wonder?"

We moved to the window and looked out on the sill. A set of distinct, though smeared impressions on the new paint gave unneeded confirmation and showed that the intruder had approached from the left side, close to which was a cast-iron stack-pipe, now covered with fresh green paint.

"So," said Foxton, "the presence or absence of the ladder is of no significance. The man got into the window somehow, and that's all that matters."

"On the contrary," said I, "the point may be of considerable importance in identification. It isn't everyone who could climb up a stack-pipe, whereas most people could make shift to climb a ladder, even if it were guarded by a plank. But the fact that the man took off his boots and socks suggests that he came up by the pipe. If he had merely aimed at silencing his footfalls, he would probably have removed his boots only."

From the window we turned to examine more closely the footprints on the floor, and, while I took a series of measurements with my spring tape, Foxton entered them in my notebook.

"Doesn't it strike you as rather odd, Jervis," said he, "that neither of the little toes has made any mark?"

"It does indeed," I replied. "The appearances suggest that the little toes were absent, but I have never met with such a condition. Have you?"

"Never. Of course one is acquainted with the supernumerary toe deformity, but I have never heard of congenitally deficient little toes."

Once more we scrutinised the footprints, and even examined those on the window-sill, obscurely marked on the fresh paint; but, exquisitely distinct as were those on the linoleum, showing every wrinkle and minute skin-marking, not the faintest hint of a little toe was to be seen on either foot.

"It's very extraordinary," said Foxton. "He has certainly lost his little toes, if he ever had any. They couldn't have failed to make some mark. But it's a queer affair. Quite a windfall for the police, by the way; I mean for purposes of identification."

"Yes," I agreed, "and having regard to the importance of the footprints, I think it would be wise to get a photograph of them."

"Oh, the police will see to that," said Foxton. "Besides, we haven't got a camera, unless you thought of using that little toy snap-shotter of yours."

As Foxton was no photographer I did not trouble to explain that my camera, though small, had been specially made for scientific purposes.

"Any photograph is better than none," I said, and with this I opened the tripod and set it over one of the most distinct of the footprints, screwed the camera to the goose-neck, carefully framed the footprint in the finder and adjusted the focus, finally making the exposure by means of an Antinous release. This process I repeated four times, twice on a right footprint and twice on a left.

"Well," Foxton remarked, "with all those photographs the police ought to be able to pick up the scent."

"Yes, they've got something to go on; but they'll have to catch their hare before they can cook him. He won't be walking about barefooted, you know."

"No. It's a poor clue in that respect. And now, we may as well be off as we've seen all there is to see. I think we won't have much to say to Mrs Beddingfield. This is a police case, and the less I'm mixed up in it the better it will be for my practice."

I was faintly amused at Foxton's caution when considered by the light of his utterances at the breakfast table. Apparently his appetite for mystery and romance was easily satisfied. But that was no affair of mine. I waited on the doorstep while he said a few – probably evasive – words to the landlady and then, as we started off together in the direction of the police station, I began to turn over in my mind the salient features of the case. For some time we walked on in silence, and must have been pursuing a parallel train of thought for, when he at length spoke, he almost put my reflections into words.

"You know, Jervis," said he, "there ought to be a clue in those footprints. I realise that you can't tell how many toes a man has by looking at his booted feet. But those unusual footprints ought to give an expert a hint as to what sort of man to look for. Don't they convey any hint to you?"

I felt that Foxton was right; that if my brilliant colleague, Thorndyke, had been in my place, he would have extracted from those footprints some leading fact that would have given the police a start along some definite line of inquiry; and that belief, coupled with Foxton's challenge, put me on my mettle.

"They offer no particular suggestions to me at this moment," said I, "but I think that, if we consider them systematically, we may be able to draw some useful deductions."

"Very well," said Foxton, "then let us consider them systematically. Fire away. I should like to hear how you work these things out."

Foxton's frankly spectatorial attitude was a little disconcerting, especially as it seemed to commit me to a result that I was by no means confident of attaining. I therefore began a little diffidently.

"We are assuming that both the feet that made those prints were from some cause devoid of little toes. That assumption — which is almost certainly correct — we treat as a fact, and, taking it as our starting point, the first step in the inquiry is to find some explanation of it. Now there are three possibilities, and only three: deformity, injury and disease. The toes may have been absent from birth, they may have been lost as a result of mechanical injury, or they may have been lost by disease. Let us take those possibilities in order.

"Deformity we exclude since such a malformation is unknown to us.

"Mechanical injury seems to be excluded by the fact that the two little toes are on opposite sides of the body and could not conceivably be affected by any violence which left the intervening feet uninjured. This seems to narrow the possibilities down to

10

disease; and the question that arises is, what diseases are there which might result in the loss of both little toes?"

I looked inquiringly at Foxton, but he merely nodded encouragingly. His rôle was that of listener.

"Well," I pursued, "the loss of both toes seems to exclude local disease, just as it excluded local injury; and as to general diseases, I can think only of three which might produce this condition — Raynaud's disease, ergotism, and frostbite."

"You don't call frostbite a general disease, do you?" objected Foxton.

"For our present purpose, I do. The effects are local, but the cause — low external temperature — affects the whole body and is a general cause. Well, now, taking the diseases in order, I think we can exclude Raynaud's disease. It does, it is true, occasionally cause the fingers or toes to die and drop off, and the little toes would be especially liable to be affected as being most remote from the heart. But in such a severe case the other toes would be affected. They would be shrivelled and tapered, whereas, if you remember, the toes of these feet were quite plump and full, to judge by the large impressions they made. So I think we may safely reject Raynaud's disease. There remain ergotism and frostbite; and the choice between them is just a question of relative frequency. Frostbite is more common; therefore frostbite is more probable."

"Do they tend equally to affect the little toes?" asked Foxton.

"As a matter of probability, yes. The poison of ergot acting from within, and intense cold acting from without, contract the small blood-vessels and arrest the circulation. The feet, being the most distant parts of the body from the heart, are the first to feel the effects; and the little toes, which are the most distant parts of the feet, are the most susceptible of all."

Foxton reflected awhile, and then remarked:

"This is all very well, Jervis, but I don't see that you are much forrarder. This man has lost both his little toes, and on your showing, the probabilities are that the loss was due either to chronic ergot poisoning or to frostbite, with a balance of probability in favour of frostbite. That's all. No proof, no verification. Just the law of probability applied to a particular case, which is always unsatisfactory. He may have lost his toes in some totally different way. But even if the probabilities work out correctly, I don't see what use your conclusions would be to the police. They wouldn't tell them what sort of man to look for."

There was a good deal of truth in Foxton's objection. A man who has suffered from ergotism or frostbite is not externally different from any other man. Still, we had not exhausted the case, as I ventured to point out.

"Don't be premature, Foxton," said I. "Let us pursue our argument a little farther. We have established a probability that this unknown man has suffered either from ergotism or frostbite. That, as you say, is of no use by itself; but supposing we can show that these conditions tend to affect a particular class of persons, we shall have established a fact that will indicate a line of investigation. And I think we can. Let us take the case of ergotism first.

"Now how is chronic ergot poisoning caused? Not by the medicinal use of the drug, but by the consumption of the diseased rye in which ergot occurs. It is therefore peculiar to countries in which rye is used extensively as food. Those countries, broadly speaking, are the countries of North Eastern Europe, and especially Russia and Poland.

"Then take the case of frostbite. Obviously, the most likely person to get frost-bitten is the inhabitant of a country with a cold climate. The most rigorous climates inhabited by white people are North America and North Eastern Europe, especially Russia and Poland. So you see, the areas associated with ergotism and frostbite overlap to some extent. In fact they do more than overlap; for a person even slightly affected by ergot would be specially liable, to frostbite, owing to the impaired circulation. The conclusion is that, racially, in both ergotism and frostbite, the balance of probability is in favour of a Russian, a Pole or a Scandinavian.

"Then in the case of frostbite there is the occupation factor. What class of men tend most to become frost-bitten? Well, beyond all doubt, the greatest sufferers from frostbite are sailors, especially those on sailing ships, and, naturally, on ships trading to arctic and subarctic countries. But the bulk of such sailing ships are those engaged in the Baltic and Archangel trade; and the crews of those ships are almost exclusively Scandinavians, Finns, Russians and Poles. So, that, again, the probabilities point to a native of North-Eastern Europe, and, taken as a whole, by the overlapping of factors, to a Russian, a Pole, or a Scandinavian."

Foxton smiled sardonically. "Very ingenious, Jervis," said he. "Most ingenious. As an academic statement of probabilities, quite excellent. But for practical purposes absolutely useless. However, here we are at the police station. I'll just run in and give them the facts and then go on to the coroner's office."

"I suppose I'd better not come in with you?" I said.

"Well, no," he replied. "You see, you have no official connection with the case and they mightn't like it. You'd better go and amuse yourself while I get the morning's visits done. We can talk things over at lunch."

With this he disappeared into the police station, and I turned away with a smile of grim amusement. Experience is apt to make us a trifle uncharitable, and experience had taught me that those who are the most scornful of academic reasoning are often not above retailing it with some reticence as to its original authorship. I had a shrewd suspicion that Foxton was at this very moment disgorging my despised "academic statement of probabilities" to an admiring police inspector.

My way towards the sea lay through Ethelred Road, and I had traversed about half its length and was approaching the house of the tragedy when I observed Mrs Beddingfield at the bay window. Evidently she recognised me, for a few moments later she appeared in outdoor clothes on the doorstep and advanced to meet me.

"Have you seen the police?" she asked as we met.

I replied that Dr Foxton was even now at the police station.

"Ah!" she said, "it's a dreadful affair most unfortunate, too, just at the beginning of the season. A scandal is absolute ruin to a boarding house. What do you think of the case? Will it be possible to hush it up? Dr Foxton said you were a lawyer, I think, Dr Jervis?"

"Yes. I am a lawyer, but really I know nothing of the circumstances of this case. Did I understand that there had been something in the nature of a love affair?"

"Yes – at least – well, perhaps I oughtn't to have said that. But hadn't I better tell you the whole story? – that is, if I am not taking up too much of your time."

"I should be interested to hear what led to the disaster," said I.

"Then," she said, "I will tell you all about it. Will you come indoors, or shall I walk a little way with you?"

As I suspected that the police were at that moment on their way to the house, I chose the latter alternative and led her away seawards at a pretty brisk pace.

"Was this poor lady a widow?" I asked as we started up the street.

"No, she wasn't," replied Mrs Beddingfield, "and that was the trouble. Her husband was abroad – at least, he had been, and he was just coming home. A pretty home-coming it will be for him, poor man. He is an officer in the civil police at Sierra Leone, but he hasn't been there long. He went there for his health."

"What! To Sierra Leone!" I exclaimed, for the "White Man's Grave" seemed a queer health resort.

"Yes. You see, Mr Toussaint is a French Canadian, and it seems that he has always been somewhat of a rolling stone. For some time he was in the Klondyke, but he suffered so much from the cold that he had to come away. It injured his health very severely; I don't quite know in what way, but I do know that he was quite a cripple for a time. When he got better he looked out for a post in a warm climate and eventually obtained the appointment of Inspector of Civil Police at Sierra Leone. That was about ten months ago, and when he sailed for Africa his wife came to stay with me and has been here ever since."

"And this love affair that you spoke of?"

"Yes, but I oughtn't to have called it that. Let me explain what happened. About three months ago a Swedish gentleman – a Mr Bergson came to stay here, and he seemed to be very much smitten with Mrs Toussaint."

"And she?"

"Oh, she liked him well enough. He is a tall, good-looking man – though for that matter he is no taller than her husband, nor any better looking. Both men are over six feet. But there was no harm so far as she was concerned, excepting that she didn't see the position quite soon enough. She wasn't very discreet, in fact I thought it necessary to give her a little advice. However, Mr Bergson left here and went to live at Ramsgate to superintend the unloading of the ice ships (he came from Sweden in one), and I thought the trouble was at an end. But it wasn't, for he took to coming over to see Mrs Toussaint, and of course I couldn't have that. So at last I had to tell him that he mustn't come to the house again. It was very unfortunate, for on that occasion I think he had been 'tasting,' as they say in Scotland. He wasn't drunk but he was excitable and noisy, and when I told him he mustn't come again he made such a disturbance that two of the gentlemen boarders – Mr Wardale and Mr Macauley – had to interfere. And then he was most insulting to them, especially to Mr Macauley, who is a coloured gentleman; called him a 'buck nigger' and all sorts of offensive names."

"And how did the coloured gentleman take it?"

"Not very well, I am sorry to say, considering that he is a gentleman – a law student with chambers in the Temple. In fact, his language was so objectionable that Mr Wardale insisted on my giving him notice on the spot. But I managed to get him taken in next door but one; you see, Mr Wardale had been a Commissioner at Sierra Leone – it was through him that Mr Toussaint got his appointment – so I suppose he was rather on his dignity with coloured people."

"And was that the last you heard of Mr Bergson?"

15

"He never came here again, but he wrote several times to Mrs Toussaint, asking her to meet him. At last, only a few days ago, she wrote to him and told him that the acquaintance must cease."

"And has it ceased?"

"As far as I know, it has."

"Then, Mrs Beddingfield," said I, "what makes you connect the affair with – with what has happened?"

"Well, you see," she explained, "there is the husband. He was coming home, and is probably in England already."

"Indeed!" said I.

"Yes," she continued. "He went up into the bush to arrest some natives belonging to one of these gangs of murderers – Leopard Societies, I think they are called – and he got seriously wounded. He wrote to his wife from hospital, saying that he would be sent home as soon as he was fit to travel, and about ten days ago she got a letter from him saying that he was coming by the next ship.

"I noticed that she seemed very nervous and upset when she got the letters from hospital, and still more so when the last letter came. Of course, I don't know what he said to her in those letters. It may be that he had heard something about Mr Bergson, and threatened to take some action. Of course, I can't say. I only know that she was very nervous and restless, and when we saw in the paper four days ago that the ship he would be coming by had arrived in Liverpool, she seemed dreadfully upset. And she got worse and worse until – well last night."

"Has anything been heard of the husband since the ship arrived?" I asked.

"Nothing whatever," replied Mrs Beddingfield, with a meaningful look at me which I had no difficulty in interpreting. "No letter, no telegram, not a word. And you see, if he hadn't come by that ship, he would almost certainly have sent a letter by her. He must have arrived in England, but why hasn't he turned up, or at least sent a wire? What is he doing? Why is he staying away? Can he have heard something? And what does he mean to do? That's what kept the poor thing on wires, and that, I feel certain, is what drove her to make away with herself."

It was not my business to contest Mrs Beddingfield's erroneous deductions. I was seeking information – it seemed that I had nearly exhausted the present source. But one point required amplifying.

"To return to Mr Bergson, Mrs Beddingfield," said I. "Do I understand that he is a seafaring man?"

"He was," she replied. "At present he is settled at Ramsgate as manager of a company in the ice trade, but formerly he was a sailor. I have heard him say that he was one of the crew of an exploring ship that went in search the North Pole and that he was locked up in the ice for months and months. I should have thought he would have had enough of ice after that."

With this view I expressed warm agreement, and having now obtained all the information that appeared to be available, I proceeded to bring the interview to an end.

"Well, Mrs. Beddingfield," I said, "it is a rather mysterious affair. Perhaps more light may be thrown on it at the inquest. Meanwhile, I should think that it will be wise of you to keep your own counsel as far as outsiders are concerned."

The remainder of the morning I spent pacing the smooth stretch of sand that lies to the east of the jetty, and reflecting on the evidence that I had acquired in respect of this singular crime. Evidently there was no lack of clues in this case. On the contrary, there were two quite obvious lines of inquiry, for both the Swede and the missing husband presented the characters of the hypothetical murderer. Both had been exposed to the conditions which tend to produce frostbite; one of them had probably been a consumer of rye meal, and both might be said to have a motive – though, to be sure, it was a very insufficient one – for committing the crime. Still, in both cases the evidence was merely speculative; it suggested a line of investigation, but it did nothing more.

When I met Foxton at lunch I was sensible of a curious change in his manner. His previous expansiveness had given place to marked reticence and a certain official secretiveness.

"I don't think, you know, Jervis," he said, when I opened the subject, "that we had better discuss this affair. You see, I am the principal witness, and while the case is *sub judice* – well, in fact, the police don't want the case talked about."

"But surely I am a witness, too, and an expert witness, moreover – "

"That isn't the view of the police. They look on you as more or less of an amateur, and as you have no official connection with the case, I don't think they propose to subpœna you. Superintendent Platt, who is in charge of the case, wasn't very pleased at my having taken you to the house. Said it was quite irregular. Oh, and by the way, he says you must hand over those photographs."

"But isn't Platt going to have the footprints photographed on his own account?" I objected.

"Of course he is. He is going to have a set of proper photographs taken by an expert photographer – he was mightily amused when he heard about your little snapshot affair. Oh, you can trust Platt. He is a great man. He has had a course of instruction at the Fingerprint Department in London."

"I don't see how that is going to help him as there aren't any fingerprints in this case." This was a mere fly-cast on my part, but Foxton rose at once at the rather clumsy bait.

"Oh, aren't there?" he exclaimed. "You didn't happen to spot them, but they were there. Platt has got the prints of a complete right hand. This is in strict confidence, you know," he added, with somewhat belated caution.

Foxton's sudden reticence restrained me from uttering the obvious comment on the superintendent's achievement. I returned to the subject of the photographs.

"Supposing I decline to hand over my film?" said I.

"But I hope you won't – and in fact you mustn't. I am officially connected with the case, and I've got to live with these people. As the police surgeon, I am responsible for the medical evidence, and Platt expects me to get those photographs from you. Obviously you can't keep them. It would be most irregular."

It was useless to argue. Evidently the police did not want me to be introduced into the case, and after all, the superintendent was within his rights, if he chose to regard me as a private individual and to demand the surrender of the film.

Nevertheless I was loath to give up the photographs, at least, until I had carefully studied them. The case was within my own speciality of practice, and was a strange and interesting one. Moreover, it appeared to be in unskilful hands, judging from the fingerprint episode, and then experience had taught me to treasure up small scraps of chance evidence, since one never knew when one might be drawn into a case in a professional capacity.

In effect, I decided not to give up the photographs, though that decision committed me to a ruse that I was not very willing to adopt. I would rather have acted quite straightforwardly.

"Well, if you insist, Foxton," I said, "I will hand over the film or, if you like, I will destroy it in your presence."

"I think Platt would rather have the film uninjured," said Foxton. "Then he'll know, you know," he added, with a sly grin.

In my heart, I thanked Foxton for that grin. It made my own guileful proceedings so much easier; for a suspicious man invites you to get the better of him if you can.

After lunch I went up to my room, locked the door and took the little camera from my pocket. Having fully wound up the film, I extracted it, wrapped it up carefully and bestowed it in my inside breast-pocket. Then I inserted a fresh film, and going to the open window, took four successive snapshots of the sky. This done, I closed the camera, slipped it into my pocket and went downstairs. Foxton was in the hall, brushing his hat, as I descended, and at once renewed his demand.

"About those photographs, Jervis," said he, "I shall be looking in at the police station presently, so if you wouldn't mind – "

"To be sure," said I. "I will give you the film now, if you like."

Taking the camera from my pocket, I solemnly wound up the remainder of the film, extracted it, stuck down the loose end with ostentatious care, and handed it to him.

"Better not expose it to the light," I said, going the whole hog of deception, "or you may fog the exposures."

Foxton took the spool from me as if it were hot – he was not a photographer – and thrust it into his bag. He was still thanking me quite profusely when the front-door bell rang.

The visitor who stood revealed when Foxton opened the door was a small, spare gentleman with a complexion of the peculiar brown-papery quality that suggests long residence in the Tropics. He stepped in briskly and introduced, himself and his business without preamble.

"My name is Wardale – boarder at Beddingfield's. I've called with reference to the tragic event which – "

Here Foxton interposed in his frostiest official tone. "I am afraid, Mr Wardale, I can't give you any information about the case at present."

"I saw you two gentlemen at the house this morning," Mr Wardale continued, but Foxton again cut him short.

"You did. We were there – or at least, I was – as the representative of the Law, and while the case is *sub judice* – "

"It, isn't yet," interrupted Wardale.

"Well, I can't enter into any discussion of it – "

"I am not asking you to," said Wardale, a little impatiently. "But I understand that one of you is Dr Jervis."

"I am," said I.

"I must really warn you," Foxton began again; but Mr Wardale interrupted testily:

"My dear sir, I am a lawyer and a magistrate and understand perfectly well what is and what is not permissible. I have come simply to make a professional engagement with Dr Jervis."

"In what way can I be of service to you?" I asked.

"I will tell you," said Mr Wardale. "This poor lady, whose death has occurred in so mysterious a manner, was the wife of a man who was, like myself, a servant of the Government of Sierra Leone. I was the friend of both of them; and in the absence of the husband, I should like to have the inquiry into the circumstances of this lady's death watched by a competent lawyer with the necessary special knowledge of medical evidence. Will you or your colleague, Dr Thorndyke, undertake to watch the case for me?"

Of course I was willing to undertake the case and said so.

"Then," said Mr Wardale, "I will instruct my solicitor to write to you and formally retain you in the case. Here is my card. You will find my name in the Colonial Office List, and you know my address here."

He handed me his card, wished us both good afternoon, and then, with a stiff little bow, turned and took his departure.

"I think I had better run up to town and confer with Thorndyke," said I. "How do the trains run?"

"There is a good train in about three-quarters of an hour," replied Foxton.

"Then I will go by it, but I shall come down again tomorrow or the next day, and probably Thorndyke will come down with me."

"Very well," said Foxton. "Bring him in to lunch or dinner, but I can't put him up, I am afraid."

"It would be better not," said I. "Your friend, Platt, wouldn't like it. He won't want Thorndyke – or me either for that matter. And what about those photographs? Thorndyke will want them, you know."

"He can't have them," said Foxton doggedly, "unless Platt is willing to hand them back; which I don't suppose he will be."

I had private reasons for thinking otherwise, but I kept them to myself; and as Foxton went forth on his afternoon round, I returned upstairs to pack my suitcase and write the telegram to Thorndyke informing him of my movements.

It was only a quarter past five when I let myself into our chambers in King's Bench Walk.

To my relief I found my colleague at home and our laboratory assistant, Polton, in the act of laying tea for two.

"I gather," said Thorndyke as we shook hands, "that my learned brother brings grist to the mill?"

"Yes," I replied. "Nominally a watching brief, but I think you will agree with me that it is a case for independent investigation."

"Will there be anything in my line, sir?" inquired Polton, who was always agog at the word "investigation."

"There is a film to be developed. Four exposures of white footprints on a dark ground."

"Ah!" said Polton, "you'll want good strong negatives and they ought to be enlarged if they are from the little camera. Can you give me the dimensions?"

I wrote out the measurements from my notebook and handed him the paper together with the spool of film, with which he retired gleefully to the laboratory.

"And now, Jervis," said Thorndyke, "while Polton is operating on the film and we are discussing our tea, let us have a sketch of the case."

I gave him more than a sketch, for the events were recent and I had carefully sorted out the facts during my journey to town, making rough notes which I now consulted. To my rather lengthy recital he listened in his usual attentive manner, without any comment, excepting in regard to my manœuvre to retain possession of the exposed film.

"It's almost a pity you didn't refuse," said he. "They could hardly have enforced their demand, and my feeling is that it is more convenient as well as more dignified to avoid direct deception unless one is driven to it. But perhaps you considered that you were."

As a matter of fact I had at the time, but I had since come to Thorndyke's opinion. My little manoeuvre was going to be a source of inconvenience presently.

"Well," said Thorndyke, when I had finished my recital, "I think we may take it that the police theory is, in the main, your own theory derived from Foxton."

"I think so, excepting that I learn from Foxton that Superintendent Platt has obtained the complete fingerprints of a right hand."

Thorndyke raised his eyebrows. "Fingerprints!" he exclaimed. "Why the fellow must be a mere simpleton. But there," he added, "everybody – police, lawyers, judges, even Galton himself – seems to lose every vestige of common sense as soon as the subject of fingerprints is raised. But it would be interesting to know how he got them and what they are like. We must try to find that out. However, to return to your case, since your theory and the police theory are probably the same, we may as well consider the value of your inferences.

"At present we are dealing with the case in the abstract. Our data are largely assumptions, and our inferences are largely derived from an application of the mathematical laws of probability. Thus we assume that a murder has been committed, whereas it may turn out to have been suicide. We assume the murder to have been committed by the person who made the footprints, and we assume that that person has no little toes, whereas he may have retracted little toes which do not touch the ground and so leave no impression. Assuming the little toes to be absent, we account for their absence by considering known causes in the order of their probability. Excluding – quite properly, I think – Raynaud's disease, we arrive at frostbite and ergotism. But two persons, both of whom are of a stature corresponding to the size of the footprints, may have had a motive – though a very inadequate one – for committing the crime, and both have been exposed to the conditions which tend to produce frostbite, while one of them has probably been exposed to the conditions which tend to produce ergotism. The laws of probability point to both of these two men; and the chances in favour of the Swede being the murderer rather than the Canadian would be represented by the common factor – frostbite – multiplied by the additional factor, ergotism. But this is purely speculative at present. There is no evidence that either man has ever been frost-bitten or has ever eaten spurred rye.

Nevertheless, it is a perfectly sound method at this stage. It indicates a line of investigation. If it should transpire that either man has suffered from frostbite or ergotism, a definite advance would have been made. But here is Polton with a couple of finished prints. How on earth did you manage it in the time, Polton?"

"Why, you see, sir, I just dried the film with spirit," replied Polton. "It saves a lot of time. I will let you have a pair of enlargements in about a quarter of an hour."

Handing us the two wet prints, each stuck on a glass plate, he retired to the laboratory, and Thorndyke and I proceeded to scrutinise the photographs with the aid of our pocket lenses. The promised enlargements were really hardly necessary excepting for the purpose of comparative measurements, for the image of the white footprint, fully two inches long, was so microscopically sharp that, with the assistance of the lens, the minutest detail could be clearly seen.

"There is certainly not a vestige of little toe," remarked Thorndyke, "and the plump appearance of the other toes supports your rejection of Raynaud's disease. Does the character of the footprint convey any other suggestion to you, Jervis?"

"It gives me the impression that the man had been accustomed to go barefooted in early life and had only taken to boots comparatively recently. The position of the great toe suggests this, and the presence of a number of small scars on the toes and ball of the foot, seems to confirm it. A person walking barefoot would sustain innumerable small wounds from treading on small, sharp objects."

Thorndyke looked dissatisfied. "I agree with you," he said, "as to the suggestion offered by the undeformed state of the great toes; but those little pits do not convey to me the impression of scars produced as you suggest. Still, you may be right."

Here our conversation was interrupted by a knock on the outer oak. Thorndyke stepped out through the lobby and I heard him open the door. A moment or two later he re-entered, accompanied by a short, brown-faced gentleman whom I instantly recognised as Mr Wardale.

"I must have come up by the same train as you," he remarked as we shook hands, "and to a certain extent, I suspect, on the same errand. I thought I would like to put our arrangement on a business footing, as I am a stranger to both of you."

"What do you want us to do?" asked Thorndyke.

"I want you to watch the case, and, if necessary, to look into the facts independently."

"Can you give us any information that may help us?"

Mr Wardale reflected. "I don't think I can," he said at length. "I have no facts that you have not, and any surmises of mine might be misleading. I had rather you kept an open mind. But perhaps we might go into the question of costs."

This, of course, was somewhat difficult, but Thorndyke contrived to indicate the probable liabilities involved to Mr Wardale's satisfaction.

"There is one other little matter," said Wardale as he rose to depart. "I have got a suitcase here which Mrs Beddingfield lent me to bring some things up to town. It is one that Mr Macauley left behind when he went away from the boarding house. Mrs Beddingfield suggested that I might leave it at his chambers when I had finished with it; but I don't know his address, excepting that it is somewhere in the Temple, and I don't want to meet the fellow if he should happen to have come up to town."

"Is it empty?" asked Thorndyke.

"Excepting for a suit of pyjamas and a pair of shocking old slippers." He opened the suitcase as he spoke and exhibited its contents with a grin.

"Characteristic of a negro, isn't it? Pink silk pyjamas and slippers about three sizes too small."

"Very well," said Thorndyke. "I will get my man to find out the address and leave it there."

As Mr Wardale went out, Polton entered with the enlarged photographs, which showed the footprints the natural size.

Thorndyke handed them to me, and as I sat down to examine them he followed his assistant to the laboratory. He returned in a few minutes, and after a brief inspection of the photographs, remarked:

"They show us nothing more than we have seen, though they may be useful later. So your stock of facts is all we have to go on at present. Are you going home tonight?"

"Yes, I shall go back to Margate tomorrow."

"Then, as I have to call at Scotland Yard, we may as well walk to Charing Cross together."

As we walked down the Strand we gossiped on general topics, but before we separated at Charing Cross, Thorndyke reverted to the case.

"Let me know the date of the inquest," said he, "and try to find out what the poison was – if it was really a poison."

"The liquid that was left in the bottle seemed to be a watery solution of some kind," said I, "as I think I mentioned."

"Yes," said Thorndyke. "Possibly a watery infusion of strophanthus."

"Why strophanthus?" I asked.

"Why not?" demanded Thorndyke. And with this and an inscrutable smile, he turned and walked down Whitehall.

Three days later I found myself at Margate sitting beside Thorndyke in a room adjoining the Town Hall, in which the inquest on the death of Mrs Toussaint was to be held. Already the coroner was in his chair, the jury were in their seats and the witnesses assembled in a group of chairs apart. These included Foxton, a stranger who sat by him – presumably the other medical witness – Mrs Beddingfield, Mr Wardale, the police superintendent and a well-dressed coloured man, whom I correctly assumed to be Mr Macauley.

As I sat by my rather sphinx-like colleague my mind recurred for the hundredth time to his extraordinary powers of mental synthesis. That parting remark of his as to the possible nature of the poison had brought home to me in a flash the fact that he already had a definite theory of this crime, and that his theory was not mine nor that of the police. True, the poison might not be strophanthus, after all, but that would not alter the position. He had a theory of the crime, but yet he was in possession of no facts excepting those with which I had supplied him. Therefore those facts contained the material for a theory, whereas I had deduced from them nothing but the bald, ambiguous mathematical probabilities.

The first witness called was naturally Dr Foxton, who described the circumstances already known to me. He further stated that he had been present at the autopsy, that he had found on the throat and limbs of the deceased, bruises that suggested a struggle and violent restraint. The immediate cause of death was heart failure but whether that failure was due to shock, terror, or the action of a poison, he could not positively say.

The next witness was a Dr Prescott, an expert pathologist and toxicologist. He had made the autopsy and agreed with Dr Foxton as to the cause of death. He had examined the liquid contained in the bottle taken from the hand of the deceased and found it to be a watery infusion or decoction of strophanthus seeds. He had analysed the fluid contained in the stomach and found it to consist largely of the same infusion.

"Is infusion of strophanthus seeds used in medicine?" the coroner asked.

"No," was the reply. "The tincture is the form in which strophanthus is administered unless it is given in the form of strophanthine."

"Do you consider that the strophanthus caused, or contributed to death?"

"It is difficult to say," replied Dr Prescott. "Strophanthus is a heart poison, and there was a very large poisonous dose. But very little had been absorbed, and the appearances were not inconsistent with death from shock."

"Could death have been self-produced by the voluntary taking of the poison?" asked the coroner.

"I should say, decidedly not. Dr Foxton's evidence shows that the bottle was almost certainly placed in the hands of the deceased after death, and this is in complete agreement with the enormous dose, and small absorption."

"Would you say that appearances point to suicidal or homicidal poisoning?"

"I should say that they point to homicidal poisoning, but that death was probably due mainly to shock."

This concluded the expert's evidence. It was followed by that of Mrs Beddingfield, which brought out nothing new to me but the fact that a trunk had been broken open and a small attaché case belonging to the deceased abstracted and taken away.

"Do you know what the deceased kept in that case?" the coroner asked.

"I have seen her put her husband's letters into it. She had quite a number of them. I don't know what else she kept in it except, of course, her cheque book."

"Had she any considerable balance at the bank?"

"I believe she had. Her husband used to send most of his pay home and she used to pay it in and leave it with the bank. She might have two or three hundred pounds to her credit."

As Mrs Beddingfield concluded Mr Wardale was called, and he was followed by Mr Macauley. The evidence of both was quite brief and concerned entirely with the disturbance made by Bergson, whose absence from the court I had already noted.

The last witness was the police superintendent, and he, as I had expected, was decidedly reticent. He did refer to the footprints but, like Foxton – who presumably hid his instructions – he abstained from describing their peculiarities. Nor did he say anything about fingerprints. As to the identity of the criminal, that had to be further inquired into. Suspicion had at first fastened upon Bergson, but it had since transpired that the Swede sailed from Ramsgate on an ice-ship two days before the occurrence of the tragedy. Then suspicion had pointed to the husband, who was known to have landed at Liverpool four days before the death of his wife and who had mysteriously disappeared. But he (the superintendent) had only that morning received a telegram from the Liverpool police informing him that the body of Toussaint had been found floating in the Mersey, and that it bore a number of wounds, of an apparently homicidal character. Apparently he had been murdered and his corpse thrown into the river.

"This is very terrible," said the coroner. "Does this second murder throw any light on the case which we are investigating?"

"I think it does," replied the officer, without any great conviction, however, "but it is not advisable to go into details."

"Quite so," agreed the coroner. "Most inexpedient. But are we to understand that you have a clue to the perpetrator of this crime – assuming, a crime to have been committed?"

"Yes," replied Platt. "We have several important clues."

"And do they point to any particular individual?"

The superintendent hesitated. "Well – " he began, with some embarrassment, but the coroner interrupted him.

"Perhaps the question is indiscreet. We mustn't hamper the police, gentlemen, and the point is not really material to our inquiry. You would rather we waived that question, superintendent?"

"If you please, sir," was the emphatic reply.

"Have any cheques from the deceased woman's cheque-book been presented at the bank?"

"Not since her death. I inquired at the bank only this morning."

This concluded the evidence, and after a brief but capable summing-up by the coroner, the jury returned a verdict of "wilful murder against some person unknown."

As the proceedings terminated, Thorndyke rose and turned round, and then to my surprise I perceived Superintendent Miller, of the Criminal Investigation Department, who had come in unperceived by me and was sitting immediately behind us.

"I have followed your instructions, sir," said he, addressing Thorndyke, "but before we take any definite action I should like to have a few words with you."

He led the way to an adjoining room and, as we entered, we were followed by Superintendent Platt and Dr Foxton.

"Now, doctor," said Miller, carefully closing the door, "I have carried out your suggestions. Mr Macauley is being detained, but before we commit ourselves to an arrest, we must have something to go upon. I shall want you to make out a prima facie case."

"Very well," said Thorndyke, laying upon the table the small, green suitcase that was his almost invariable companion.

"I've seen that prima facie case before," Miller remarked with a grin, as Thorndyke unlocked it and drew out a large envelope. "Now, what have you got there?"

As Thorndyke extracted from the envelope Polton's enlargements of my small photographs, Platt's eyes appeared to bulge, while Foxton gave me a quick glance of reproach.

"These," said Thorndyke, "are the full-sized photographs of the footprints of the suspected murderer. Superintendent Platt can probably verify them."

Rather reluctantly Platt produced from his pocket a pair of whole-plate photographs, which he laid beside the enlargements.

"Yes," said Miller, after comparing them, "they are the same footprints. But you say, doctor, that they are Macauley's footprints. Now, what evidence have you?"

Thorndyke again had recourse to the green case, from which he produced two copper plates mounted on wood and coated with printing ink.

"I propose," said he, lifting the plates out of their protecting frame, "that we take prints of Macauley's feet and compare them with the photographs."

"Yes," said Platt. "And then there are the fingerprints that we've got. We can test those, too."

"You don't want fingerprints if you've got a set of toe-prints," objected Miller.

"With regard to those fingerprints," said Thorndyke. "May I ask if they were obtained from the bottle?"

"They were," Platt admitted.

"And were there any other fingerprints?"

"No," replied Platt. "These were the only ones."

As he spoke he laid on the table a photograph showing the prints of the thumb and fingers of a right hand.

Thorndyke glanced at the photograph and, turning to Miller, said:

"I suggest that those are Dr Foxton's fingerprints."

"Impossible!" exclaimed Platt, and then suddenly fell silent.

"We can soon see," said Thorndyke, producing from the case a pad of white paper. "If Dr Foxton will lay the finger-tips of his right hand first on this inked plate and then on the paper, we can compare the prints with the photograph."

Foxton placed his fingers on the blackened plate and then pressed them on the paper pad, leaving on the latter four beautifully clear, black fingerprints. These Superintendent Platt scrutinised eagerly, and as his glance travelled from the prints to the photographs, he broke into a sheepish grin.

"Sold again!" he muttered. "They are the same prints."

"Well," said Miller in a tone of disgust, "you must have been a mug not to have thought of that when you knew that Dr Foxton had handled the bottle."

"The fact, however, is important," said Thorndyke. "The absence of any fingerprints but Dr Foxton's not only suggests that the murderer took the precaution to wear gloves, but especially it proves that the bottle was not handled by the deceased during life. A suicide's hands will usually be pretty moist and would leave conspicuous, if not very clear, impressions."

"Yes," agreed Miller, "that is quite true. But with regard to these footprints. We can't compel this man to let us examine his feet without arresting him. Don't think, Dr Thorndyke, that I suspect you of guessing. I've known you too long for that. You've got your facts all right, I don't doubt, but you must let us have enough to justify our arrest."

Thorndyke's answer was to plunge once more into the inexhaustible green case, from which he now produced two objects wrapped in tissue paper. The paper being removed, there was revealed what looked like a model of an excessively shabby pair of brown shoes.

"These," said Thorndyke, exhibiting the "models" to Superintendent Miller – who viewed them with an undisguised grin – "are plaster casts of the interiors of a pair of slippers – very old and much too tight – belonging to Mr Macauley. His name was written inside them. The casts have been waxed and painted with raw umber, which has been lightly rubbed off, thus accentuating the prominences and depressions. You will notice that the impressions of the toes on the soles and of the 'knuckles' on the uppers appear as prominences; in fact we have in these casts a sketchy reproduction of the actual feet.

"Now, first as to dimensions. Dr Jervis' measurements of the footprints give us ten inches and three-quarters as the extreme length and four inches and five-eighths as the extreme width at the heads of the metatarsus. On these casts, as you see, the extreme length is ten inches and five-eighths – the loss of one eighth being accounted for by the curve of the sole – and the extreme width is four inches and a quarter – three-eighths being accounted for by the lateral compression of a tight slipper. The agreement of the dimensions is remarkable, considering the unusual size. And now as to the peculiarities of the feet. You notice that each toe has made a perfectly distinct impression on the sole, excepting the little toe; of which there is no trace in either cast. And, turning to the uppers, you notice that the knuckles of the toes appear quite distinct and prominent – again excepting the little toes, which have made no impression at all. Thus it is not a case of retracted little toes, for they would appear as an extra prominence. Then, looking at the feet as a whole, it is evident that the little toes are absent; there is a distinct hollow where there should be a prominence."

"M'yes," said Miller dubiously, "it's all very neat. But isn't it just a bit speculative?"

"Oh, come, Miller," protested Thorndyke; "just consider the facts. Here is a suspected murderer known to have feet of an unusual size and presenting a very rare deformity; and here are a pair of feet of that same unusual size and presenting that same rare deformity; and they are the feet of a man who had actually lived in the same house as the murdered woman and who, at the date of the crime, was living only two doors away. What more would you have?"

"Well, there is the question of motive," objected Miller.

"That hardly belongs to a prima facie case," said Thorndyke. "But even if it did, is there not ample matter for suspicion? Remember who the murdered woman was, what her husband was, and who this Sierra Leone gentleman is."

"Yes, yes; that's true," said Miller somewhat hastily, either perceiving the drift of Thorndyke's argument (which I did not), or being unwilling to admit that he was still in the dark. "Yes, we'll have the fellow in and get his actual footprints."

He went to the door and, putting his head out, made some sign, which was almost immediately followed by a trampling of feet, and Macauley entered the room, followed by two large plain-clothes policemen. The negro was evidently alarmed, for he looked about him with the wild expression of a hunted animal. But his manner was aggressive and truculent.

"Why am I being interfered with in this impertinent manner?" he demanded in the deep, buzzing voice characteristic of the male negro.

"We want to have a look at your feet, Mr Macauley," said Miller. "Will you kindly take off your shoes and socks?"

"No," roared Macauley. "I'll see you damned first."

"Then," said Miller, "I arrest you on charge of having murdered – "

The rest of the sentence was drowned in a sudden uproar. The tall, powerful negro, bellowing like an angry bull, had whipped out a large, strangely shaped knife and charged furiously at the Superintendent. But the two plain-clothes men had been watching him from behind and now sprang upon him, each seizing an arm. Two sharp, metallic clicks in quick succession, a thunderous crash and an earsplitting yell, and the formidable barbarian lay prostrate on the floor with one massive constable sitting astride his chest and the other seated on his knees.

"Now's your chance, doctor," said Miller. "I'll get his shoes and socks off."

As Thorndyke re-inked his plates, Miller and the local superintendent expertly removed the smart patent shoes and the green silk socks from the feet of the writhing, bellowing negro. Then Thorndyke rapidly and skilfully applied the inked plates to the soles of the feet – which I steadied for the purpose – and followed up with a dexterous pressure of the paper pad, first to one foot and then – having torn off the printed sheet – to the other. In spite of the difficulties occasioned by Macauley's struggles, each sheet presented a perfectly clear and sharp print of the sole of the foot, even the ridge-patterns of the toes and ball of the foot being quite distinct. Thorndyke laid each of the new prints on the table beside the corresponding large photograph and invited the two superintendents to compare them.

"Yes," said Miller – and Superintendent Platt nodded his acquiescence – "there can't be a shadow of a doubt. The ink-prints and the photographs are identical, to every line and skin-marking. You've made out your case, doctor, as you always do."

"So you see," said Thorndyke, as we smoked our evening pipes on the old stone pier, "your method was a perfectly sound one, only you didn't apply it properly. Like too many mathematicians, you started on your calculations before you had secured your data. If you had applied the simple laws of probability to the real data, they would have pointed straight to Macauley."

"How do you suppose he lost his little toes?" I asked.

"I don't suppose at all. Obviously it was a case of double ainhum."

"Ainhum!" I exclaimed with a sudden flash of recollection.

"Yes; that was what you overlooked. You compared the probabilities of three diseases either of which only very rarely causes the loss of even one little toe and infinitely rarely causes the loss of both, and none of which conditions is confined to any definite class of persons; and you ignored ainhum, a disease which attacks almost exclusively the little toe, causing it to drop off, and quite commonly destroys both little toes − a disease, moreover, which is confined to the black-skinned races. In European practice ainhum is unknown, but in Africa, and to a less extent, in India, it is quite common. If you were to assemble all the men in the world who have lost both little toes, more than nine-tenths of them would be suffering from ainhum; so that, by the laws of probability, your footprints were, by nine chances to one, those of a man who had suffered from ainhum, and therefore a black-skinned man. But as soon as you had established a black man as the probable criminal, you opened up a new field of corroborative evidence. There was a black man on the spot. That man was a native of Sierra Leone and almost certainly a man of importance there. But the victim's husband had deadly enemies in the native secret societies of Sierra Leone. The letters of the husband to the wife probably contained matter incriminating certain natives of Sierra Leone. The evidence became cumulative, you see. Taken as a whole, it pointed plainly to Macauley, apart from the new fact of the murder of Toussaint in Liverpool, a city with a considerable floating population of West Africans."

"And I gather from your reference to the African poison, strophanthus, that you fixed on Macauley at once when I gave you my sketch of the case?"

"Yes; especially when I saw your photographs of the footprints with the absent little toes and those characteristic chigger-scars on the toes that remained. But it was sheer luck that enabled me to fit the keystone into its place and turn mere probability into virtual certainty. I could have embraced the magician Wardale when he brought us the magic slippers. Still, It isn't an absolute certainty, even now, though I expect it will be by tomorrow."

And Thorndyke was right. That very evening the police entered Macauley's chambers in Tanfield Court, where they discovered the dead woman's attaché case. It still contained Toussaint's letters to his wife, and one of those letters mentioned by name, as members of a dangerous secret society, several prominent Sierra Leone men, including the accused David Macauley.

The Blue Scarab

Medico-legal practice is largely concerned with crimes against the person, the details of which are often sordid, gruesome and unpleasant. Hence the curious and romantic case of the Blue Scarab (though really outside our specialty) came as somewhat of a relief. But to me it is of interest principally as illustrating two of those remarkable gifts which made my friend, Thorndyke, unique as an investigator: his uncanny power of picking out the one essential fact at a glance, and his capacity to produce, when required, inexhaustible stores of unexpected knowledge of the most out-of-the-way subjects.

It was late in the afternoon when Mr James Blowgrave, arrived, by appointment, at our chambers, accompanied by his daughter, a rather strikingly pretty girl of about twenty-two; and when we had mutually introduced ourselves, the consultation began without preamble.

"I didn't give any details in my letter to you," said Mr Blowgrave. "I thought it better not to, for fear you might decline the case. It is really a matter of a robbery, but not quite an ordinary robbery. There are some unusual and rather mysterious features in the case. And as the police hold out very little hope, I have come to ask if you will give me your opinion on the case and perhaps look into it for me. But first I had better tell you how the affair happened.

"The robbery occurred just a fortnight ago, about half-past nine o'clock in the evening. I was sitting in my study with my daughter, looking over some things that I had taken from a small deedbox, when a servant rushed in to tell us that one of the outbuildings was on fire. Now my study opens by a French window on the garden at the back, and, as the outbuilding was in a meadow at the side of the garden, I went out that way, leaving the French window open; but before going I hastily put the things back in the deedbox and locked it.

"The building – which I used partly as a lumber store and partly as a workshop – was well alight and the whole household was already on the spot, the boy working the pump and the two maids carrying the buckets and throwing water on the fire. My daughter and I joined the party and helped to carry the buckets and take out what goods we could reach from the burning building. But it was nearly half an hour before we got the fire completely extinguished, and then my daughter and I went to our rooms to wash and tidy ourselves up. We returned to the study together, and when I had shut the French window my daughter proposed that we should resume our interrupted occupation. Thereupon I took out of my pocket the key of the deedbox and turned to the cabinet on which the box always stood.

"But there was no deedbox there!

"For a moment I thought I must have moved it, and cast my eyes round the room in search of it. But it was nowhere to be seen, and a moment's reflection reminded me that I had left it in its usual place. The only possible conclusion was that during our absence at the fire, somebody must have come in by the window and taken it. And it looked as if that somebody had deliberately set fire to the outbuilding for the express purpose of luring us all out of the house."

"That is what the appearances suggest," Thorndyke agreed. "Is the study window furnished with a blind or curtains?"

"Curtains," replied Mr Blowgrave. "But they were not drawn. Anyone in the garden could have seen into the room; and the garden is easily accessible to an active person who could climb over a low wall."

"So far, then," said Thorndyke, "the robbery might be the work of a casual prowler who had got into the garden and watched you through the window, and assuming that the things you had taken from the box were of value, seized an easy opportunity to make off with them. Were the things of any considerable value?"

"To a thief they were of no value at all. There were a number of share certificates, a lease, one or two agreements, some family photographs and a small box containing an old letter and a scarab. Nothing worth stealing, you see, for the certificates were made out in my name and were therefore unnegotiable."

"And the scarab?"

"That may have been lapis lazuli, but more probably it was a blue glass imitation. In any case it was of no considerable value. It was about an inch and a half long. But before you come to any conclusion, I had better finish the story. The robbery was on Tuesday, the 7th of June. I gave information to the police, with a description of the missing property, but nothing happened until Wednesday, the 15th, when I received a registered parcel bearing the Southampton postmark. On opening it I found, to my astonishment, the entire contents of the deedbox, with the exception of the scarab, and this rather mysterious communication."

He took from his pocket-book and handed to Thorndyke an ordinary envelope addressed in typewritten characters, and sealed with a large, elliptical seal, the face of which was covered with minute hieroglyphics.

"This," said Thorndyke, "I take to be an impression of the scarab; and an excellent impression it is."

"Yes," replied Mr Blowgrave, "I have no doubt that it is the scarab. It is about the same size."

Thorndyke looked quickly at our client with an expression of surprise. "But," he asked, "don't you recognise the hieroglyphics on it?"

Mr Blowgrave smiled deprecatingly. "The fact is," said he, "I don't know anything about hieroglyphics, but I should say, as far as I can judge, these look the same. What do you think, Nellie?"

Miss Blowgrave looked at the seal – rather vaguely – and replied, "I am in the same position. Hieroglyphics are to me just funny looking things that don't mean anything. But these look the same to me as those on our scarab, though I expect any other hieroglyphics would, for that matter."

Thorndyke made no comment on this statement, but examined the seal attentively through his lens. Then he drew out the contents of the envelope, consisting of two letters, one typewritten and the other in a faded brown handwriting. The former he read through and then inspected the paper closely, holding it up to the light to observe the watermark.

"The paper appears to be of Belgian manufacture," he remarked, passing it to me. I confirmed this observation and then read the letter, which was headed "Southampton" and ran thus: –

Dear old Pal,

I am sending you back some trifles removed in error. The ancient document is enclosed with this, but the curio is at present in the custody of my respected uncle. Hope its temporary loss will not inconvenience you, and that I may be able to return it to you later. Meanwhile, believe me,

Your ever affectionate,

Rudolpho.

"Who is Rudolpho?" I asked.

"The Lord knows," replied Mr Blowgrave. "A pseudonym of our absent friend, I presume. He seems to be a facetious sort of person."

"He does," agreed Thorndyke. "This letter and the seal appear to be what the schoolboys would call a leg-pull. But still, this is all quite normal. He has returned you the worthless things and has kept the one thing that has any sort of negotiable value. Are you quite clear that the scarab is not more valuable than you have assumed?"

"Well," said Mr Blowgrave, "I have had an expert opinion on it. I showed it to M. Fouquet, the Egyptologist, when he was over here from Brussels a few months ago, and his opinion was that it was a worthless imitation. Not only was it not a genuine scarab, but the inscription was a sham, too; just a collection of hieroglyphic characters jumbled together without sense or meaning."

"Then," said Thorndyke, taking another look at the seal through his lens, "it would seem that Rudolpho, or Rudolpho's uncle, has got a bad bargain. Which doesn't throw much light on the affair."

At this point Miss Blowgrave intervened. "I think, father," said she, "you have not given Dr Thorndyke quite all the facts about the scarab. He ought to be told about its connection with Uncle Reuben."

As the girl spoke Thorndyke looked at her with a curious expression of suddenly awakened interest. Later I understood the meaning of that look, but at the time there seemed to me nothing particularly arresting in her words.

"It is just a family tradition," Mr Blowgrave said deprecatingly. "Probably it is all nonsense."

"Well, let us have it, at any rate," said Thorndyke. "We may get some light from it."

Thus urged, Mr Blowgrave hemmed a little shyly and began:

"The story concerns my great-grandfather, Silas Blowgrave, and his doings during the war with France. It seems that he commanded a privateer, of which he and his brother Reuben were the joint owners, and that in the course of their last cruise, they acquired a very remarkable and valuable collection of jewels. Goodness knows how they got them; not very honestly, I suspect, for they appear to have been a pair of precious rascals. Something has been said about the loot from a South American church or cathedral, but there is really nothing known about the affair. There are no documents. It is mere oral tradition and very vague and sketchy. The story goes that when they had sold off the ship, they came down to live at Shawstead in Hertfordshire, Silas occupying the manor house – in which I live at present – and Reuben a farmhouse adjoining. The bulk of the loot they shared out at the end of the cruise, but the jewels were kept apart to be dealt with later – perhaps when the circumstances under which they had been acquired had been forgotten. However, both men were inveterate gamblers, and it seems – according to the testimony of a servant of Reuben's who overheard them – that on a certain night when they had been playing heavily, they decided to finish up by playing for the whole collection of jewels as a single stake. Silas, who had the jewels in his custody was seen to go to the manor house and return to Reuben's house carrying a small, iron-bound chest.

"Apparently they played late into the night, after every one else but the servant had gone to bed, and the luck was with Reuben, though it seems probable that he gave luck some assistance. At any rate, when the play was finished and the chest handed over, Silas roundly accused him of cheating, and we may assume that a pretty serious quarrel took place. Exactly what happened is not clear, for when the quarrel began Reuben dismissed the servant, who retired to her bedroom in a distant part of the house. But in the morning it was discovered that Reuben and the chest of jewels had both disappeared, and there were distinct traces of blood in the room in which the two men had been playing. Silas professed to know nothing about the disappearance; but a strong – and probably just – suspicion arose that he had murdered his brother and made away with the jewels. The result was that Silas also disappeared, and for a long time his whereabouts was not known even by his wife. Later it transpired that he had taken up his abode, under an assumed name, in Egypt, and that he had developed an enthusiastic interest in the then new science of Egyptology – the Rosetta Stone had been deciphered only a few years previously. After a time he resumed communication with his wife, but never made any statement as to the mystery of his brother's disappearance. A few months before his death he visited his home in disguise and he then handed to his wife a little sealed packet which was to be delivered to his only son, William, on his attaining the age of twenty-one. That packet contained the scarab and the letter which you have taken from the envelope."

"Am I to read it?" asked Thorndyke.

"Certainly, if you think it worthwhile," was the reply.

Thorndyke opened the yellow sheet of paper and, glancing through the brown and faded writing, read aloud:

Cairo, 4th March, 1833.

My dear Son,

I am sending you, as my last gift, a valuable scarab, and a few words of counsel on which I would bid you meditate. Believe me, there is much wisdom in the lore of Old Egypt. Make it your own. Treasure the scarab as a precious inheritance. Handle it often but show it to none. Give your Uncle Reuben Christian burial. It is your duty, and you will have your reward. He robbed your father, but he shall make restitution.

Farewell!

Your affectionate father,

Silas Blowgrave.

As Thorndyke laid down the letter he looked inquiringly at our client.

"Well," he said, "here are some plain instructions. How have they been carried out?"

"They haven't been carried out at all," replied Mr Blowgrave. "As to his son William, my grandfather, he was not disposed to meddle in the matter. This seemed to be a frank admission that Silas killed his brother and concealed the body, and William didn't choose to reopen the scandal. Besides, the instructions are not so very plain. It is all very well to say 'Give your Uncle Reuben Christian burial,' but where the deuce is Uncle Reuben?"

"It is plainly hinted," said Thorndyke, "that whoever gives the body Christian burial will stand to benefit, and the word 'restitution' seems to suggest a clue to the whereabouts of the jewels. Has no one thought it worth while to find out where the body is deposited?"

"But how could they?" demanded Blowgrave. "He doesn't give the faintest clue. He talks as if his son knew where the body was. And then, you know even supposing Silas did not take the jewels with him, there was the question, whose property were they? To begin with, they were pretty certainly stolen property, though no one knows where they came from. Then Reuben apparently got them from Silas by fraud, and Silas got them back by robbery and murder. If William had discovered them, he would have had to give them up to Reuben's sons, and yet they weren't strictly Reuben's property. No one had an undeniable claim to them, even if they could have found them."

"But that is not the case now," said Miss Blowgrave.

"No," said Mr Blowgrave, in answer to Thorndyke's look of inquiry. "The position is quite clear now. Reuben's grandson, my cousin Arthur, has died recently, and as he had no children, he has dispersed his property. The old farmhouse and the bulk of his estate he has left to a nephew, but he made a small bequest to my daughter and named her as the residuary legatee. So that whatever rights Reuben had to the jewels are now vested in her, and on my death she will be Silas' heir, too. As a matter of fact," Mr Blowgrave continued, "we were discussing this very question on the night of the robbery – I may as well tell you that my girl will be left pretty poorly off when I go, for there is a heavy mortgage on our property and mighty little capital. Uncle Reuben's jewels would have made the old home secure for her if we could have laid our hands on them. However, I mustn't take up your time with our domestic affairs."

"Your domestic affairs are not entirely irrelevant," said Thorndyke. "But what is it that you want me to do in the matter?"

"Well," said Blowgrave, "my house has been robbed and my premises set fire to. The police can apparently do nothing. They say there is no clue at all unless the robbery was committed by somebody in the house which is absurd, seeing that the servants were all engaged in putting out the fire. But I want the robber traced and punished, and I want to get the scarab back. It may be intrinsically valueless, as M. Fouquet said, but Silas' testamentary letter seems to indicate that it had some value. At any rate, it is an heirloom, and I am loath to lose it. It seems a presumptuous thing to ask you to investigate a trumpery robbery, but I should take it as a great kindness if you would look into the matter."

"Cases of robbery pure and simple," replied Thorndyke, "are rather alien to my ordinary practice, but in this one there are certain curious features that seem to make an investigation worth while. Yes, Mr Blowgrave, I will look into the case, and I have some hope that we may be able to lay our hands on the robber, in spite of the apparent absence of clues. I will ask you to leave both these letters for me to examine more minutely, and I shall probably want to make an inspection of the premises – perhaps tomorrow."

"Whenever you like," said Blowgrave. "I am delighted that you are willing to undertake the inquiry. I have heard so much about you from my friend Stalker, of the Griffin Life Assurance Company, for whom you have acted on several occasions."

"Before you go," said Thorndyke, "there is one point that we must clear up. Who is there besides yourselves that knows of the existence of the scarab and this letter and the history attaching to them?"

"I really can't say," replied Blowgrave. "No one has seen them but my cousin Arthur. I once showed them to him, and he may have talked about them in the family. I didn't treat the matter as a secret."

When our visitors had gone we discussed the bearings of the case.

"It is quite a romantic story," said I, "and the robbery has its points of interest, but I am rather inclined to agree with the police – there is mighty little to go on."

"There would have been less," said Thorndyke, "if our sporting friend hadn't been so pleased with himself. That typewritten letter was a piece of gratuitous impudence. Our gentleman overrated his security and crowed too loud."

"I don't see that there is much to be gleaned from the letter, all the same," said I.

"I am sorry to hear you say that, Jervis," he exclaimed, "because I was proposing to hand the letter over to you to examine and report on."

"I was only referring to the superficial appearances," I said hastily. "No doubt a detailed examination will bring something more distinctive into view."

"I have no doubt it will," he said, "and as there are reasons for pushing on the investigation as quickly as possible, I suggest that you get to work at once. I shall occupy myself with the old letter and the envelope."

On this I began my examination without delay, and as a preliminary I proceeded to take a facsimile photograph of the letter by putting it in a large printing-frame with a sensitive plate and a plate of clear glass. The resulting negative showed not only the typewritten lettering, but also the watermark and wire lines of the paper, and a faint grease spot. Next I turned my attention to the lettering itself, and here I soon began to accumulate quite a number of identifiable peculiarities. The machine was apparently a Corona, fitted with the small "Elite" type, and the alignment was markedly defective. The "lower case" – or small – "a" was well below the line, although the capital "A" appeared to be correctly placed; the "u" was slightly above the line, and the small "m" was partly clogged with dirt.

Up to this point I had been careful to manipulate the letter with forceps (although it had been handled by at least three persons, to my knowledge), and I now proceeded to examine it for finger-prints. As I could detect none by mere inspection, I dusted the back of the paper with finely-powdered fuchsin, and distributed the powder by tapping the paper lightly. This brought into view quite a number of fingerprints, especially round the edges of the letter, and though most of them were very faint and shadowy, it was possible to make out the ridge pattern well enough for our purpose. Having blown off the excess of powder, I took the letter to the room where the large copying camera was set up, to photograph it before developing the fingerprints on the front. But here I found our laboratory assistant, Polton, in possession, with the sealed envelope fixed to the copying easel.

"I shan't be a minute, sir," said he. "The doctor wants an enlarged photograph of this seal. I've got the plate in."

I waited while he made his exposure and then proceeded to take the photograph of the letter, or rather of the fingerprints on the back of it. When I had developed the negative I powdered the front of the letter and brought out several more fingerprints – mostly thumbs this time. They were a little difficult to see where they were imposed on the lettering, but, as the latter was bright blue and the fuchsin powder was red, this confusion disappeared in the photograph, in which the lettering was almost invisible while the fingerprints were more distinct than they had appeared to the eye. This completed my examination, and when I had verified the make of typewriter by reference to our album of specimens of typewriting, I left the negatives for Polton to dry and print and went down to the sitting-room to draw up my little report. I had just finished this and was speculating on what had become of Thorndyke, when I heard his quick step on the stair and a few moments later he entered with a roll of paper in his hand. This he unrolled on the table, fixing it open with one or two lead paperweights, and I came round to inspect it, when I found it to be a sheet of the Ordnance map on the scale of twenty-five inches to the mile.

"Here is the Blowgraves' place," said Thorndyke, "nearly in the middle of the sheet. This is his house – Shawstead Manor – and that will probably be the outbuilding that was on fire. I take it that the house marked Dingle Farm is the one that Uncle Reuben occupied."

"Probably," I agreed. "But I don't see why you wanted this map if you are going down to the place itself tomorrow."

"The advantage of a map," said Thorndyke, "is that you can see all over it at once and get the lie of the land well into your mind; and you can measure all distances accurately and quickly with a scale and a pair of dividers. When we go down tomorrow, we shall know our way about as well as Blowgrave himself."

"And what use will that be?" I asked. "Where does the topography come into the case?"

"Well, Jervis," he replied, "there is the robber, for instance; he came from somewhere and he went somewhere. A study of the map may give us a hint as to his movements. But here comes Polton 'with the documents,' as poor Miss Flite would say. What have you got for us, Polton?"

"They aren't quite dry, sir," said Polton, laying four large bromide prints on the table.

"There's the enlargement of the seal – ten by eight, mounted – and three unmounted prints of Dr Jervis'."

Thorndyke looked at my photographs critically. "They're excellent," said he.

"The fingerprints are perfectly legible, though faint. I only hope some of them are the right ones. That is my left thumb. I don't see yours. The small one is presumably Miss Blowgrave's. We must take her fingerprints tomorrow, and her father's too. Then we shall know if we have got any of the robber's." He ran his eye over my report and nodded approvingly. "There is plenty there to enable us to identify the typewriter if we can get hold of it, and the paper is very distinctive. What do you think of the seal?" he added, laying the enlarged photograph before me.

"It is magnificent," I replied, with a grin. "Perfectly monumental."

"What are you grinning at?" he demanded.

"I was thinking that you seem to be counting your chickens in pretty good time," said I. "You are making elaborate preparations to identify the scarab, but you are rather disregarding the classical advice of the prudent Mrs Glasse."

"I have a presentiment that we shall get that scarab," said he. "At any rate we ought to be in a position to identify it instantly and certainly if we are able to get a sight of it."

"We are not likely to," said I. "Still, there is no harm in providing for the improbable."

This was evidently Thorndyke's view, and he certainly made ample provision for this most improbable contingency; for, having furnished himself with a drawing-board and sheet of tracing-paper, he pinned the latter over the photograph on the board and proceeded, with a fine pen and hectograph ink, to make a careful and minute tracing of the intricate and bewildering hieroglyphic inscription on the seal. When he had finished it he transferred it to a clay duplicator and took off half a dozen copies, one of which he handed to me. I looked at it dubiously and remarked: "You have said that the medical jurist must make all knowledge his province. Has he got to be an Egyptologist, too?"

"He will be the better medical jurist if he is," was the reply, of which I made a mental note for my future guidance. But meanwhile Thorndyke's proceedings were, to me, perfectly incomprehensible. What was his object in making this minute tracing? The seal itself was sufficient for identification. I lingered awhile hoping that some fresh development might throw a light on the mystery But his next proceeding was like to have reduced me to stupefaction. I saw him go to the bookshelves and take down a book. As he laid it on the table I glanced at the title, and when I saw that it was Raper's *Navigation Tables* I stole softly out into the lobby, put on my hat and went for a walk.

When I returned the investigation was apparently concluded, for Thorndyke was seated in his easy chair, placidly reading *The Compleat Angler*. On the table lay a large circular protractor, a straight-edge, an architect's scale and a sheet of tracing paper on which was a tracing in hectograph ink of Shawstead Manor.

"Why did you make this tracing?" I asked. "Why not take the map itself?"

"We don't want the whole of it," he replied, "and I dislike cutting up maps."

By taking an informal lunch in the train, we arrived at Shawstead Manor by half-past two. Our approach up the drive had evidently been observed, for Blowgrave and his daughter were waiting at the porch to receive us. The former came forward with outstretched hand, but a distinctly woebegone expression, and exclaimed: "It is most kind of you to come down; but alas! you are too late."

"Too late for what?" demanded Thorndyke.

"I will show you," replied Blowgrave, and seizing my colleague by the arm, he strode off excitedly to a little wicket at the side of the house, and, passing through it, hurried along a narrow alley that skirted the garden wall and ended in a large meadow, at one end of which stood a dilapidated windmill. Across this meadow he bustled, dragging my colleague with him, until he reached a heap of freshly-turned earth, where he halted and pointed tragically to a spot where the turf had evidently been raised and untidily replaced.

"There!" he exclaimed, stooping to pull up the loose turfs and thereby exposing what was evidently a large hole, recently and hastily filled in. "That was done last night or early this morning, for I walked over this meadow only yesterday evening and there was no sign of disturbed ground then."

Thorndyke stood looking down at the hole with a faint smile. "And what do you infer from that?" he asked.

"Infer!" shrieked Blowgrave. "Why, I infer that whoever dug this hole was searching for Uncle Reuben and the lost jewels!"

"I am inclined to agree with you," Thorndyke said calmly. "He happened to search in the wrong place, but that is his affair."

"The wrong place!" Blowgrave and his daughter exclaimed in unison. "How do you know it is the wrong place?"

"Because," replied Thorndyke, "I believe I know the right place, and this is not it. But we can put the matter to the test, and we had better do so. Can you get a couple of men with picks and shovels? Or shall we handle the tools ourselves?"

"I think that would be better," said Blowgrave, who was quivering with excitement. "We don't want to take anyone into our confidence if we can help it."

"No," Thorndyke agreed. "Then I suggest that you fetch the tools while I locate the spot."

Blowgrave assented eagerly and went off at a brisk trot, while the young lady remained with us and watched Thorndyke with intense curiosity.

"I mustn't interrupt you with questions," said she, "but I can't imagine how you found out where Uncle Reuben was buried."

"We will go into that later," he replied; "but first we have got to find Uncle Reuben." He laid his research-case down on the ground, and opening it, took out three sheets of paper, each bearing a duplicate of his tracing of the map; and on each was marked a spot on this meadow from which a number of lines radiated like the spokes of a wheel.

"You see, Jervis," he said, exhibiting them to me, "the advantage of a map. I have been able to rule off these sets of bearings regardless of obstructions, such as those young trees, which have arisen since Silas' day, and mark the spot in its correct place. If the recent obstructions prevent us from taking the bearings we can still find the spot by measurements with the land-chain or tape."

"Why have you got three plans?" I asked.

"Because there are three imaginable places. No. 1 is the most likely; No. 2, less likely, but possible; No. 3 is impossible. That is the one that our friend tried last night. No. 1 is among those young trees, and we will now see if we can pick up the bearings in spite of them."

We moved on to the clump of young trees, where Thorndyke took from the research-case a tall, folding camera tripod and a large prismatic compass with an aluminium dial. With the latter he took one or two trial bearings and then, setting up the tripod, fixed the compass on it. For some minutes Miss Blowgrave and I watched him as he shifted the tripod from spot to spot, peering through the sight-vane of the compass and glancing occasionally at the map. At length he turned to us and said:

"We are in luck. None of these trees interferes with our bearings." He took from the research-case a surveyor's arrow, and sticking it in the ground under the tripod, added: "That is the spot. But we may have to dig a good way round it, for a compass is only a rough instrument."

At this moment Mr Blowgrave staggered up, breathing hard, and flung down on the ground three picks, two shovels and a spade. "I won't hinder you, doctor, by asking for explanations," said he, "but I am utterly mystified. You must tell us what it all means when we have finished our work."

This Thorndyke promised to do, but meanwhile he took off his coat, and rolling up his shirt sleeves, seized the spade and began cutting out a large square of turf. As the soil was uncovered, Blowgrave and I attacked it with picks and Miss Blowgrave shovelled away the loose earth.

"Do you know how far down we have to go?" I asked.

"The body lies six feet below the surface," Thorndyke replied; and as he spoke he laid down his spade, and taking a telescope from the research-case, swept it round the margin of the meadow and finally pointed it at a farmhouse some six hundred yards distant, of which he made a somewhat prolonged inspection, after which he took the remaining pick and fell to work on the opposite corner of the exposed square of earth.

For nearly half an hour we worked on steadily, gradually eating our way downwards, plying pick and shovel alternately, while Miss Blowgrave cleared the loose earth away from the edges of the deepening pit. Then a halt was called and we came to the surface, wiping our faces.

"I think, Nellie," said Blowgrave, divesting himself of his waistcoat, "a jug of lemonade and four tumblers would be useful, unless our visitors would prefer beer."

We both gave our votes for lemonade, and Miss Nellie tripped away towards the house, while Thorndyke, taking up his telescope, once more inspected the farmhouse.

"You seem greatly interested in that house," I remarked.

"I am," he replied, handing me the telescope. "Just take a look at the window in the right hand gable, but keep under the tree."

I pointed the telescope at the gable and there observed an open window at which a man was seated. He held a binocular glass to his eyes and the instrument appeared to be directed at us.

"We are being spied on, I fancy," said I, passing the telescope to Blowgrave, "but I suppose it doesn't matter. This is your land, isn't it?"

"Yes," replied Blowgrave, "but still, we didn't want any spectators. That is Harold Bowker," he added, steadying the telescope against a tree, "my cousin Arthur's nephew, whom I told you about as having inherited the farmhouse. He seems mighty interested in us; but small things interest one in the country."

Here the appearance of Miss Nellie, advancing across the meadow with an inviting looking basket, diverted our attention from our inquisitive watcher. Six thirsty eyes were riveted on that basket until it drew near and presently disgorged a great glass jug and four tumblers, when we each took off a long and delicious draught and then jumped down into the pit to resume our labours.

Another half-hour passed. We had excavated in some places to nearly the full depth and were just discussing the advisability of another short rest when Blowgrave, who was working in one corner, uttered a loud cry and stood up suddenly, holding something in his fingers. A glance at the object showed it to be a bone, brown and earth-stained, but evidently a bone. Evidently too, a human bone, as Thorndyke decided when Blowgrave handed it to him triumphantly.

"We have been very fortunate," said he, "to get so near at the first trial. This is from the right great toe, so we may assume that the skeleton lies just outside this pit, but we had better excavate carefully in your corner and see exactly how the bones lie." This he proceeded to do himself, probing cautiously with the spade and clearing the earth away from the corner. Very soon the remaining bones of the right foot came into view and then the ends of the two leg-bones and a portion of the left foot.

"We can see now," said he, "how the skeleton lies, and all we have to do is to extend the excavation in that direction. But there is only room for one to work down here. I think you and Mr Blowgrave had better dig down from the surface."

On this, I climbed out of the pit, followed reluctantly by Blowgrave, who still held the little brown bone in his hand and was in a state of wild excitement and exultation that somewhat scandalised his daughter.

"It seems rather ghoulish," she remarked, "to be gloating over poor Uncle Reuben's body in this way."

"I know," said Blowgrave, "it isn't reverent. But I didn't kill Uncle Reuben, you know, whereas – well it was a long time ago." With this rather inconsequent conclusion he took a draught of lemonade, seized his pick and fell to work with a will. I, too, indulged in a draught and passed a full tumbler down to Thorndyke. But before resuming my labours I picked up the telescope and once more inspected the farmhouse. The window was still open, but the watcher had apparently become bored with the not very thrilling spectacle. At any rate he had disappeared.

From this time onward every few minutes brought some discovery. First, a pair of deeply rusted steel shoe buckles; then one or two buttons, and presently a fine gold watch with a fob-chain and a bunch of seals, looking uncannily new and fresh and seeming more fraught with tragedy than even the bones themselves. In his cautious digging, Thorndyke was careful not to disturb the skeleton; and looking down into the narrow trench that was growing from the corner of the pit, I could see both legs, with only the right foot missing, projecting from the miniature cliff. Meanwhile our part of the trench was deepening rapidly, so that Thorndyke presently warned us to stop digging and bade us come down and shovel away the earth as he disengaged it.

At length the whole skeleton, excepting the head, was uncovered, though it lay undisturbed as it might have lain in its coffin. And now, as Thorndyke picked away the earth around the head, we could see that the skull was propped forward as if it rested on a high pillow. A little more careful probing with the pick-point served to explain this appearance. For as the earth fell away and disclosed the grinning skull, there came into view the edge and ironbound corners of a small chest.

It was an impressive spectacle; weird, solemn and rather dreadful. There for over a century the ill-fated gambler had lain, his mouldering head pillowed on the booty of unrecorded villainy, booty that had been won by fraud, retrieved by violence, and hidden at last by the final winner with the witness of his crime.

"Here is a fine text for a moralist who would preach on the vanity of riches," said Thorndyke.

We all stood silent for a while, gazing, not without awe, at the stark figure that lay guarding the ill-gotten treasure. Miss Blowgrave – who had been helped down when we descended – crept closer to her father and murmured that it was "rather awful"; while Blowgrave himself displayed a queer mixture of exultation and shuddering distaste.

Suddenly the silence was broken by a voice from above, and we all looked up with a start. A youngish man was standing on the brink of the pit, looking down on us with very evident disapproval.

"It seems that I have come just in the nick of time," observed the newcomer. "I shall have to take possession of that chest, you know, and of the remains, too, I suppose. That is my ancestor, Reuben Blowgrave."

"Well, Harold," said Blowgrave, "you can have Uncle Reuben if you want him. But the chest belongs to Nellie."

Here Mr Harold Bowker – I recognised him now as the watcher from the window – dropped down into the pit and advanced with something of a swagger.

"I am Reuben's heir," said he, "through my Uncle Arthur, and I take possession of this property and the remains."

"Pardon me, Harold," said Blowgrave, "but Nellie is Arthur's residuary legatee, and this is the residue of the estate."

"Rubbish!" exclaimed Bowker. "By the way, how did you find out where he was buried?"

"Oh, that was quite simple," replied Thorndyke with unexpected geniality. "I'll show you the plan." He climbed up to the surface and returned in a few moments with the three tracings and his letter-case. "This is how we located the spot." He handed the plan numbered 3 to Bowker, who took it from him and stood looking at it with a puzzled frown.

"But this isn't the place," he said at length.

"Isn't it?" queried Thorndyke. "No, of course; I've given you the wrong one. This is the plan." He handed Bowker the plan marked No. 1, and took the other from him, laying it down on a heap of earth. Then, as Bowker pored gloomily over No. 1, he took a knife and a pencil from his pocket, and with his back to our visitor, scraped the lead of the pencil, letting the black powder fall on the plan that he had just laid down. I watched him with some curiosity; and when I observed that the black scrapings fell on two spots near the edges of the paper, a sudden suspicion flashed into my mind, which was confirmed when I saw him tap the paper lightly with his pencil, gently blow away the powder, and quickly producing my photograph of the typewritten letter from his case, hold it for a moment beside the plan.

"This is all very well," said Bowker, looking up from the plan, "but how did you find out about these bearings?"

Thorndyke swiftly replaced the letter in his case, and turning round, replied, "I am afraid I can't give you any further information."

"Can't you, indeed!" Bowker exclaimed insolently. "Perhaps I shall compel you to. But, at any rate, I forbid any of you to lay hands on my property."

Thorndyke looked at him steadily and said in an ominously quiet tone:

"Now listen to me, Mr Bowker. Let, us have an end of this nonsense. You have played a risky game and you have lost. How much you have lost I can't say until I know whether Mr Blowgrave intends to prosecute."

"To prosecute!" shouted Bowker. "What the deuce do you mean by prosecute?"

"I mean," said Thorndyke, "that on the 7th of June, after nine o'clock at night, you entered the dwelling-house of Mr Blowgrave and stole and carried away certain of his goods and chattels. A part of them you have restored, but you are still in possession of some of the stolen property, to wit a scarab and a deedbox."

As Thorndyke made this statement in his calm, level tones, Bowker's face blanched to a tallowy white, and he stood staring at my colleague, the very picture of astonishment and dismay. But he fired a last shot.

"This is sheer midsummer madness," he exclaimed huskily; "and you know it."

Thorndyke turned to our host. "It is for you to settle, Mr Blowgrave," said he. "I hold conclusive evidence that Mr Bowker stole your deedbox. If you decide to prosecute, I shall produce that evidence in court and he will certainly be convicted."

Blowgrave and his daughter looked at the accused man with an embarrassment almost equal to his own.

"I am astounded," the former said at length; "but I don't want to be vindictive. Look here, Harold, hand over the scarab and we'll say no more about it."

"You can't do that," said Thorndyke. "The law doesn't allow you to compound a robbery. He can return the property if he pleases and you can do as you think best about prosecuting. But you can't make conditions."

There was silence for some seconds; then, without another word, the crestfallen adventurer turned, and scrambling up out of the pit, took a hasty departure.

It was nearly a couple of hours later that, after a leisurely wash and a hasty, nondescript meal, we carried the little chest from the dining-room to the study. Here, when he had closed the French window and drawn the curtains, Mr Blowgrave produced a set of tools and we fell to work on the iron fastenings of the chest. It was no light task, though a century's rust had thinned the stout bands, but at length the lid yielded to the thrust of a long case-opener and rose with a protesting creak. The chest was lined with a double thickness of canvas, apparently part of a sail, and contained a number of small leather bags, which, as we lifted them out, one by one, felt as if they were filled with pebbles. But when we untied the thongs of one and emptied its contents into a wooden bowl, Blowgrave heaved a sigh of ecstasy and Miss Nellie uttered a little scream of delight. They were all cut stones, and most of them of exceptional size; rubies, emeralds, sapphires, and a few diamonds. As to their value, we could form but the vaguest guess; but Thorndyke, who was a fair judge of gemstones, gave it as his opinion that they were fine specimens of their kind, though roughly cut, and that they had probably formed the enrichment of some shrine.

"The question is," said Blowgrave, gazing gloatingly on the bowl of sparkling gems, "what are we to do with them?"

"I suggest," said Thorndyke, "that Dr Jervis stays here tonight to help you to guard them and that in the morning you take them up to London and deposit them at your bank."

Blowgrave fell in eagerly with this suggestion, which I seconded. "But," said he, "that chest is a queer-looking package to be carrying abroad. Now, if we only had that confounded deed-box – "

"There's a deedbox on the cabinet behind you," said Thorndyke.

58

Blowgrave turned round sharply. "God bless us!" he exclaimed. "It has come back the way it went. Harold must have slipped in at the window while we were at tea. Well, I'm glad he has made restitution. When I look at that bowl and think what he must have narrowly missed, I don't feel inclined to be hard on him. I suppose the scarab is inside – not that it matters much now."

The scarab was inside in an envelope; and as Thorndyke turned it over in his hand and examined the hieroglyphics on it through his lens, Miss Blowgrave asked: "Is it of any value, Dr Thorndyke? It can't have any connection with the secret of the hiding place, because you found the jewels without it."

"By the way, doctor, I don't know whether it is permissible for me to ask, but how on earth *did* you find out where the jewels were hidden? To me it looks like black magic."

Thorndyke laughed in a quiet, inward fashion.

"There is nothing magical about it," said he. "It was a perfectly simple, straightforward problem. But Miss Nellie is wrong. We had the scarab; that is to say we had the wax impression of it, which is the same thing. And the scarab was the key to the riddle. You see," he continued, "Silas' letter and the scarab formed together a sort of intelligence test."

"Did they?" said Blowgrave. "Then he drew a blank every time."

Thorndyke chuckled. "His descendants were certainly a little lacking in enterprise," he admitted. "Silas' instructions were perfectly plain and explicit. Whoever would find the treasure must first acquire some knowledge of Egyptian lore and must study the scarab attentively. It was the broadest of hints, but no one – excepting Harold Bowker, who must have heard about the scarab from his Uncle Arthur – seems to have paid any attention to it.

Now it happens that I have just enough elementary knowledge of the hieroglyphic characters to enable me to spell them out when they are used alphabetically; and as soon as I saw the seal, I could see that these hieroglyphics formed English words. My attention was first attracted by the second group of signs, which spelled the word 'Reuben,' and then I saw that the first group spelled 'Uncle.' Of course, the instant I heard Miss Nellie speak of the connection between the scarab and Uncle Reuben, the murder was out. I saw at a glance that the scarab contained all the required information. Last night I made a careful tracing of the hieroglyphics and then rendered them into our own alphabet. This is the result."

He took from his letter-case and spread out on the table a duplicate of the tracing which I had seen him make, and of which he had given me a copy. But since I had last seen it, it had received an addition; under each group of signs the equivalents in modern Roman lettering had been written, and these made the following words:

"UNKL RUBN IS IN TH MILL FIELD SKS FT DOWN CHURCH SPIR NORTH TEN THIRTY EAST DINGL SOUTH GABL NORTH ATY FORTY-FIF WEST GOD SAF KING JORJ."

Our two friends gazed at Thorndyke's transliteration in blank astonishment. At length Blowgrave remarked: "But this translation must have demanded a very profound knowledge of the Egyptian writing."

"Not at all," replied Thorndyke. "Any intelligent person could master the Egyptian alphabet in an hour. The language, of course, is quite another matter. The spelling of this is a little crude, but it is quite intelligible and does Silas great credit, considering how little was known in his time."

"How do you suppose M. Fouquet came to overlook this?" Blowgrave asked.

"Naturally enough," was the reply. "He was looking for an Egyptian inscription. But this is not an Egyptian inscriptions. Does he speak English?"

"Very little. Practically not at all."

"Then, as the words are English words and imperfectly spelt, the hieroglyphics must have appeared to him mere nonsense. And he was right as to the scarab being an imitation."

"There is another point," said Blowgrave. "How was it that Harold made that extraordinary mistake about the place? The directions are clear enough. All you had to do was to go out there with a compass and take the bearings just as they were given."

"But," said Thorndyke, "that is exactly what he did, and hence the mistake. He was apparently unaware of the phenomenon known as the Secular Variation of the Compass. As you know, the compass does not – usually – point to true north, but to the Magnetic North; and the Magnetic North is continually changing its position. When Reuben was buried – about 1810 – it was twenty-four degrees, twenty-six minutes west of true north; at the present time it is fourteen degrees, forty-eight minutes west of true north. So Harold's bearings would be no less than ten degrees out, which, of course, gave him a totally wrong position. But Silas was a shipmaster, a navigator, and of course, knew all about the vagaries of the compass; and, as his directions were intended for use at some date unknown to him, I assumed that the bearings that he gave were true bearings – that when he said 'north' he meant true north, which is always the same; and this turned out to be the case. But I also prepared a plan with magnetic bearings corrected up to date. Here are the three plans: No. 1 – the one we used – showing true bearings; No. 2, showing corrected magnetic bearings which might have given us the correct spot; and No. 3, with uncorrected magnetic bearings, giving us the spot where Harold dug, and which could not possibly have been the right spot."

On the following morning I escorted the deedbox, filled with the booty and tied up and sealed with the scarab, to Mr Blowgrave's bank. And that ended our connection with the case; excepting that, a month or two later, we attended by request the unveiling in Shawstead churchyard of a fine monument to Reuben Blowgrave. This took the slightly inappropriate form of an obelisk, on which were cut the name and approximate dates, with the added inscription: "Cast thy bread upon the waters and it shall return after many days"; concerning which Thorndyke remarked dryly that he supposed the exhortation applied equally even if the bread happened to belong to someone else.

The New Jersey Sphinx

"A rather curious neighbourhood this, Jervis," my friend Thorndyke remarked as we turned into Upper Bedford Place; "a sort of temporary aviary for cosmopolitan birds of passage, especially those of the Oriental variety. The Asiatic and African faces that one sees at the windows of these Bloomsbury boarding houses almost suggest an overflow from the ethnographical galleries of the adjacent British Museum."

"Yes," I agreed, "there must be quite a considerable population of Africans, Japanese and Hindus in Bloomsbury; particularly Hindus."

As I spoke, and as if in illustration of my statement, a dark-skinned man rushed out of one of the houses farther down the street and began to advance towards us in a rapid, bewildered fashion, stopping to look at each street door as he came to it. His hatless condition – though he was exceedingly well dressed – and his agitated manner immediately attracted my attention, and Thorndyke's too, for the latter remarked, "Our friend seems to be in trouble. An accident, perhaps, or a case of sudden illness."

Here the stranger, observing our approach, ran forward to meet us and asked in an agitated tone, "Can you tell me, please, where I can find a doctor?"

"I am a medical man," replied Thorndyke, "and so is my friend."

Our acquaintance grasped Thorndyke's sleeve and exclaimed eagerly:

"Come with me, then, quickly if you please. A most dreadful thing has happened."

He hurried us along at something between a trot and a quick walk, and as we proceeded he continued excitedly, "I am quite confused and terrified; it is all so strange and sudden and terrible."

"Try," said Thorndyke, "to calm yourself a little and tell us what has happened."

"I will," was the agitated reply. "It is my cousin, Dinanath Byramji – his surname is the same as mine. Just now I went to his room and was horrified to find him lying on the floor, staring at the ceiling and blowing like this," and he puffed out his cheeks with a soft blowing noise. "I spoke to him and shook his hand, but he was like a dead man. This is the house." He darted up the steps to an open door at which a rather scared page-boy was on guard, and running along the hall, rapidly ascended the stairs. Following him closely, we reached a rather dark first-floor landing where, at a half-open door, a servant-maid stood listening with an expression of awe to a rhythmical snoring sound that issued from the room.

The unconscious man lay as Mr Byramji had said, staring fixedly at the ceiling with wide-open, glazy eyes, puffing out his cheeks slightly at each breath. But the breathing was shallow and slow, and it grew perceptibly slower, with lengthening pauses. And even as I was timing it with my watch while Thorndyke examined the pupils with the aid of a wax match, it stopped. I laid my finger on the wrist and caught one or two slow, flickering beats. Then the pulse stopped too.

"He is gone," said I. "He must have burst one of the large arteries."

"Apparently," said Thorndyke, "though one would not have expected it at his age. But wait! What is this?"

He pointed to the right ear, in the hollow of which a few drops of blood had collected, and as he spoke he drew his hand gently over the dead man's head and moved it slightly from side to side.

"There is a fracture of the base of the skull," said he, "and quite distinct signs of contusion of the scalp." He turned to Mr Byramji, who stood wringing his hands and gazing incredulously at the dead man, and asked:

"Can you throw any light on this?"

The Indian looked at him vacantly. The sudden tragedy seemed to have paralysed his brain. "I don't understand," said he. "What does it mean?"

"It means," replied Thorndyke, "that he has received a heavy blow on the head."

For a few moments Mr Byramji continued to stare vacantly at my colleague. Then he seemed suddenly to realise the import of Thorndyke's reply, for he started up excitedly and turned to the door, outside which the two servants were hovering.

"Where is the person gone who came in with my cousin?" he demanded.

"You saw him go out, Albert," said the maid. "Tell Mr Byramji where he went to."

The page tiptoed into the room with a fearful eye fixed on the corpse, and replied falteringly. "I only see the back of him as he went out, and all I know is that he turned to the left. P'raps he's gone for a doctor."

"Can you give us any description of him?" asked Thorndyke.

"I only see the back of him," repeated the page. "He was a shortish gentleman and he had on a dark suit of clothes and a soft felt hat. That's all I know."

"Thank you," said Thorndyke. "We may want to ask you some more questions presently," and having conducted the page to the door, he shut it and turned to Mr Byramji.

"Have you any idea who it was that was with your cousin?" he asked.

"None at all," was the reply. "I was sitting in my room opposite, writing, when I heard my cousin come up the stairs with another person, to whom he was talking. I could not hear what he was saying. They went into his room – this room – and I could occasionally catch the sound of their voices. In about a quarter of an hour I heard the door open and shut, and then someone went downstairs, softly and rather quickly. I finished the letter that I was writing, and when I had addressed it I came in here to ask my cousin who the visitor was. I thought it might be someone who had come to negotiate for the ruby."

"The ruby!" exclaimed Thorndyke. "What ruby do you refer to?"

"The great ruby," replied Byramji. "But of course you have not – " He broke off suddenly and stood for a few moments staring at Thorndyke with parted lips and wide-open eyes; then abruptly he turned, and kneeling beside the dead man he began, in a curious, caressing, half-apologetic manner, first to pass his hand gently over the body at the waist and then to unfasten the clothes. This brought into view a handsome, soft leather belt, evidently of native workmanship, worn next to the skin and furnished with three pockets. Mr Byramji unbuttoned and explored them in quick succession, and it was evident that they were all empty.

"It is gone!" he exclaimed in low, intense tones. "Gone! Ah! But how little would it signify! But thou, dear Dinanath, my brother, my friend, thou art gone, too!"

He lifted the dead man's hand and pressed it to his cheek, murmuring endearments in his own tongue. Presently he laid it down reverently, and sprang up, and I was startled at the change in his aspect. The delicate, gentle, refined face had suddenly become the face of a Fury – fierce, sinister, vindictive.

"This wretch must die!" he exclaimed huskily. "This sordid brute who without compunction, has crushed out a precious life as one would carelessly crush a fly for the sake of a paltry crystal – he must die, if I have to follow him and strangle him with my own hands!"

Thorndyke laid his hand on Byramji's shoulder. "I sympathise with you most cordially," said he, "if it is as you think, and, appearances suggest, that your cousin has been murdered as a mere incident of robbery, the murderer's life is forfeit, and Justice cries aloud for retribution. The fact of murder will be determined, for or against, by a proper inquiry. Meanwhile we have to ascertain

THE NEW JERSEY SPHINX

who this unknown man is and what happened while he was with your cousin."

Byramji made a gesture of despair. "But the man has disappeared, and nobody has seen him! What can we do?"

"Let us look around us," replied Thorndyke, "and see if we can judge what has happened in this room. What, for instance, is this?"

He picked up from a corner near the door a small leather object, which he handed to Mr Byramji. The Indian seized it eagerly, exclaiming:

"Ah! It is the little bag in which my cousin used to carry the ruby. So he had taken it from his belt."

"It hasn't been dropped, by any chance?" I suggested.

In an instant Mr Byramji was down on his knees, peering and groping about the floor, and Thorndyke and I joined in the search. But, as might have been expected, there was no sign of the ruby, nor, indeed, of anything else – excepting a hat which I picked up from under the table.

"No," said Mr Byramji, rising with a dejected air. "It is gone – of course it is gone, and the murderous villain – "

Here his glance fell on the hat, which I had laid on the table, and he bent forward to look at it.

"Whose hat is this?" he demanded, glancing at the chair on which Thorndyke's hat and mine had been placed.

"Is it not your cousin's?" asked Thorndyke.

"No, certainly not. His hat was like mine – we bought them both together. It had a white silk lining with his initials, D.B., in gold. This has no lining and is a much older hat. It must be the murderer's hat."

"If it is," said Thorndyke, "that is a most important fact – important in two respects. Could you let us see your hat?"

"Certainly," replied Byramji, walking quickly, but with a soft tread to the door. As he went out, shutting the door silently behind him, Thorndyke picked up the derelict hat and swiftly tried it on the head of the dead man. As far as I could judge, it appeared to fit, and this Thorndyke confirmed as he replaced it on the table.

67

"As you see," said he, "it is at least a practicable fit, which is a fact of some significance."

Here Mr Byramji returned with his own hat, which he placed on the table by the side of the other, and thus placed, crown uppermost, the two hats were closely similar. Both were black, hard felts of the prevalent "bowler" shape, and of good quality, and the difference in their age and state of preservation was not striking; but when Byramji turned them over and exhibited their interiors it was seen that whereas the strange hat was unlined save for the leather headband, Byramji's had a white silk lining and bore the owner's initials in embossed gilt letters.

"What happened," said Thorndyke, when he had carefully compared the two hats, "seems fairly obvious. The two men, on entering, placed their hats crown upwards on the table. In some way – perhaps during a struggle – the visitor's hat was knocked down and rolled under the table. Then the stranger, on leaving, picked up the only visible hat almost identically similar to his own – and put it on."

"Is it not rather singular," I asked, "that he should not have noticed the different feel of a strange hat?"

"I think not," Thorndyke replied. "If he noticed anything unusual he would probably assume that he had put it on the wrong way round. Remember that he would be extremely hurried and agitated. And once he had left the house he would not dare to take the risk of returning, though he would doubtless realise the gravity of the mistake. And now," he continued, "would you mind giving us a few particulars? You have spoken of a great ruby, which your cousin had, and which seems to be missing."

"Yes. You shall come to my room and I will tell you about it; but first let us lay my poor cousin decently on his bed."

"I think," said Thorndyke, "the body ought not to be moved until the police have seen it."

"Perhaps you are right," Byramji agreed reluctantly, "though it seems callous to leave him lying there." With a sigh he turned to the door, and Thorndyke followed, carrying the two hats.

"My cousin and I," said our host, when we were seated in his own large bed-sitting room, "were both interested in gemstones. I deal in all kinds of stones that are found in the East, but Dinanath dealt almost exclusively in rubies. He was a very fine judge of those beautiful gems, and he used to make periodical tours in Burma in search of uncut rubies of unusual size or quality. About four months ago he acquired at Mogok, in Upper Burma, a magnificent specimen over twenty-eight carats in weight, perfectly flawless and of the most gorgeous colour. It had been roughly cut, but my cousin was intending to have it recut unless he should receive an advantageous offer for it in the meantime."

"What would be the value of such a stone?" I asked.

"It is impossible to say. A really fine large ruby of perfect colour is far, far more valuable than the finest diamond of the same size. It is the most precious of all gems, with the possible exception of the emerald. A fine ruby of five carats is worth about three thousand pounds, but of course, the value rises out of all proportion with increasing size. Fifty thousand pounds would be a moderate price for Dinanath's ruby."

During this recital I noticed that Thorndyke, while listening attentively, was turning the stranger's hat over in his hands, narrowly scrutinising it both inside and outside. As Byramji concluded, he remarked:

"We shall have to let the police know what has happened, but, as my friend and I will be called as witnesses, I should like to examine this hat a little more closely before you hand it over to them. Could you let me have a small, hard brush? A dry nail-brush would do."

Our host complied readily – in fact eagerly. Thorndyke's authoritative, purposeful manner had clearly impressed him, for he said as he handed my colleague a new nail-brush: "I thank you for your help and value it. We must not depend on the police only."

Accustomed as I was to Thorndyke's methods, his procedure was not unexpected, but Mr Byramji watched him with breathless interest and no little surprise as, laying a sheet of notepaper on the table, he brought the hat close to it and brushed firmly but slowly, so that the dust dislodged should fall on it. As it was not a very well-kept hat, the yield was considerable, especially when the brush was drawn under the curl of the brim, and very soon the paper held quite a little heap. Then Thorndyke folded the paper into a small packet and having written "outside" on it, put it in his pocketbook.

"Why do you do that?" Mr Byramji asked. "What will the dust tell you?"

"Probably nothing," Thorndyke replied. "But this hat is our only direct clue to the identity of the man who was with your cousin, and we must make the most of it. Dust, you know, is only a mass of fragments detached from surrounding objects. If the objects are unusual, the dust may be quite distinctive. You could easily identify the hat of a miller or a cement worker." As he was speaking he reversed the hat and turned down the leather head-lining, whereupon a number of strips of folded paper fell down into the crown.

"Ah!" exclaimed Byramji, "perhaps we shall learn something now."

He picked out the folded slips and began eagerly to open them out, and we examined them systematically, one by one. But they were singularly disappointing and uninforming. Mostly they consisted of strips of newspaper, with one or two circulars, a leaf from a price list of gas stoves, a portion of a large envelope on which were the remains of an address which read " – n – don, W.C.," and a piece of paper, evidently cut down vertically and bearing the right-hand half of some kind of list. This read:

> " – el 3 oz. 5 dwts.
> – eep 9 $1/2$ oz."

"Can you make anything of this?" I asked, handing the paper to Thorndyke.

He looked at it reflectively, and answered, as he copied it into his notebook: "It has, at least, some character. If we consider it with the other data, we should get some sort of hint from it. But these scraps of paper don't tell us much. Perhaps their most suggestive feature is their quantity and the way in which, as you have no doubt noticed, they were arranged at the sides of the hat. We had better replace them as we found them for the benefit of the police."

The nature of the suggestion to which he referred was not very obvious to me, but the presence of Mr Byramji rendered discussion inadvisable; nor was there any opportunity, for we had hardly reconstituted the hat when we became aware of a number of persons ascending the stairs, and then we heard the sound of rather peremptory rapping at the door of the dead man's room.

Mr Byramji opened the door and went out on to the landing, where several persons had collected, including the two servants and a constable.

"I understand," said the policeman, "that there is something wrong here. Is that so?"

"A very terrible thing has happened," replied Byramji. "But the doctors can tell you better than I can." Here he looked appealingly at Thorndyke, and we both went out and joined him.

"A gentleman – Mr Dinanath Byramji – has met with his death under somewhat suspicious circumstances," said Thorndyke, and, glancing at the knot of naturally curious persons on the landing, he continued: "If you will come into the room where the death occurred, I will give you the facts so far as they are known to us."

With this he opened the door and entered the room with Mr Byramji, the constable, and me. As the door opened, the bystanders craned forward and a middle-aged woman uttered a cry of horror and followed us into the room.

"This is dreadful!" she exclaimed, with a shuddering glance at the corpse. "The servants told me about it when I came in just now and I sent Albert for the police at once. But what does it mean? You don't think poor Mr Dinanath has been murdered?"

"We had better get the facts, ma'am," said the constable, drawing out a large black notebook and laying his helmet on the table. He turned to Mr Byramji, who had sunk into a chair and sat, the picture of grief, gazing at his dead cousin. "Would you kindly tell me what you know about how it happened?"

Byramji repeated the substance of what he had told us, and when the constable had taken down his statement, Thorndyke and I gave the few medical particulars that we could furnish and handed the constable our cards. Then having helped to lay the corpse on the bed and cover it with a sheet, we turned to take our leave.

"You have been very kind," Mr Byramji said as he shook our hands warmly. "I am more than grateful. Perhaps I may be permitted to call on you and hear if – if you have learned anything fresh," he concluded discreetly.

"We shall be pleased to see you," Thorndyke replied, "and to give you any help that we can"; and with this we took our departure, watched inquisitively down the stairs by the boarders and the servants who still lurked in the vicinity of the chamber of death.

"If the police have no more information than we have," I remarked as we walked homeward, "they won't have much to go on."

"No," said Thorndyke. "But you must remember that this crime – as we are justified in assuming it to be – is not an isolated one. It is the fourth of practically the same kind within the last six months. I understand that the police have some kind of information respecting the presumed criminal, though it can't be worth much, seeing that no arrest has been made. But there is some new evidence this time. The exchange of hats may help the police considerably."

"In what way? What evidence does it furnish?"

"In the first place it suggests a hurried departure, which seems to connect the missing man with the crime. Then, he is wearing the dead man's hat, and though he is not likely to continue wearing it, it may be seen and furnish a clue. We know that that

hat fits him fairly and we know its size, so that we know the size of his head. Finally, we have the man's own hat."

"I don't fancy the police will get much information from that," said I.

"Probably not," he agreed. "Yet it offered one or two interesting suggestions, as you probably observed."

"It made no suggestions whatever to me," said I.

"Then," said Thorndyke, "I can only recommend you to recall our simple inspection and consider the significance of what we found."

This I had to accept as closing the discussion for the time being, and as I had to make a call at my bookseller's concerning some reports that I had left to be bound, I parted from Thorndyke at the corner of Chichester Rents and left him to pursue his way alone.

My business with the bookseller took me longer than I had expected, for I had to wait while the lettering on the backs was completed, and when I arrived at our chambers in King's Bench Walk, I found Thorndyke apparently at the final stage of some experiment evidently connected with our late adventure. The microscope stood on the table with one slide on the stage and a second one beside it; but Thorndyke had apparently finished his microscopical researches, for as I entered he held in his hand a test-tube filled with a smoky-coloured fluid.

"I see that you have been examining the dust from the hat," said I. "Does it throw any fresh light on the case?"

"Very little," he replied. "It is just common dust — assorted fibres and miscellaneous organic and mineral particles. But there are a couple of hairs from the inside of the hat — both lightish brown, and one of the atrophic, note-of-exclamation type that one finds at the margin of bald patches; and the outside dust shows minute traces of lead, apparently in the form of oxide. What do you make of that?"

"Perhaps the man is a plumber or a painter," I suggested.

"Either is possible and worth considering," he replied; but his tone made clear to me that this was not his own inference; and a row of five consecutive Post Office Directories, which I had already noticed ranged along the end of the table, told me that he had not only formed a hypothesis on the subject, but had probably either confirmed or disproved it. For the Post Office Directory was one of Thorndyke's favourite books of reference; and the amount of curious and recondite information that he succeeded in extracting from its matter-of-fact pages would have surprised no one more than it would the compilers of the work.

At this moment the sound of footsteps ascending our stairs became audible. It was late for business callers, but we were not unaccustomed to late visitors; and a familiar rat-tat of our little brass knocker seemed to explain the untimely visit.

"That sounds like Superintendent Miller's knock," said Thorndyke, as he strode across the room to open the door. And the Superintendent it turned out to be. But not alone.

As the door opened the officer entered with two gentlemen, both natives of India, and one of whom was our friend Mr Byramji.

"Perhaps," said Miller, "I had better look in a little later."

"Not on my account," said Byramji. "I have only a few words to say and there is nothing secret about my business. May I introduce my kinsman, Mr Khambata, a student of the Inner Temple?"

Byramji's companion bowed ceremoniously.

"Byramji came to my chambers just now," he explained, "to consult me about this dreadful affair, and he chanced to show me your card. He had not heard of you, but supposed you to be an ordinary medical practitioner. He did not realise that he had entertained an angel unawares. But I, who knew of your great reputation, advised him to put his affairs in your hands – without prejudice to the official investigations," Mr Khambata added hastily, bowing to the Superintendent.

"And I," said Mr Byramji, "instantly decided to act on my kinsman's advice. I have come to beg you to leave no stone unturned to secure the punishment of my cousin's murderer.

Spare no expense. I am a rich man and my poor cousin's property will come to me. As to the ruby, recover it if you can, but it is of no consequence. Vengeance – justice is what I seek. Deliver this wretch into my hands, or into the hands of justice, and I give you the ruby or its value, freely – gladly."

"There is no need," said Thorndyke, "of such extraordinary inducement. If you wish me to investigate this case, I will do so and will use every means at my disposal, without prejudice, as your friend says, to the proper claims of the officers of the law. But you understand that I can make no promises. I cannot guarantee success."

"We understand that," said Mr Khambata. "But we know that if you undertake the case, everything that is possible will be done. And now we must leave you to your consultation."

As soon as our clients had gone, Miller rose from his chair with his hand in his breast pocket. "I dare say, doctor," said he, "you can guess what I have come about. I was sent for to look into this Byramji case, and I heard from Mr Byramji that you had been there and that you had made a minute examination of the missing man's hat. So have I; and I don't mind telling you that I could learn nothing from it."

"I haven't learnt much myself," said Thorndyke.

"But you've picked up something," urged Miller, "if it is only a hint; and we have just a little clue. There is very small doubt that this is the same man – 'The New Jersey Sphinx,' as the papers call him – that committed those other robberies; and a very difficult type of criminal he is to get hold of. He is bold, he is wary, he plays a lone hand, and he sticks at nothing. He has no confederates, and he kills every time. The American police never got near him but once; and that once gives us the only clues we have."

"Fingerprints?" inquired Thorndyke.

"Yes, and very poor ones, too. So rough that you can hardly make out the pattern. And even those are not absolutely guaranteed to be his; but in any case, fingerprints are not much use until you've got the man. And there is a photograph of the fellow himself. But it is only a snapshot, and a poor one at that. All it shows is that he has a mop of hair and a pointed beard – or at least he had, when the photograph was taken. But for identification purposes it is practically worthless. Still, there it is; and what I propose is this: we want this man and so do you; we've worked together before and can trust one another. I am going to lay my cards on the table and ask you to do the same."

"But my dear Miller," said Thorndyke, "I haven't any cards. I haven't a single, solid fact."

The detective was visibly disappointed. Nevertheless, he laid two photographs on the table and pushed them towards Thorndyke, who inspected them through his lens and passed them to me.

"The pattern is very indistinct and broken up," he remarked.

"Yes," said Miller; "the prints must have been made on a very rough surface, though you get prints something like those from fitters or other men who use files and handle rough metal. And now, doctor, can't you, give us a lead of any kind?"

Thorndyke reflected a few moments. "I really have not a single real fact," said he, "and I am unwilling to make merely speculative suggestions."

"Oh, that's all right," Miller replied cheerfully. "Give us a start. I shan't complain if it comes to nothing."

"Well," Thorndyke said reluctantly, "I was thinking of getting a few particulars as to the various tenants of No. 51, Clifford's Inn. Perhaps you could do it more easily and it might be worth your while."

"Good!" Miller exclaimed gleefully. "He 'gives to airy nothing a local habitation and a name.' "

"It is probably the wrong name," Thorndyke reminded him.

"I don't care," said Miller. "But why shouldn't we go together? It's too late tonight, and I can't manage tomorrow morning. But say tomorrow afternoon. Two heads are better than one, you know, especially when the second one is yours. Or perhaps," he added, with a glance at me, "three would be better still."

Thorndyke considered for a moment or two and then looked at me.

"What do you say, Jervis?" he asked.

As my afternoon was unoccupied, I agreed with enthusiasm, being as curious as the Superintendent to know how Thorndyke had connected this particular locality with the vanished criminal, and Miller departed in high spirits with an appointment for the morrow at three o'clock in the afternoon.

For some time after the Superintendent's departure I sat wrapped in profound meditation. In some mysterious way the address, 51 Clifford's Inn, had emerged from the formless data yielded by the derelict hat. But what had been the connection? Apparently the fragment of the addressed envelope had furnished the clue. But how had Thorndyke extended " – n" into "51, Clifford's Inn"? It was to me a complete mystery.

Meanwhile, Thorndyke had seated himself at the writing table, and I noticed that of the two letters which he wrote, one was written on our headed paper and the other on ordinary plain notepaper. I was speculating on the reason for this when he rose, and as he stuck on the stamps, said to me, "I am just going out to post these two letters. Do you care for a short stroll through the leafy shades of Fleet Street? The evening is still young."

"The rural solitudes of Fleet Street attract me at all hours," I replied, fetching my hat from the adjoining office, and we accordingly sallied forth together, strolling up King's Bench Walk and emerging into Fleet Street by way of Mitre Court. When Thorndyke had dropped his letters into the post office box he stood awhile gazing up at the tower of St Dunstan's Church.

"Have you ever been in Clifford's Inn, Jervis?" he inquired.

"Never," I replied (we passed through it together on an average a dozen times a week), "but it is not too late for an exploratory visit."

We crossed the road, and entering Clifford's Inn Passage, passed through the still half open gate, crossed the outer court and threaded the tunnel-like entry by the hall to the inner court, near the middle of which Thorndyke halted, and looking up at one of the ancient houses, remarked, "No. 51."

"So that is where our friend hangs out his flag," said I.

"Oh come, Jervis," he protested, "I am surprised at you; you are as bad as Miller. I have merely suggested a possible connection between these premises and the hat that was left at Bedford Place. As to the nature of that connection I have no idea, and there may be no connection at all. I assure you, Jervis, that I am on the thinnest possible ice. I am working on a hypothesis which is in the highest degree speculative, and I should not have given Miller a hint, but that he was so eager and so willing to help – and also that I wanted his fingerprints. But we are really only at the beginning, and may never get any farther."

I looked up at the old house. It was all in darkness excepting the top floor, where a couple of lighted windows showed the shadow of a man moving rapidly about the room. We crossed to the entry and inspected the names painted on the doorposts. The ground floor was occupied by a firm of photo-engravers, the first floor by a Mr Carrington, whose name stood out conspicuously on its oblong of comparatively fresh white paint, while the tenants of the second floor – old residents, to judge by the faded and discoloured paint in which their names were announced – were Messrs Burt & Highley, metallurgists.

"Burt has departed," said Thorndyke, as I read out the names; and he pointed to two red lines of erasure which I had not noticed in the dim light, "so the active gentleman above is presumably Mr Highley, and we may take it that he has residential as well as business premises. I wonder who and what Mr Carrington is – but I dare say we shall find out tomorrow."

With this he dismissed the professional aspects of Clifford's Inn, and changing the subject to its history and associations, chatted in his inimitable, picturesque manner until our leisurely perambulations brought us at length to the Inner Temple Gate.

On the following morning we bustled through our work in order to leave the afternoon free, making several joint visits to solicitors from whom we were taking instructions. Returning from the last of these – a City lawyer – Thorndyke turned into St Helen's Place and halted at a doorway bearing the brass plate of a firm of essayists and refiners. I followed him into the outer office where, on his mentioning his name, an elderly man came to the counter.

"Mr Grayson has put out some specimens for you, sir," said he. "They are about thirty grains to the ton – you said that the content was of no importance – and I am to tell you that you need not return them. They are not worth treating." He went to a large safe from which he took a canvas bag, and returning to the counter, turned out on it the contents of the bag, consisting of about a dozen good-sized lumps of quartz and a glittering yellow fragment, which Thorndyke picked out and dropped in his pocket.

"Will that collection do?" our friend inquired.

"It will answer my purpose perfectly," Thorndyke replied, and when the specimens had been replaced in the bag, and the latter deposited in Thorndyke's hand-bag, my colleague thanked the assistant and we went on our way.

"We extend our activities into the domain of mineralogy," I remarked.

Thorndyke smiled an inscrutable smile. "We also employ the suction pump as an instrument of research," he observed. "However, the strategic uses of chunks of quartz – otherwise than as missiles – will develop themselves in due course, and the interval may be used for reflection."

It was. But my reflections brought no solution. I noticed, however, that when at three o'clock we set forth in company with the Superintendent, the bag went with us; and having offered to carry it and having had my offer accepted with a sly twinkle, its weight assured me that the quartz was still inside.

"Chambers and Offices to let," Thorndyke read aloud as we approached the porter's lodge. "That let us in, I think. And the porter knows Dr Jervis and me by sight so he will talk more freely."

"He doesn't know me," said the Superintendent, "but I'll keep in the background, all the same."

A pull at the bell brought out a clerical-looking man in a tall hat and a frock coat, who regarded Thorndyke and me through his spectacles with an amiable air of recognition.

"Good afternoon, Mr Larkin," said Thorndyke. "I am asked to get particulars of vacant chambers. What have you got to let?"

Mr Larkin reflected. "Let me see. There's a ground floor at No. 5 – rather dark – and a small second-pair set at No. 12. And then there is – oh, yes, there is a good first floor set at No. 51. They wouldn't have been vacant until Michaelmas, but Mr Carrington, the tenant, has had to go abroad suddenly. I had a letter from him this morning, enclosing the key. Funny letter, too." He dived into his pocket, and hauling out a bundle of letters, selected one and handed it to Thorndyke with a broad smile.

Thorndyke glanced at the postmark ("London, E."), and having taken out the key, extracted the letter, which he opened and held so that Miller and I could see it. The paper bore the printed heading, "Baltic Shipping Company, Wapping," and the further written heading, "S.S. *Gothenburg,*" and the letter was brief and to the point:

> *Dear Sir,*
> I *am giving up my chambers at No. 51, as I have been suddenly called abroad. I enclose the key, but am not troubling with the rent. The sale of my costly furniture will more than cover it, and the surplus can be expended on painting the garden railings.*
> *Yours sincerely,*
> A. *Carrington.*

Thorndyke smilingly replaced the letter and the key in the envelope and asked:

"What is the furniture like?"

"You'll see," chuckled the porter, "if you care to look at the rooms. And I think they might suit. They're a good set."

"Quiet?"

"Yes, pretty quiet. There's a metallurgist overhead – Highley – used to be Burt & Highley, but Burt has gone to the City, and I don't think Highley does much business now."

"Let me see," said Thorndyke, "I think I used to meet Highley sometimes – a tall, dark man, isn't he?"

"No, that would be Burt. Highley is a little, fairish man, rather bald, with a pretty rich complexion" – here Mr Larkin tapped his pose knowingly and raised his little finger – "which may account for the falling off of business."

"Hadn't we better have a look at the rooms?" Miller interrupted a little impatiently.

"Can we see them, Mr Larkin?" asked Thorndyke.

"Certainly," was the reply. "You've got the key. Let me have it when you've seen the rooms; and whatever you do," he added with a broad grin, "be careful of the furniture."

"It looks," the Superintendent remarked as we crossed the inner court, "as if Mr Carrington had done a mizzle. That's hopeful. And I see," he continued, glancing at the fresh paint on the doorpost as we passed through the entry, "that he hasn't been here long. That's hopeful too."

We ascended to the first floor, and as Thorndyke unlocked and threw open the door, Miller laughed aloud. The "costly furniture" consisted of a small kitchen table, a Windsor chair and a dilapidated deckchair. The kitchen contained a gas ring, a small saucepan and a frying pan, and the bedroom was furnished with a camp bed devoid of bedclothes, a wash hand basin on a packing case, and a water can.

"Hallo!" exclaimed the Superintendent. "He's left a hat behind. Quite a good hat, too." He took it down from the peg, glanced at its exterior and then turning it over, looked inside. And then his mouth opened with a jerk.

"Great Solomon Eagle!" he gasped. "Do you see, doctor? It's *the* hat."

He held it out to us, and sure enough on the white silk lining of the crown were the embossed, gilt letters, D.B., just as Mr Byramji had described them.

"Yes," Thorndyke agreed, as the Superintendent snatched up a greengrocer's paper bag from the kitchen floor and persuaded the hat into it, "it is undoubtedly the missing link. But what are you going to do now?"

"Do!" exclaimed Miller. "Why, I am going to collar the man. These Baltic boats put in at Hull and Newcastle – perhaps he didn't know that – and they are pretty slow boats, too. I shall wire to Newcastle to have the ship detained and take Inspector Badger down to make the arrest. I'll leave you to explain to the porter, and I owe you a thousand thanks for your valuable tip."

With this he bustled away, clasping the precious hat, and from the window we saw him hurry across the court and dart out through the postern into Fetter Lane.

"I think Miller was rather precipitate," said Thorndyke. "He should have got a description of the man and some further particulars."

"Yes," said I. "Miller had much better have waited until you had finished with Mr Larkin. But you can get some more particulars when we take back the key."

"We shall get more information from the gentleman who lives on the floor above, and I think we will go up and interview him now. I wrote to him last night and made a metallurgical appointment, signing myself W Polton. Your name, if he should ask, is Stevenson."

As we ascended the stairs to the next floor, I meditated on the rather tortuous proceedings of my usually straightforward colleague. The use of the lumps of quartz was now obvious; but why these mysterious tactics? And why, before knocking at the door, did Thorndyke carefully take the reading of the gas meter on the landing?

The door was opened in response to our knock by a shortish, alert-looking, clean-shaved man in a white overall, who looked at us keenly and rather forbiddingly. But Thorndyke was geniality personified.

"How do you do, Mr Highley?" said he, holding out his hand, which the metallurgist shook coolly. "You got my letter, I suppose?"

"Yes. But I am not Mr Highley. He's away and I am carrying on. I think of taking over his business, if there is any to take over. My name is Sherwood. Have you got the samples?"

Thorndyke produced the canvas bag, which Mr Sherwood took from him and emptied out on a bench, picking up the lumps of quartz one by one and examining them closely. Meanwhile Thorndyke took a rapid survey of the premises. Against the wall were two cupel furnaces and a third larger furnace like a small pottery kiln. On a set of narrow shelves were several rows of bone-ash cupels, looking like little white flowerpots, and near them was the cupel-press – an appliance into which powdered bone-ash was fed and compressed by a plunger to form the cupels – while by the side of the press was a tub of bone-ash – a good deal coarser, I noticed, than the usual fine powder. This coarseness was also observed by Thorndyke, who edged up to the tub and dipped his hand into the ash and then wiped his fingers on his handkerchief.

"This stuff doesn't seem to contain much gold," said Mr Sherwood. "But we shall see when we make the assay."

"What do you think of this?" asked Thorndyke, taking from his pocket the small lump of glittering, golden-looking mineral that he had picked out at the assayist's. Mr Sherwood took it from him and examined it closely. "This looks more hopeful," said he; "rather rich, in fact."

Thorndyke received this statement with an unmoved countenance; but as for me, I stared at Mr Sherwood in amazement. For this lump of glittering mineral was simply a fragment of common iron pyrites! It would not have deceived a schoolboy, much less a metallurgist.

Still holding the specimen, and taking a watchmaker's lens from a shelf, Mr Sherwood moved over to the window. Simultaneously, Thorndyke stepped softly to the cupel shelves and quickly ran his eye along the rows of cupels. Presently he paused at one, examined it more closely, and then, taking it from the shelf, began to pick at it with his fingernail.

At this moment Mr Sherwood turned and observed him; and instantly there flashed into the metallurgist's face an expression of mingled anger and alarm.

"Put that down!" he commanded peremptorily, and then, as Thorndyke continued to scrape with his fingernail, he shouted furiously, "Do you hear? Drop it!"

Thorndyke took him literally at his word and let the cupel fall on the floor, when it shattered into innumerable fragments, of which one of the largest separated itself from the rest. Thorndyke pounced upon it and in an instantaneous glance as he picked it up, I recognised it as a calcined tooth.

Then followed a few moments of weird, dramatic silence. Thorndyke, holding the tooth between his finger and thumb, looked steadily into the eyes of the metallurgist; and the latter, pallid as a corpse, glared at Thorndyke and furtively unbuttoned his overall.

Suddenly the silence broke into a tumult as bewildering as the crash of a railway collision. Sherwood's right hand darted under his overall. Instantly, Thorndyke snatched up another cupel and hurled it with such truth of aim that it shattered on the metallurgist's forehead. And as he flung the missile, he sprang forward, and delivered a swift upper-cut. There was a thunderous crash, a cloud of white dust, and an automatic pistol clattered along the floor.

I snatched up the pistol and rushed to my friend's assistance. But there was no need. With his great strength and his uncanny skill – to say nothing of the effects of the knock-out blow – Thorndyke had the man pinned down immovably.

"See if you can find some cord, Jervis," he said in a calm quiet tone that seemed almost ridiculously out of character with the circumstances.

There was no difficulty about this, for several corded boxes stood in a corner of the laboratory. I cut off two lengths, with one of which I secured the prostrate man's arms and with the other fastened his knees and ankles.

"Now," said Thorndyke, "if you will take charge of his hands, we will make a preliminary inspection. Let us first see if he wears a belt."

Unbuttoning the man's waistcoat, he drew up the shirt, disclosing a broad, webbing belt furnished with several leather pockets, the buttoned flaps of which he felt carefully, regardless of the stream of threats and imprecations that poured from our victim's swollen lips. From the front pockets he proceeded to the back, passing an exploratory hand under the writhing body.

"Ah!" he exclaimed suddenly, "just turn him over, and look out for his heels."

We rolled our captive over and Thorndyke "skinned the rabbit," a centre pocket came into view, into which, when he had unbuttoned it, he inserted his fingers. "Yes," he continued, "I think this is what we are looking for." He withdrew his fingers, between which he held a small packet of Japanese paper, and with feverish excitement I watched him open out layer after layer of the soft wrapping. As he turned back the last fold a wonderful crimson sparkle told me that the "great ruby" was found.

"There, Jervis," said Thorndyke, holding the magnificent gem towards me in the palm of his hand, "look on this beautiful, sinister thing, charged with untold potentialities of evil – and thank the gods that it is not yours."

He wrapped it up again carefully and, having bestowed it in an inner pocket, said, "And now give me the pistol and run down to the telegraph office and see if you can stop Miller. I should like him to have the credit for this."

I handed him the pistol and made my way out into Fetter Lane and so down to Fleet Street, where at the post office my urgent message was sent off to Scotland Yard immediately. In a few minutes the reply came that Superintendent Miller had not yet left and that he was starting immediately for Clifford's Inn. A quarter of an hour later he drove up in a hansom to the Fetter Lane gate and I conducted him up to the second floor, where Thorndyke introduced him to his prisoner and witnessed the official arrest.

"You don't see how I arrived at it," said Thorndyke as we walked homeward after returning the key. "Well, I am not surprised. The initial evidence was of the weakest; it acquired significance only by cumulative effect. Let us reconstruct it as it developed.

"The derelict hat was, of course, the starting point. Now the first thing one noticed was that it appeared to have had more than one owner. No man would buy a new hat that fitted so badly as to need all that packing; and the arrangement of the packing suggested a long-headed man wearing a hat that had belonged to a man with a short head. Then there were the suggestions offered by the slips of paper. The fragmentary address referred to a place the name of which ended in 'n' and the remainder was evidently 'London, W.C.' Now what West Central place names end in 'n.' It was not a street, a square or a court, and Barbican is not in the W.C. district. It was almost certainly one of the half-dozen surviving Inns of Court or Chancery. But, of course, it was not necessarily the address of the owner of the hat.

"The other slip of paper bore the end of a word ending in 'el,' and another word ending 'eep,' and connected with these were quantities stated in ounces and pennyweights troy weight.

"But the only persons who use troy weight, are those who deal in precious metals. I inferred therefore that the 'el' was part of 'lemel.' and that the 'eep', was part of 'floor-sweep,' an inference that was supported by the respective quantities, three ounces five pennyweights of lemel and nine and a half ounces of floor-sweep."

"What is lemel?" I asked.

"It is the trade name for the gold or silver filings that collect in the 'skin' of a jeweller's bench. Floor-sweep is, of course, the dust swept up on the floor of a jeweller's or goldsmith's workshop. The lemel is actual metal, though not of uniform fineness, but the 'sweep' is a mixture of dirt and metal. Both are saved and sent to the refiners to have the gold and silver extracted.

This paper, then, was connected either with a goldsmith or a gold refiner – who might call himself an assayist or a metallurgist. The connection was supported by the leaf of a price list of gas stoves. A metallurgist would be kept well supplied with lists of gas stoves and furnaces. The traces of lead in the dust from the hat gave us another straw blowing in the same direction, for gold assayed by the dry process is fused in the cupel furnace with lead; and as the lead oxidises and the oxide is volatile, traces of lead would tend to appear in the dust deposited in the laboratory.

The next thing to do was to consult the directory; and when I did so, I found that there were no goldsmiths in any of the Inns and only one assayist – Mr Highley, of Clifford's Inn. The probabilities, therefore, slender as they were, pointed to some connection between this stray hat and Mr Highley. And this was positively all the information that we had when we came out this afternoon.

As soon as we got to Clifford's Inn, however, the evidence began to grow like a rolling snowball. First there was Larkin's contribution; and then there was the discovery of the missing hat. Now, as soon as I saw that hat my suspicions fell upon the man upstairs. I felt a conviction that the hat had been left there purposely and that the letter to Larkin was just a red herring to create a false trail. Nevertheless, the presence of that hat completely confirmed the other evidence. It showed that the apparent connection was a real connection."

"But," I asked, "what made you suspect the man upstairs?"

"My dear Jervis!" he exclaimed, "consider the facts. That hat was enough to hang the man who left it there. Can you imagine this astute, wary villain making such an idiot's mistake – going away and leaving the means of his conviction for anyone to find? But you are forgetting that whereas the missing hat was found on the first floor, the murderer's hat was connected with the second floor. The evidence suggested that it was Highley's hat. And now, before we go on to the next stage, let me remind you of those finger-prints. Miller thought that their rough appearance was due to the surface on which they had been made. But it was not. They were the prints of a person who was suffering from ichthyosis, palmar psoriasis or some dry dermatitis.

"There is one other point. The man we were looking for was a murderer. His life was already forfeit. To such a man another murder more or less is of no consequence. If this man, having laid the false trail, had determined to take sanctuary in Highley's rooms, it was probable that he had already got rid of Highley. And remember that a metallurgist has an unrivalled means of disposing of a body; for not only is each of his muffle furnaces a miniature crematorium, but the very residue of a cremated body – bone-ash – is one of the materials of his trade.

"When we went upstairs, I first took the reading of the gas meter and ascertained that a large amount of gas had been used recently. Then, when we entered I took the opportunity to shake hands with Mr Sherwood, and immediately I became aware that he suffered from a rather extreme form of ichthyosis. That was the first point of verification. Then we discovered that he actually could not distinguish between iron pyrites and auriferous quartz. He was not a metallurgist at all. He was a masquerader. Then the bone-ash in the tub was mixed with fragments of calcined bone, and the cupels all showed similar fragments.

"In one of them I could see part of the crown of a tooth. That was pure luck. But observe that by that time I had enough evidence to justify an arrest. The tooth served only to bring the affair to a crisis; and his response to my unspoken accusation saved us the trouble of further search for confirmatory evidence."

"What is not quite clear to me," said I, "is, when and why he made away with Highley. As the body has been completely reduced to bone-ash, Highley must have been dead at least some days."

"Undoubtedly," Thorndyke agreed. "I take it that the course of events was somewhat like this: The police have been searching eagerly for this man, and every new crime must have made his position more unsafe – for a criminal can never be sure that he has not dropped some clue. It began to be necessary for him to make some arrangements for leaving the country and meanwhile to have a retreat in case his whereabouts should chance to be discovered. Highley's chambers were admirable for both purposes. Here was a solitary man who seldom had a visitor, and who would probably not be missed for some considerable time; and in those chambers were the means of rapidly and completely disposing of the body. The mere murder would be a negligible detail to this ruffian.

"I imagine that Highley was done to death at least a week ago, and that the murderer did not take up his new tenancy until the body was reduced to ash. With that large furnace in addition to the small ones, this would not take long. When the new premises were ready, he could make a sham disappearance to cover his actual flight later; and you must see how perfectly misleading that sham disappearance was. If the police had discovered that hat in the empty room only a week later, they would have been certain that he had escaped to one of the Baltic ports; and while they were following his supposed tracks, he could have gone off comfortably via Folkestone or Southampton."

"Then you think he had only just moved into Highley's rooms?"

"I should say he moved in last night. The murder of Byramji was probably planned on some information that the murderer had picked up, and as soon as it was accomplished he began forthwith to lay down the false tracks. When he reached his rooms yesterday afternoon, he must have written the letter to Larkin and gone off at once to the East End to post it. Then he probably had his bushy hair cut short and shaved off his beard and moustache – which would render him quite unrecognisable by Larkin – and moved into Highley's chambers, from which he would have quietly sallied forth in a few days' time to take his passage to the Continent. It was quite a good plan and but for the accident of taking the wrong hat, would almost certainly have succeeded."

Once every year, on the second of August, there is delivered with unfailing regularity at No. 5A, King's Bench Walk, a large box of carved sandalwood filled with the choicest Trichinopoly cheroots and accompanied by an affectionate letter from our late client, Mr Byramji. For the second of August is the anniversary of the death (in the execution shed at Newgate) of Cornelius Barnett, otherwise known as the "New Jersey Sphinx."

The Touchstone

It happened not uncommonly that the exigencies of practice committed my friend Thorndyke to investigations that lay more properly within the province of the police. For problems that had arisen as secondary consequences of a criminal act could usually not be solved until the circumstances of that act were fully elucidated, and, incidentally, the identity of the actor established. Such a problem was that of the disappearance of James Harewood's will, a problem that was propounded to us by our old friend, Mr Marchmont, when he called on us, by appointment, with the client of whom he had spoken in his note.

It was just four o'clock when the solicitor arrived at our chambers, and as I admitted him he ushered in a gentlemanly-looking man of about thirty-five, whom he introduced as Mr William Crowhurst.

"I will just stay," said he, with an approving glance at the tea-service on the table, "and have a cup of tea with you, and give you an outline of the case. Then I must run away and leave Mr Crowhurst to fill in the details."

He seated himself in an easy chair within comfortable reach of the table, and as Thorndyke poured out the tea, he glanced over a few notes scribbled on a sheet of paper.

"I may say," he began, stirring his tea thoughtfully, "that this is a forlorn hope. I have brought the case to you, but I have not the slightest expectation that you will be able to help us."

"A very wholesome frame of mind," Thorndyke commented with a smile. "I hope it is that of your client also."

"It is indeed," said Mr Crowhurst; "in fact, it seems to me a waste of your time to go into the matter. Probably you will think so too, when you have heard the particulars."

"Well, let us hear the particulars," said Thorndyke. "A forlorn hope has, at least, the stimulating quality of difficulty. Let us have your outline sketch, Marchmont."

The solicitor, having emptied his cup and pushed it towards the tray for replenishment, glanced at his notes and began:

"The simplest way in which to present the problem is to give a brief recital of the events that have given rise to it, which are these: The day before yesterday – that is last Monday – at a quarter to two in the afternoon, Mr James Harewood executed a will at his house at Merbridge, which is about two miles from Welsbury. There were present four persons: two of his servants, who signed as witnesses, and the two principal beneficiaries – Mr Arthur Baxfield, a nephew of the testator, and our friend here, Mr William Crowhurst. The will was a holograph written on the two pages of a sheet of letter-paper. When the witnesses signed, the will was covered by another sheet of paper so that only the space for the signatures was exposed. Neither of the witnesses read the will, nor did either of the beneficiaries; and so far as I am aware, no one but the testator knew what were its actual provisions, though, after the servants had left the room, Mr Harewood explained its general purport to the beneficiaries."

"And what was its general purport?" Thorndyke asked.

"Broadly speaking," replied Marchmont, "it divided the estate in two very unequal portions between Mr Baxfield and Mr Crowhurst. There were certain small legacies of which neither the amounts nor the names of the legatees are known. Then, to Baxfield was given a thousand pounds to enable him either to buy a partnership or to start a small factory – he is a felt hat manufacturer by trade – and the remainder to Crowhurst, who was made executor and residuary legatee. But, of course, the residue of the estate is an unknown quantity, since we don't know either the number or the amounts of the legacies.

"Shortly after the signing of the will, the parties separated. Mr Harewood folded up the will and put it in a leather wallet which he slipped into his pocket, stating his intention of taking the will forthwith to deposit with his lawyer at Welsbury. A few minutes after his guests had departed, he was seen by one of the servants to leave the house, and afterwards was seen by a neighbour walking along a footpath which, after passing through a small wood, joins the main road about a mile and a quarter from Welsbury. From that time, he was never again seen alive. He never visited the lawyer nor did anyone see him at or near Welsbury or elsewhere.

"As he did not return home that night, his housekeeper (he was a widower and childless) became extremely alarmed, and in the morning she communicated with the police. A search party was organised, and, following the path on which he was last seen, explored the wood – which is known locally as Gilbert's Copse – and here, at the bottom of an old chalk-pit they found him lying dead with a fractured skull and a dislocated neck. How he came by these injuries is not at present known; but as the body had been robbed of all valuables, including his watch, purse, diamond ring and the wallet containing the will, there is naturally a strong suspicion that he has been murdered. That, however, is not our immediate concern – at least not mine. I am concerned with the will, which, as you see, has disappeared, and as it has presumably been carried away by a thief who is under suspicion of murder, it is not likely to be returned."

"It is almost certainly destroyed by this time," said Mr, Crowhurst.

"That certainly seems probable," Thorndyke agreed. "But what do you want me to do? You haven't come for counsel's opinion?"

"No." replied Marchmont. "I am pretty clear about the legal position. I shall claim, as the will has presumably been destroyed, to have the testator's wishes carried out in so far as they are known. But I am doubtful as to the view the Court may take. It may decide that the testators wishes are not known, that the provisions of the will are too uncertain to admit of administration."

"And what would be the effect of that decision?" asked Thorndyke.

"In that case," said Marchmont, "the entire estate would go to Baxfield as he is the next of kin, and there was no previous will."

"And what is it that you want me to do?"

Marchmont chuckled deprecatingly. "You have to pay the penalty of being a prodigy, Thorndyke. We are asking you to do an impossibility – but we don't really expect you to bring it off. We ask you to help us to recover the will."

"If the will has been completely destroyed, it can't be recovered," said Thorndyke. "But we don't know that it has been destroyed. The matter is, at least, worth investigating; and if you wish me to look into it, I will."

The solicitor rose with an air of evident relief. "Thank you, Thorndyke," said he. "I expect nothing – at least, I tell myself that I do – but I can now feel that everything that is possible will be done. And now I must be off. Crowhurst can give you any details that you want."

When Marchmont had gone, Thorndyke turned to our client and asked, "What do you suppose Baxfield will do, if the will is irretrievably lost? Will he press his claim as next of kin?"

"I should say yes," replied Crowhurst. "He is a business man and his natural claims are greater than mine. He is not likely to refuse what the law assigns to him as his right. As a matter of fact, I think he felt that his uncle had treated him unfairly in alienating the property."

"Was there any reason for this diversion of the estate?"

"Well," replied Crowhurst, "Harewood and I had been very good friends and he was under some obligations to me; and then Baxfield had not made himself very acceptable to his uncle. But the principal factor, I think, was a strong tendency of Baxfield's to gamble. He had lost quite a lot of money by backing horses, and a careful, thrifty man like James Harewood doesn't care to leave his savings to a gambler. The thousand pounds that he did leave to Baxfield was expressly for the purpose of investment in a business."

"Is Baxfield in business now?"

"Not on his own account. He is a sort of foreman or shop-manager in a factory just outside Welsbury, and I believe he is a good worker and knows his trade thoroughly."

"And now," said Thorndyke, "with regard to Mr Harewood's death. The injuries might, apparently, have been either accidental or homicidal. What are the probabilities of accident – disregarding the robbery?"

"Very considerable, I should say. It is a most dangerous place. The footpath runs close beside the edge of a disused chalk-pit with perpendicular or overhanging sides, and the edge is masked by bushes and brambles. A careless walker might easily fall over – or be pushed over, for that matter."

"Do you know when the inquest is to take place?"

"Yes. The day after tomorrow. I had the subpœna this morning for Friday afternoon at 2.30, at the Welsbury Town Hall."

At this moment footsteps were heard hurriedly ascending the stairs and then came a loud and peremptory rat-tat at our door. I sprang across to see who our visitor was, and as I flung open the door, Mr Marchmont rushed in, breathing heavily and flourishing a newspaper.

"Here is a new development," he exclaimed. "It doesn't seem to help us much, but I thought you had better know about it at once." He sat down, and putting on his spectacles, read aloud as follows: "A new and curious light has been thrown on the mystery of the death of Mr James Harewood, whose body was found yesterday in a disused chalk-pit near Merbridge. It appears that on Monday – the day on which Mr Harewood almost certainly was killed – a passenger alighting from a train at Barwood Junction before it had stopped, slipped and fell between the train and the platform. He was quickly extricated and as he had evidently sustained internal injuries, he was taken to the local hospital, where he was found to be suffering from a fractured pelvis. He gave his name as Thomas Fletcher, but refused to give any address, saying that he had no relatives. This morning he died, and on his clothes being searched for an address, a parcel, formed of two handkerchiefs tied up with string, was found in his pocket. When it was opened it was found to contain five watches, three watch-chains, a tie-pin and a number of banknotes. Other pockets contained a quantity of loose money – gold and silver mixed – and a card of the Welsbury Races, which were held on Monday. Of the five watches, one has been identified as the one taken from Mr Harewood; and the banknotes have been identified as a batch handed to him by the cashier of his bank at Welsbury last Thursday and presumably carried in the leather wallet which was stolen from his pocket. This wallet, by the way, has also been found. It was picked up – empty – last night on the railway embankment just outside Welsbury Station. Appearances thus suggest that the man, Fletcher, when on his way to the races, encountered Mr Harewood in the lonely copse, and murdered and robbed him; or perhaps found him dead in the chalk-pit and robbed the body – a question that is now never likely to be solved."

As Marchmont finished reading, he looked up at Thorndyke: "It doesn't help us much, does it?" said he. "As the wallet was found empty, it is pretty certain that the will has been destroyed."

"Or perhaps merely thrown away," said Thorndyke. "In which case an advertisement offering a substantial reward may bring it to light."

The solicitor shrugged his shoulders sceptically, but agreed to publish the advertisement. Then, once more he turned to go; and as Mr Crowhurst had no further information to give, he departed with his lawyer.

For some time after they had gone, Thorndyke sat with his brief notes before him, silent; and deeply reflective. I, too, maintained a discreet silence, for I knew from long experience that the motionless pose and quiet, impassive face were the outward signs of a mind in swift and strenuous action. Instinctively, I gathered that this apparently chaotic case was being quietly sorted out and arranged in a logical order; that Thorndyke, like a skilful chess-player, was "trying over the moves" before he should lay his hand upon the pieces.

Presently he looked up. "Well?" he asked. "What do you think, Jervis? Is it worthwhile?"

"That," I replied, "depends on whether the will is or is not in existence. If it has been destroyed, an investigation would be a waste of our time and our client's money."

"Yes," he agreed. "But there is quite a good chance that it has not been destroyed. It was probably dropped loose into the wallet, and then might have been picked out and thrown away before the wallet was examined. But we mustn't concentrate too much on the will. If we take up the case – which I am inclined to do – we must ascertain the actual sequence of events. We have one clear day before the inquest. If we run down to Merbridge tomorrow and go thoroughly over the ground, and then go on to Barwood and find out all that we can about the man Fletcher, we may get some new light from the evidence at the inquest."

I agreed readily to Thorndyke's proposal, not that I could see any way into the case, but I felt a conviction that my colleague had isolated some leading fact and had a definite line of research in his mind. And this conviction deepened when, later in the evening, he laid his research case on the table and rearranged its contents with evident purpose.

I watched curiously the apparatus that he was packing in it and tried – not very successfully – to infer the nature of the proposed investigation. The box of powdered paraffin wax and the spirit blowpipe were obvious enough; but the "dust-aspirator" – a sort of miniature vacuum cleaner – the portable microscope, the coil of Manila line, with an eye spliced into one end, and especially the abundance of blank-labelled microscope slides, all of which I saw him pack in the case with deliberate care, defeated me utterly.

About ten o'clock on the following morning we stepped from the train in Welsbury Station, and having recovered our bicycles from the luggage van, wheeled them through the barrier and mounted. During the train journey we had both studied the one-inch Ordnance map to such purpose that we were virtually in familiar surroundings and immune from the necessity of seeking directions from the natives. As we cleared the town we glanced up the broad by-road to the left which led to the racecourse; then we rode on briskly for a mile, which brought us to the spot where the footpath to Merbridge joined the road. Here we dismounted and, lifting our bicycles over the stile, followed the path towards a small wood which we could see ahead, crowning a low hill.

"For such a good path," Thorndyke remarked as we approached the wood, "it is singularly unfrequented. I haven't seen a soul since we left the road." He glanced at the map as the path entered the wood, and when we had walked on a couple of hundred yards, he halted and stood his bicycle against a tree. "The chalk-pit should be about here," said he, "though it is impossible to see." He grasped a stem of one of the small bushes that crowded on to the path and pulled it aside. Then he uttered an exclamation.

"Just look at that, Jervis. It is a positive scandal that a public path should be left in this condition."

Certainly Mr Crowhurst had not exaggerated. It was a most dangerous place. The parted branches revealed a chasm some thirty feet deep, the brink of which, masked by the bushes, was, but a matter of inches from the edge of the path.

"We had better go back," said Thorndyke, "and find the entrance to the pit, which seems to be to the right. The first thing is to ascertain exactly where Harewood fell. Then we can come back and examine the place from above."

We turned back, and presently found a faint track, which we followed until, descending steeply, it brought us out into the middle of the pit. It was evidently an ancient pit, for the sides were blackened by age, and the floor was occupied by a number of trees, some of considerable size. Against one of these we leaned our bicycles and then walked slowly round at the foot of the frowning cliff.

"This seems to be below the path," said Thorndyke, glancing up at the grey wall which jutted out above in stages like an inverted flight of steps. "Somewhere hereabouts we should find some traces of the tragedy."

Even as he spoke my eye caught a spot of white on a block of chalk, and on the freshly fractured surface a significant brownish-red stain. The block lay opposite the mouth of an artificial cave – an old wagon-shelter, but now empty – and immediately under a markedly overhanging part of the cliff.

"This is undoubtedly the place where he fell," said Thorndyke. "You can see where the stretcher was placed – an old-pattern stretcher with wheel-runners – and there is a little spot of broken soil at the top where he came over. Well, apart from the robbery, a clear fall of over thirty feet is enough to account for a fractured skull. Will you stay here, Jervis, while I run up and look at the path?"

He went off towards the entrance, and presently I heard him above, pulling aside the bushes, and after one or two trials, he appeared directly overhead.

"There are plenty of footprints on the path," said he, "but nothing abnormal. No trampling or signs of a struggle. I am going on a little farther."

He withdrew behind the bushes, and I proceeded to inspect the interior of the cave, noting the smoke-blackened roof and the remains of a recent fire, which, with a number of rabbit bones and a discarded tea-boiler of the kind used by the professional tramp, seemed not without a possible bearing on our investigation. I was thus engaged when I heard Thorndyke hail me from above, and coming out of the cave, I saw his head thrust between the branches. He seemed to be lying down, for his face was nearly on a level with the top of the cliff.

"I want to take an impression," he called out. "Will you bring up the paraffin and the blower? And you might bring the coil of line, too."

I hurried away to the place where our bicycles were standing, and opening the research case, took out the coil of line, the tin of paraffin wax and the spirit blowpipe, and having ascertained that the container of the latter was full, I ran up the incline and made my way along the path. Some distance along, I found my colleague nearly hidden in the bushes, lying prone, with his head over the edge of the cliff.

"You see, Jervis," he said as I crawled alongside and looked over, "this is a possible way down, and someone has used it quite recently. He climbed down with his face to the cliff – you can see the clear impression of the toe of a boot in the loam on that projection, and you can even make out the shape of an iron toe-tip. Now the problem is how to get down to take the impression without dislodging the earth above it. I think I will secure myself with the line."

"It is hardly worth the risk of a broken neck," said I. "Probably the print is that of some schoolboy."

"It is a man's foot," he replied. "Most likely it has no connection with our case. But it may have, and as a shower of rain would obliterate it we ought to secure it." As he spoke, he passed the end of the cord through the eye and slipped the loop over his shoulders, drawing it tight under his arms. Then, having made the line fast to the butt of a small tree, he cautiously lowered himself over the edge and climbed down to the projection. As soon as he had a secure footing, I passed the spare cord through the ring on the lid of the wax tin and lowered it to him, and when he had unfastened it, I drew up the cord and in the same way let down the blowpipe. Then I watched his neat, methodical procedure. First he took out a spoonful of the powdered, or grated, wax and very delicately sprinkled it on the toe-print until the latter was evenly but very thinly covered. Next he lit the blowlamp, and as soon as the blue flame began to roar from the pipe, he directed it on to the toe-print. Almost instantly the powder melted, glazing the impression like a coat of varnish. Then the flame was removed and the film of wax at once solidified and became dull and opaque. A second, heavier sprinkling with the powder, followed by another application of the flame, thickened the film of wax, and this process, repeated four or five times, produced a solid cake. Then Thorndyke held the blowlamp, and securing it and the tin to the cord, directed me to pull them up. "And you might send me down the field-glasses," he added. "There is something farther down that I can't quite make out."

I slipped the glasses from my shoulder, and opening the case, tied the cord to the leather sling and lowered it down the cliff; and then I watched with some curiosity as Thorndyke stood on his insecure perch steadily gazing through the glasses (they were Zeiss 8-prismatics) at a clump of wallflowers that grew from a boss of chalk about halfway down. Presently he lowered the glasses and, slinging them round his neck by their lanyard, turned his attention to the cake of wax. It was by this time quite solid, and when he had tested it, he lifted it carefully and placed it in the empty binocular case, when I drew it up.

"I want you, Jervis," Thorndyke called up, "to steady the line. I am going down to that wallflower clump."

It looked extremely unsafe, but I knew it was useless to protest, so I hitched the line around a massive stump and took a firm grip of the "fall."

"Ready," I sang out; and forthwith Thorndyke began to creep across the face of the cliff with feet and hands clinging to almost invisible projections. Fortunately, there was at this part no overhang, and though my heart was, in my mouth as I watched, I saw him cross the perilous space in safety. Arrived at the clump, he drew an envelope from his pocket, stooped and picked up some small object, which he placed in the envelope, returning the latter to his pocket. Then he gave me another bad five minutes while he recrossed the nearly vertical surface to his starting point; but at length this, too, was safely accomplished, and when he finally climbed up over the edge and stood beside me on solid earth, I drew a deep breath and turned to revile him.

"Well?" I demanded sarcastically, "what have you gathered at the risk of your neck? Is it samphire or edelweiss?"

He drew the envelope from his pocket, and dipping into it, produced a cigarette-holder – a cheap bone affair, black and clammy with long service and still holding the butt of a hand-made cigarette – and handed it to me. I turned it over, smelled it and hastily handed it back. "For my part," said I, "I wouldn't have risked the cervical vertebrae of a yellow cat for it. What do you expect to learn from it?"

"Of course, I expect nothing. We are just collecting facts on the chance that they may turn out to be relevant. Here, for instance, we find that a man has descended within a few yards of where Harewood fell, by this very inconvenient route, instead of going round to the entrance to the pit. He must have had some reason for adopting this undesirable mode of descent. Possibly, he was in a hurry, and probably he belonged to the district, since a stranger would not know of the existence of this short cut. Then it seems likely that this was his cigarette tube. If you look over, you will see by those vertical scrapes on the chalk that he slipped and must have nearly fallen. At that moment he probably dropped the tube, for you notice that the wallflower clump is directly under the marks of his toes."

"Why do you suppose he did not recover the tube?"

"Because the descent slopes away from the position of the clump, and he had no trusty Jervis with a stout cord to help him to cross the space. And if he went down this way because he was hurried, he would not have time to search for the tube. But if the tube was not his, still it belonged to somebody who has been here recently."

"Is there anything that leads you to connect this man with the crime?"

"Nothing but time and place," he replied. "The man has been down into the pit close to where Harewood was robbed and possibly murdered, and as the traces are quite recent, he must have been there near about the time of the robbery. That is all. I am considering the traces of this man in particular because there are no traces of any other. But we may as well have a look at the path, which, as you see, yields good impressions."

We walked slowly along the path towards Merbridge, keeping at the edges and scrutinising the surface closely. In the shady hollows, the soft loam bore prints of many feet, and among them we could distinguish one with an iron toe-tip, but it was nearly obliterated by another studded with hobnails.

"We shan't get much information here," said Thorndyke as he turned about. "The search party have trodden out the important prints. Let us see if we can find out where the man with the toe-tips went to."

We searched the path on the Welsbury side of the chalk-pit, but found no trace of him. Then we went into the pit, and having located the place where he descended, sought for some other exit than the track leading to the path. Presently, halfway up the slope, we found a second track, bearing away in the direction of Merbridge. Following this for some distance, we came to a small hollow at the bottom of which was a muddy space. And here we both halted abruptly, for in the damp ground were the clear imprints of a pair of boots which we could see had, in addition to the toe-tips, half-tips to the heels.

"We had better have wax casts of these," said Thorndyke, "to compare with the boots of the man Fletcher. I will do them while you go back for the bicycles."

By the time that I returned with the machines, two of the footprints were covered with a cake each of wax, and Thorndyke had left the track and was peering among the bushes. I inquired what he was looking for.

"It is a forlorn hope, as Marchmont would say," he replied, "but I am looking to see if the will has been thrown away here. It was quite probably jettisoned at once, and this is the most probable route for the robber to have taken, if he knew of it. You see by the map that it must lead nearly directly to the racecourse, and it avoids both the path and the main road. While the wax is setting we might as well look round."

It seemed a hopeless enough proceeding and I agreed to it without enthusiasm. Leaving the track on the opposite side to that which Thorndyke was searching, I wandered among the bushes and the little open spaces, peering about me and reminding myself of that "aged, aged man" who

> "Sometimes searched the grassy knolls,
>   For wheels of hansom cabs."

I had worked my way nearly back to where I could see Thorndyke, also returning, when my glance fell on a small, brown object caught among the branches of a bush. It was a man's pigskin purse; and as I picked it out of the bush I saw that it was open and empty.

With my prize in my hand, I hastened to the spot where Thorndyke was lifting the wax casts. He looked up and asked, "No luck, I suppose?"

I held out the purse, on which he pounced eagerly. "But this is most important, Jervis," he exclaimed. "It is almost certainly Harewood's purse. You see the initials, 'J. H.', stamped on the flap. Then we were right as to the direction that the robber took. And it would pay to search this place exhaustively for the will, though we can't do that now, as we have to go on to Barwood. I wrote to say we were coming. We had better get back to the path now and make for the road. Barwood is only half an hour's run."

We packed the casts in the research case (which was strapped to Thorndyke's bicycle), and turning back, made our way to the path. As it was still deserted, we ventured to mount, and soon reached the road, along which we started at a good pace towards Barwood.

Half an hour's ride brought us into the main street of the little town, and when we dismounted at the police station we found the Chief Constable himself waiting to receive us, courteously eager to assist us, but possessed by a devouring curiosity which was somewhat inconvenient.

"I have done as you asked me in your letter, sir," he said. "Fletcher's body is, of course, in the mortuary, but I have had all his clothes and effects brought here; and I have had them put in my private office, so that you can look them over in comfort."

"It is exceedingly good of you," said Thorndyke, "and most helpful." He unstrapped the research case, and following the officer into his sanctum, looked round with deep approval. A large table had been cleared for the examination and the dead pickpocket's clothes and effects neatly arranged at one end.

Thorndyke's first proceeding was to pick up the dead man's boots – a smart but flimsy pair of light brown leather, rather down at heel and in need of re-soling. Neither toes nor heels bore any tips or even nails excepting the small fastening brads. Having exhibited them to me without remark, Thorndyke placed them on a sheet of white paper and made a careful tracing of the soles, a proceeding that seemed to surprise the Chief Constable, for he remarked, "I should hardly have thought that the question of footprints would arise in this case. You can't charge a dead man."

Thorndyke agreed that this seemed to be true; and then he proceeded to an operation that fairly made the officer's eyes bulge. Opening the research case – into which the officer cast an inquisitive glance – he took out the dust-aspirator, the nozzle of which he inserted into one after another of the pockets while I worked the pump. When he had gone through them all, he opened the receiver and extracted quite a considerable ball of dusty fluff. Placing this on a glass slide, he tore it in halves with a pair of mounted needles and passed one half to me, when we both fell to work "teasing" it out into an open mesh, portions of which we separated and laid – each in a tiny pool of glycerine – on blank-labelled glass slides, applying to each slide its cover-glass and writing on the label, "Dust from Fletcher's pockets."

When the series was complete, Thorndyke brought out the microscope, and fitting on a one-inch objective, quickly examined the slides, one after another, and then pushed the microscope to me. So far as I could see, the dust was just ordinary dust – principally made up of broken cotton fibres with a few fibres of wool, linen, wood, jute, and others that I could not name and some undistinguishable mineral particles. But I made no comment, and resigning the microscope to the Chief Constable – who glared through it, breathing hard, and remarked that the dust was "rummy-looking stuff" – watched Thorndyke's further proceedings. And very odd proceedings they were.

First he laid the five stolen watches in a row, and with a Coddington lens minutely examined the dial of each. Then he opened the back of each in turn and copied into his notebook the watch-repairers' scratched inscriptions. Next he produced from the case a number of little vulcanite rods, and laying out five labelled slides, dropped a tiny drop of glycerine on each, covering it at once with a watch-glass to protect it from falling dust. Then he stuck a little label on each watch, wrote a number on it and similarly numbered the five slides. His next proceeding was to take out the glass of watch No. 1 and pick up one of the vulcanite rods, which he rubbed briskly on a silk handkerchief and passed slowly across and around the dial of the watch, after which he held the rod close to the glycerine on slide No. 1 and tapped it sharply with the blade of his pocket-knife. Then he dropped a cover-glass on to the glycerine and made a rapid inspection of the specimen through the microscope.

This operation he repeated on the other four watches, using a fresh rod for each, and when he had finished he turned to the open-mouthed officer. "I take it," said he, "that the watch which has the chain attached to it is Mr Harewood's watch?"

"Yes, sir. That helped us to identify it."

Thorndyke looked at the watch reflectively. Attached to the bow by a short length of green tape was a small, rather elaborate key. This my friend picked up, and taking a fresh mounted needle, inserted it into the barrel of the key from which he then withdrew it with a tiny ball of fluff on its point. I hastily prepared a slide and handed it to him, when, with a pair of dissecting scissors, he cut off a piece of the fluff and let it fall into the glycerine. He repeated this manœuvre with two more slides and then labelled the three, "Key, outside," "middle" and "inside," and in that order examined them under the microscope.

My own examination of the specimens yielded very little. They all seemed to be common dust, though that from the face of watch No. 3 contained a few broken fragments of what looked like animal hairs – possibly cat's – as also did the key-fluff marked "outside." But if this had any significance, I could not guess what it was. As to the Chief Constable, he clearly looked on the whole proceeding as a sort of legerdemain with no obvious purpose, for he remarked, as we were packing up to go, "I am glad I've seen how you do it, sir. But all the same, I think you are flogging a dead horse. We know who committed this crime and we know he's beyond the reach of the law."

"Well," said Thorndyke, "one must earn one's fee, you know. I shall put Fletcher's boots and the five watches in evidence at the inquest tomorrow, and I will ask you to leave the labels on the watches."

With renewed thanks and a hearty handshake he bade the courteous officer adieu, and we rode off to catch the train to London.

That evening, after dinner, we brought out the specimens and went over them at our leisure; and Thorndyke added a further specimen by drawing a knotted piece of twine through the cigarette-holder that he had salved from the chalk-pit, and teasing out the unsavoury, black substance that came out on the string in glycerine on a slide. When he had examined it, he passed it to me. The dark, tarry liquid somewhat obscured the detail, but I could make out fragments of the same animal hairs that I had noted in the other specimens, only here they were much more numerous. I mentioned my observation to Thorndyke. "They are certainly parts of mammalian hairs," I said, "and they look like the hairs of a cat. Are they from a cat?"

"Rabbit," Thorndyke replied curtly; and even then, I am ashamed to admit, I did not perceive the drift of the investigation.

The room in the Welsbury Town Hall had filled up some minutes before the time fixed for the opening of the inquest, and in the interval, when the jury had retired to view the body in the adjacent mortuary, I looked round the assembly. Mr Marchmont and Mr Crowhurst were present, and a youngish, horsey-looking man in cord breeches and leggings, whom I correctly guessed to be Arthur Baxfield. Our friend the Chief Constable of Barwood was also there, and with him Thorndyke exchanged a few words in a retired corner. The rest of the company were strangers.

As soon as the coroner and the jury had taken their places the medical witness was called. The cause of death, he stated, was dislocation of the neck, accompanied by a depressed fracture of the skull. The fracture might have been produced by a blow with a heavy, blunt weapon, or by the deceased falling on his head. The witness adopted the latter view, as the dislocation showed that the deceased had fallen in that manner.

The next witness was Mr Crowhurst, who repeated to the Court what he had told us, and further stated that on leaving the deceased's house he went straight home, as he had an appointment with a friend. He was followed by Baxfield, who gave evidence to the same effect, and stated that on leaving the house of the deceased he went to his place of business at Welsbury. He was about to retire when Thorndyke rose to cross-examine.

"At what time did you reach your place of business?" he asked.

The witness hesitated for a few moments and then replied, "Half-past four."

"And what time did you leave the deceased's house?"

"Two o'clock," was the reply.

"What is the distance?"

"In a direct line, about two miles. But I didn't go direct. I took a round in the country by Lenfield."

"That would take you near the racecourse on the way back. Did you go to the races?"

"No. The races were just over when I returned."

There was a slight pause and then Thorndyke asked, "Do you smoke much, Mr Baxfield?"

The witness looked surprised, and so did the jury, but the former replied, "A fair amount. About fifteen cigarettes a day."

"What brand of cigarettes do you smoke and what kind of tobacco is it?"

"I make my own cigarettes. I make them of shag."

Here protesting murmurs arose from the jury, and the coroner remarked stiffly, "These questions do not appear to have much connection with the subject of this inquiry."

"You may take it, sir," replied Thorndyke, "that they have a very direct bearing on it."

Then, turning to the witness he asked, "Do you use a cigarette-tube?"

"Sometimes I do," was the reply.

"Have you lost a cigarette-tube lately?"

The witness directed a startled glance at Thorndyke and replied after some hesitation, "I believe I mislaid one a little time ago."

"When and where did you lose that tube?" Thorndyke asked.

"I – I really couldn't say," replied Baxfield, turning perceptibly pale.

Thorndyke opened his dispatch box, and taking out the tube that he had salved at so much risk, handed it to the witness. "Is that the tube that you lost?" he asked.

At this question Baxfield turned pale as death, and the hand in which he received the tube shook as if with a palsy. "It may be," he faltered. "I wouldn't swear to it. It is like the one I lost."

Thorndyke took it from him and passed it to the coroner. "I am putting this tube in evidence, sir," said he. Then, addressing the witness, he said, "You stated that you did not go to the races. Did you go on the course or inside the grounds at all?"

Baxfield moistened his lips and replied, "I just went in for a minute or two, but I didn't stay. The races were over, and there was a very rough crowd."

"While you were in that crowd, Mr Baxfield, did you have your pocket picked?"

There was an expectant silence in the Court as Baxfield replied in a low voice:

"Yes. I lost my watch."

Again Thorndyke opened the dispatch box, and taking out a watch (it was the one that had been labelled 3), handed it to the witness.

"Is that the watch that you lost?" he asked.

Baxfield held the watch in his trembling hand and replied hesitatingly, "I believe it is, but I won't swear to it."

There was a pause. Then, in grave, impressive tones, Thorndyke said, "Now, Mr Baxfield, I am going to ask you a question which you need not answer if you consider that by doing so you would prejudice your position in any way. That question is, When your pocket was picked, were any articles besides this watch taken from your person? Don't hurry. Consider your answer carefully."

For some moments Baxfield remained silent, regarding Thorndyke with a wild, affrighted stare. At length he began falteringly, "I don't remember missing anything –" and then stopped.

"Could the witness be allowed to sit down, sir?" Thorndyke asked. And when the permission had been given and a chair placed, Baxfield sat down heavily and cast a bewildered glance round the Court. "I think," he said, addressing Thorndyke, "I had better tell you exactly what happened and take my chance of the consequences. When I left my uncle's house on Monday, I took a circuit through the fields and then entered Gilbert's Copse to wait for my uncle and tell him what I thought of his conduct in leaving the bulk of his property to a stranger. I struck the path that I knew my uncle would take and walked along it slowly to meet him. I did meet him on the path, just above where he was found – and I began to say what was in my mind. But he wouldn't listen. He flew into a rage, and as I was standing in the middle of the path, he tried to push past me. In doing so he caught his foot in a bramble and staggered back, then he disappeared through the bushes and a few seconds after I heard a thud down below. I pulled the bushes aside and looked down into the chalk-pit, and there I saw him lying with his head all on one side. Now, I happened to know of a short cut down into the pit. It was rather a dangerous climb, but I took it to get down as quickly as possible. It was there that I dropped the cigarette-tube. When I got to my uncle I could see that he was dead. His skull was battered and his neck was broken. Then the devil put into my head the idea of making away with the will. But I knew that if I took the will only, suspicion would fall on me. So I took most of his valuables – the wallet, his watch and chain, his purse and his ring. The purse I emptied and threw away, and flung the ring after it. I took the will out of the wallet – it had just been dropped in loose – and put it in an inner pocket. Then I dropped the wallet and the watch and chain into my outside coat pocket.

"I struck across country, intending to make for the racecourse and drop the things among the crowd, so that they might be picked up and safely carried away. But when I got there a gang of pickpockets saved me the trouble; they mobbed and hustled me and cleared my pockets of everything but my keys and the will."

"And what has become of the will?" asked Thorndyke.

"I have it here." He dipped into his breast pocket and produced a folded paper, which he handed to Thorndyke, who opened it, and having glanced at it, passed it to the coroner.

That was practically the end of the inquest. The jury decided to accept Baxfield's statement and recorded a verdict of "Death by Misadventure," leaving Baxfield to be dealt with by the proper authorities.

"An interesting and eminently satisfactory case," remarked Thorndyke, as we sat over a rather late dinner. "Essentially simple, too. The elucidation turned, as you probably noticed, on a single illuminating fact."

"I judged that it was so," said I, "though the illumination of that fact has not yet reached me."

"Well," said Thorndyke, "let us first take the general aspect of the case as it was presented by Marchmont. The first thing, of course, that struck one was that the loss of the will might easily have converted Baxfield from a minor beneficiary to the sole heir. But even if the Court agreed to recognise the will, it would have to be guided by the statements of the only two men to whom its provisions were even approximately known, and Baxfield could have made any statement he pleased. It was impossible to ignore the fact that the loss of the will was very greatly to Baxfield's advantage.

"When the stolen property was discovered in Fletcher's possession it looked, at the first glance, as if the mystery of the crime were solved. But there were several serious inconsistencies. First, how came Fletcher to be in this solitary wood, remote from any railway or even road? He appeared to be a London pickpocket. When he was killed he was travelling to London by train. It seemed probable that he had come from London by train to ply his trade at the races. Then, as you know, criminological experience shows that the habitual criminal is a rigid specialist. The burglar, the coiner, the pickpocket, each keeps strictly to his own special line. Now, Fletcher was a pickpocket, and had evidently been picking pockets on the racecourse. The probabilities were against his being the original robber and in favour of his having picked the pocket of the person who robbed Harewood. But if this were so, who was that person? Once more the probabilities suggested Baxfield. There was the motive, as I have said, and further, the pocket-picking had apparently taken place on the racecourse, and Baxfield was known to be a frequenter of racecourses. But again, if Baxfield were the person robbed by Fletcher, then one of the five watches was probably Baxfield's watch. Whether it was so or not might have been very difficult to prove, but here came in the single illuminating fact that I have spoken of.

"You remember that when Marchmont opened the case he mentioned that Baxfield was a manufacturer of felt hats, and Crowhurst told us that he was a sort of foreman or manager of the factory."

"Yes, I remember, now you speak of it. But what is the bearing of the fact?"

"My dear Jervis!" exclaimed Thorndyke. "Don't you see that it gave us a touchstone? Consider, now. What is a felt hat? It is just a mass of agglutinated rabbits' hair. The process of manufacture consists in blowing a jet of the more or less disintegrated hair on to a revolving steel cone which is moistened by a spray of an alcoholic solution of shellac. But, of course, a quantity of the finer and more minute particles of the broken hairs miss the cone and float about in the air. The air of the factory is thus charged with the dust of broken rabbit hairs; and this dust settles on and penetrates the clothing of the workers. But when clothing becomes charged with dust, that dust tends to accumulate in the pockets and find its way into the hollows and interstices of any objects carried in those pockets. Thus, if one of the five watches was Baxfield's it would almost certainly show traces where this characteristic dust had crept under the bezel and settled on the dial. And so it turned out to be. When I inspected those five watches through the Coddington lens, on the dial of No. 3 I saw a quantity of dust of this character. The electrified vulcanite rod picked it all up neatly and transferred it to the slide, and under the microscope its nature was obvious. The owner of this watch was therefore, almost certainly, employed in a felt hat factory. But, of course, it was necessary to show not only the presence of rabbit hair in this watch, but its absence in the others and in Fletcher's pockets, which I did.

"Then with regard to Harewood's watch. There was no rabbit hair on the dial, but there was a small quantity on the fluff from the key barrel. Now, if that rabbit hair had come from Harewood's pocket, it would have been uniformly distributed through the fluff. But it was not. It was confined exclusively to the part of the fluff that was exposed. Thus it had come from some pocket other than Harewood's, and the owner of that pocket was almost certainly employed in a felt hat factory, and was most probably the owner of watch No. 3."

"Then there was the cigarette-tube. Its bore was loaded with rabbit hair. But its owner had unquestionably been at the scene of the crime. There was a clear suggestion that his was the pocket in which the stolen watch had been carried and that he was the owner of watch No. 3. The problem was to piece this evidence together and prove definitely who this person was. And that I was able to do by means of a fresh item of evidence, which I acquired when I saw Baxfield at the inquest. I suppose you noticed his boots?"

"I am afraid I didn't," I had to admit.

"Well, I did. I watched his feet constantly, and when he crossed his legs, I could see that he had iron toe-tips on his boots. That was what gave me confidence to push the cross-examination."

"It was certainly a rather daring cross-examination – and rather irregular, too," said I.

"It was extremely irregular," Thorndyke agreed. "The coroner ought not to have permitted it. But it was all for the best. If the coroner had disallowed my questions we should have had to take criminal proceedings against Baxfield, whereas now that we have recovered the will, it is possible that no one will trouble to prosecute him."

Which, I subsequently ascertained, is what actually happened.

A Fisher of Men

"The man," observed Thorndyke, "who would successfully practise the scientific detection of crime must take all knowledge for his province. There is no single fact which may not, in particular circumstances, acquire a high degree of evidential value; and in such circumstances, success or failure is determined by the possession or non-possession of the knowledge wherewith to interpret the significance of that fact."

This *obiter dictum* was thrown off apropos of our investigation of the case rather magniloquently referred to in the press as "The Blue Diamond Mystery"; and more particularly of an incident which occurred in the office of our old friend, Superintendent Miller, at Scotland Yard. Thorndyke had called to verify the few facts which had been communicated to him, and having put away his notebook and picked up his green canvas-covered research case, had risen to take his leave, when his glance fell on a couple of objects on a side-table – a leather handbag and a walking-stick, lashed together with string, to which was attached a descriptive label.

He regarded them for a few moments reflectively and then glanced at the Superintendent.

"Derelicts?" he inquired, "or jetsam?"

"Jetsam," the Superintendent replied, "literally jetsam – thrown overboard to lighten the ship."

Here Inspector Badger, who had been a party to the conference, looked up eagerly.

"Yes," he broke in. "Perhaps the doctor wouldn't mind having a look at them. It's quite a nice little, problem, doctor, and entirely in your line."

"What is the problem?" asked Thorndyke.

"It's just this," said Badger. "Here is a bag. Now the question is, whose bag is it? What sort of person is the owner? Where did he come from and where has he gone to?"

Thorndyke chuckled. "That seems quite simple," said he. "A cursory inspection ought to dispose of trivial details like those. But how did you come by the bag?"

"The history of the derelicts," said Miller, "is this: About four o'clock this morning, a constable on duty in King's Road, Chelsea, saw a man walking on the opposite side of the road, carrying a hand-bag. There was nothing particularly suspicious in this, but still the constable thought he would cross and have a closer look at him. As he did so the man quickened his pace and, of course, the constable quickened his. Then the man broke into a run, and so did the constable, and a fine, stern chase started. Suddenly the man shot down a by-street, and as the constable turned the corner he saw his quarry turn into a sort of alley. Following him into this, and gaining on him perceptibly, he saw that the alley ended in a rather high wall. When the fugitive reached the wall he dropped his bag and stick and went over like a harlequin. The constable went over after him, but not like a harlequin – he wasn't dressed for the part. By the time he got over, into a large garden with a lot of fruit trees in it, my nabs had disappeared. He traced, him by his footprints across the garden to another wall, and when he climbed over that he found himself in another by-street. But there was no sign of our agile friend. The constable ran up and down the street to the next crossings, blowing his whistle, but of course it was no go. So he went back across the garden and secured the bag and stick, which were at once sent here for examination."

"And no arrest has been made?"

"Well," replied Miller with a faint grin, "a constable in Oakley Street who had heard the whistle arrested a man who was carrying a suspicious-looking object. But he turned out to be a cornet player coming home from the theatre."

"Good," said Thorndyke. "And now let us have a look at the bag, which I take it has already been examined?"

"Yes, we've been through it," replied Miller, "but everything has been put back as we found it."

Thorndyke picked up the bag and proceeded to make a systematic inspection of its exterior.

"A good bag," he commented; "quite an expensive one originally, though it has seen a good deal of service. You noticed the muddy marks on the bottom?"

"Yes," said Miller. "Those were probably made when he dropped the bag to jump over the wall."

"Possibly," said Thorndyke, "though they don't look like street mud. But we shall probably get more information from the contents." He opened the bag, and after a glance at its interior, spread out on the table a couple of sheets of foolscap from the stationery rack, on which he began methodically to deposit the contents of the bag, accompanying the process with a sort of running commentary on their obvious characteristics.

"Item one: a small leather dressing wallet. Rather shabby, but originally of excellent quality. It contains two Swedish razors, a little Washita hone, a diminutive strop, a folding shaving-brush, which is slightly damp to the fingers and has a scent similar to that of the stick of shaving soap. You notice that the hone is distinctly concave in the middle and that the inscription on the razors, 'Arensburg, Eskilstuna, Sweden,' is partly ground away. Then there is a box containing a very dry cake of soap, a little manicure set, a well-worn toothbrush, a nailbrush, dental-brush, buttonhook, corn-razor, a small clothesbrush and a pair of small hairbrushes. It seems to me, Badger, that this wallet suggests – mind, I only say 'suggests' – a pretty complete answer to one of your questions."

"I don't see how," said the Inspector. "Tell us what it suggests to you."

"It suggests to me," replied Thorndyke, laying down the lens through which he had been inspecting the hairbrushes, "a middle- aged or elderly man with a shaven upper lip and a beard; a well-preserved, healthy man, neat, orderly, provident and careful as to his appearance; a man long habituated to travelling, and – though I don't insist on this, but the appearances suggest that he had been living for some time in a particular household, and that at the time, when he lost the bag, he was changing his residence."

"He was that," cackled the Inspector, "if the constable's account of the way he went over that wall is to be trusted. But still, I don't see how you have arrived at all those facts."

"Not facts, Badger," Thorndyke corrected. "I said suggestions. And those suggestions may be quite misleading. There may be some factor, such as change of ownership of the wallet, which we have not allowed for. But, taking the appearances at their face value, that is what they suggest. There is the wallet itself, for instance – strong, durable, but shabby with years of wear. And observe that it is a travelling wallet and would be subjected to wear only during travel. Then further, as to the time factor, there are the hone and the razors. It takes a good many years to wear a Washita hone hollow or to wear away the blade of a Swedish razor until the maker's mark is encroached on. The state of health, and to some extent the age, are suggested by the toothbrush and the dental-brush. He has lost some teeth, since he wears a plate, but not many; and he is free from pyorrhea and alveolar absorption. You don't wear a toothbrush down like this on half a dozen rickety survivors. But a man whose teeth will bear hard brushing is probably well preserved and healthy."

"You say that he shaves his upper lip but wears a beard," said the Inspector. "How do you arrive at that?"

"It is fairly obvious," replied Thorndyke. "We see that he has razors and uses them, and we also see that he has a beard."

"Do we?" exclaimed Badger. "How do we?"

Thorndyke delicately picked a hair from one of the hairbrushes and held it up. "That is not a scalp hair," said he. "I should say that it came from the side of the chin."

Badger regarded the hair with evident disfavour. "Looks to me," he remarked, "as if a small-tooth comb might have been useful."

"It does," Thorndyke agreed, "but the appearance is deceptive. This is what is called a moniliform hair – like a string of beads. But the bead-like swellings are really parts of the hair. It is a diseased, or perhaps we should say an abnormal, condition." He handed me the hair together with his lens, through which I examined it and easily recognised the characteristic swellings.

"Yes," said I, "it is an early case of *trichorrexis nodosa.*"

"Good Lord!" murmured the Inspector. "Sounds like a Russian nobleman. Is it a common complaint?"

"It is not a rare disease – if you can call it a disease," I replied, "but it is a rare condition, taking the population as a whole."

"It is rather a remarkable coincidence that it should happen to occur in this particular case," the Superintendent observed.

"My dear Miller," exclaimed Thorndyke, "surely your experience must have impressed on you the astonishing frequency of the unusual and the utter failure of the mathematical laws of probability in practice. Believe me, Miller, the Bread-and-butterfly was right. It is, the exceptional that always happens."

Having discharged this paradox, he once more dived into the bag, and this time handed out a singular and rather unsavoury-looking parcel, the outer investment of which formed by what looked like an excessively dirty towel, but which, as Thorndyke delicately unrolled it, was seen to be only half a towel which was supplemented by a still dirtier and excessively ragged coloured handkerchief. This, too, being opened out, disclosed an extremely soiled and rather frayed collar (which, like the other articles, bore no name or mark), and a mass of grass, evidently used as packing material.

The Inspector picked up the collar and quoted reflectively, "He is a man, neat, orderly and careful as to his appearance," after which he dropped the collar and ostentatiously wiped his fingers.

Thorndyke smiled grimly but refrained from repartee as he carefully separated the grass from the contained objects, which turned out to be a small telescopic jemmy, a jointed augur, a screwdriver and a bunch of skeleton keys.

"One understands his unwillingness to encounter the constable with these rather significant objects in his possession," Thorndyke remarked. "They would have been difficult to explain away." He took up the heap of grass between his hands and gently compressed it to test its freshness. As he did so a tiny, cigar-shaped object dropped on the paper.

"What is that?" asked the Superintendent. "It looks like a chrysalis."

"It isn't," said Thorndyke. "It is a shell, a species of *Clausilia*, I think." He picked up the little shell and closely examined its mouth through his lens. "Yes," he continued, "it is a *Clausilia*. Do you study our British molluscs, Badger?"

"No, I don't," the Inspector replied with emphasis.

"Pity," murmured Thorndyke. "If you did, you would be interested to learn that the name of this little shell is *Clausilia biplicata.*"

"I don't care what its beastly name is," said Badger. "I want to know whose bag this is; what the owner is like; and where he came from and where he has gone to. Can you tell us that?"

Thorndyke regarded the Inspector with wooden gravity. "It is all very obvious," said he, "very obvious. But still I think I should like to fill in a few details before making a definite statement. Yes, I think I will reserve my judgment until I have considered the matter a little further."

The Inspector received this statement with a dubious grin. He was in somewhat of a dilemma. My colleague was addicted to a certain dry facetiousness, and was probably "pulling" the Inspector's "leg." But, on the other hand, I knew, and so did both the detectives, that it was perfectly conceivable that he had actually solved Badger's problem, impossible as it seemed, and was holding back his knowledge until he had seen whither it led.

"Shall we take a glance at the stick?" said he, picking it up as he spoke and running his eye over its not very distinctive features. It was a common ash stick, with a crooked handle polished and darkened by prolonged contact with an apparently ungloved hand, and it was smeared for about three inches from the tip with a yellowish mud. The iron shoe of the ferrule was completely worn away and the deficiency had been made good by driving a steel boot-stud into the exposed end.

"A thrifty gentleman, this," Thorndyke remarked, pointing to the stud as he measured the diameter of the ferrule with his pocket calliper-gauge. "Twenty-three thirty-seconds is the diameter," he added, looking gravely at the Inspector. "You had better make a note of that, Badger."

The Inspector smiled sourly as Thorndyke laid down the stick, and once more picking up the little green canvas case that contained his research outfit, prepared to depart.

"You will hear from us, Miller," he said, "if we pick up anything that will be useful to you. And now, Jervis, we must really take ourselves off."

As the hansom bore us down Whitehall towards Waterloo, I remarked, "Badger half suspects you of having withheld from him some valuable information in respect of that bag."

"He does," Thorndyke agreed with a mischievous smile; "and he doesn't in the least suspect me of having given him a most illuminating hint."

"But did you?" I asked, rapidly reviewing the conversation and deciding that the facts elicited from the dressing wallet could hardly be described as hints.

"My learned friend," he replied, "is pleased to counterfeit obtuseness. It won't do, Jervis. I've known you too long."

I grinned with vexation. Evidently I had missed the point of a subtle demonstration, and I knew that it was useless to ask further questions; and for the remainder of our journey in the cab I struggled vainly to recover the "illuminating hint" that the detectives – and I – had failed to note. Indeed, so preoccupied was I with this problem that I rather overlooked the fact that the jettisoned bag was really no concern of ours and that we were actually engaged in the investigation of a crime of which, at present, I knew practically nothing. It was not until we had secured an empty compartment and the train had begun to move that this suddenly dawned on me; whereupon I dismissed the bag problem and applied to Thorndyke for details of the "Brentford Train Mystery."

"To call it a mystery," said he, "is a misuse of words. It appears to be a simple train robbery. The identity of the robber is unknown, but there is nothing very mysterious in that; and the crime otherwise is quite commonplace. The circumstances are these: Some time ago, Mr Lionel Montague, of the firm, Lyons, Montague & Salaman, art dealers, bought from a Russian nobleman a very valuable diamond necklace and pendant. The peculiarity of this necklace was that the stones were all of a pale blue colour and pretty accurately matched, so that in addition to the aggregate value of the stones – which were all of large size and some very large – there was the value of the piece as a whole due to this uniformity of colour. Mr Montague gave £70,000 for it, and considered that he had made an excellent bargain. I should mention that Montague was the chief buyer for the firm, and that he spent most of his time travelling about the Continent in search of works of art and other objects suitable for the purposes of his firm, and that, naturally, he was an excellent judge of such things. Now, it seems that he was not satisfied with the settings of this necklace, and as soon as he had purchased it he handed it over to Messrs Binks, of Old Bond Street to have the settings replaced by others of better design. Yesterday morning he was notified by Binks that the resetting was completed, and in the afternoon he called to inspect the work and take the necklace away if it was satisfactory. The interview between Binks and Montague took place in a room behind the shop, but it appears that Montague came out into the shop to get a better light for his inspection; and Mr Binks states that as his customer stood facing the door, examining the new settings, he, Binks, noticed a man standing by the doorway furtively watching Mr Montague."

"There is nothing very remarkable in that," said I. "If a man stands at a shop door with a necklace of blue diamonds in his hand, he is rather likely to attract attention."

"Yes," Thorndyke agreed. "But the significance of an antecedent is apt to be more appreciated after the consequences have developed. Binks is now very emphatic about the furtive watcher. However, to continue: Mr Montague, being satisfied with the new settings, replaced the necklace in its case, put the latter into his bag – which he had brought with him from the inner room – and a minute or so later left the shop. That was about 5 p.m.; and he seems to have gone direct to the flat of his partner, Mr Salaman, with whom he had been staying for a fortnight, at Queen's Gate. There he remained until about half-past eight, when he came out accompanied by Mr Salaman. The latter carried a small suitcase, while Montague carried a handbag in which was the necklace. It is not known whether it contained anything else.

"From Queen's Gate the two men proceeded to Waterloo, walking part of the way and covering the remainder by omnibus."

"By omnibus!" I exclaimed, "with seventy thousand pounds of diamonds about them!"

"Yes, it sounds odd. But people who habitually handle portable property of great value seem to resemble those who habitually handle explosives. They gradually become unconscious of the risks. At any rate, that is how they went, and they arrived safely at Waterloo in time to catch the 9.15 train for Isleworth. Mr Salaman saw his partner established in an empty first-class compartment and stayed with him, chatting, until the train started.

"Mr Montague's destination was Isleworth, in which rather unlikely neighbourhood Mr Jacob Lowenstein, late of Chicago, and now of Berkeley Square, has a sort of riverside villa with a motor boat-house attached. Lowenstein had secured the option of purchasing the blue diamond necklace, and Montague was taking it down to exhibit it and carry out the deal. He was proposing to stay a few days with Lowenstein, and then he was proceeding to Brussels on one of his periodic tours. But he never reached Isleworth. When the train stopped at Brentford, a porter noticed a suitcase on the luggage-rack of an apparently empty first-class compartment. He immediately entered to take possession of it, and was in the act of reaching up to the rack when his foot came in contact with something soft under the seat. Considerably startled, he stooped and peered under, when, to his horror, he perceived the body of a man, quite motionless and apparently dead. Instantly he darted out and rushed up the platform in a state of wild panic until he, fortunately, ran against the station master, with whom and another porter he returned to the compartment. When they drew the body out from under the seat it was found to be still breathing, and they proceeded at once to apply such restoratives as cold water and fresh air, pending the arrival of the police and the doctor, who had been sent for.

"In a few minutes the police arrived accompanied by the police surgeon, and the latter, after a brief examination, decided that the unconscious man was suffering from the effects of a large dose of chloroform, violently and unskilfully administered, and ordered him to be carefully removed to a local nursing home. Meanwhile, the police had been able, by inspecting the contents of his pockets. to identify him as Mr Lionel Montague."

"The diamonds had vanished, of course?" said I.

"Yes. The handbag was not in the compartment, and later an empty handbag was picked up on the permanent way between Barnes and Chiswick, which seems to indicate the locality where the robbery took place."

"And what is our present objective?"

"We are going, on instructions from Mr Salaman, to the nursing home to see what information we can pick up. If Montague has recovered sufficiently to give an account of the robbery, the police will have a description of the robber, and there may not be much for us to do. But you will have noticed that they do not seem to have any information at Scotland Yard at present, beyond what I have given you. So there is a chance yet that we may earn our fees."

Thorndyke's narrative of this somewhat commonplace crime, with the discussion which followed it, occupied us until the train stopped at Brentford Station. A few minutes later we halted in one of the quiet by-streets of this old-world town, at a soberly painted door on which was a brass plate inscribed "St Agnes Nursing Home." Our arrival had apparently been observed, for the door was opened by a middle-aged lady in a nurse's uniform.

"Dr Thorndyke?" she inquired; and as my colleague bowed assent she continued: "Mr Salaman told me you would probably call. I am afraid I haven't very good news for you. The patient is still quite unconscious."

"That is rather remarkable," said Thorndyke.

"It is. Dr Kingston, who is in charge of the case, is somewhat puzzled by this prolonged stupor. He is inclined to suspect a narcotic – possibly a large dose of morphine – in addition to the effects of the chloroform and the shock."

"He is probably right," said I, "and the marvel is that the man is alive at all after such outrageous treatment."

"Yes," Thorndyke agreed. "He must be pretty tough. Shall we be able to see him?"

"Oh, yes," the matron replied. "I am instructed to give you every assistance. Dr Kingston would like to have your opinion on the case."

With this she conducted us to a pleasant room on the first floor where, in a bed placed opposite a large window – purposely left uncurtained – with the strong light falling full on his face, a man lay with closed eyes, breathing quietly and showing no sign of consciousness when we somewhat noisily entered the room. For some time Thorndyke stood by the bedside, looking down at the unconscious man, listening to the breathing and noting its frequency by his watch. Then he felt the pulse, and raising both eyelids, compared the two pupils.

"His condition doesn't appear alarming," was his conclusion. "The breathing is rather shallow, but it is quite regular, and the pulse is not bad though slow. The contracted pupils strongly suggest opium, or more probably morphine. But that could easily be settled by a chemical test. Do you notice the state of the face, Jervis?"

"You mean the chloroform burns? Yes, the handkerchief or pad must have been saturated. But I was also noticing that he corresponds quite remarkably with the description you were giving Badger of the owner of the dressing wallet. He is about the age you mentioned – roughly about fifty – and he has the same old-fashioned treatment of the beard, the shaven upper lip and the monkey-fringe under the chin. It is rather an odd coincidence."

Thorndyke looked at me keenly. "The coincidence is closer than that, Jervis. Look at the beard itself."

He handed me his lens, and, stooping down, I brought it to bear on the patient's beard. And then I started back in astonishment; for by the bright light I could see plainly that a considerable proportion of the hairs were distinctly moniliform. This man's beard, too, was affected by an early stage of *trichorrexis nodosa!*

"Well!" I exclaimed, "this is really an amazing coincidence. I wonder if it is anything more."

"I wonder," said Thorndyke. "Are those Mr Montague's things, Matron?"

"Yes," she replied, turning to the side table on which the patient's effects were neatly arranged. "Those are his clothes and the things which were taken from his pockets, and that is his bag. It was found on the line and sent on here a couple of hours ago. There is nothing in it."

Thorndyke looked over the various objects – keys, card-case, pocketbook, etc. – that had been turned out of the patient's pockets, and then picked up the bag, which he turned over curiously and then opened to inspect the interior. There was nothing distinctive about it. It was just a plain, imitation leather bag, fairly new, though rather the worse for its late vicissitudes, lined with coarse linen to which two large, wash-leather pockets had been roughly stitched. As he laid the bag down and picked up his own canvas case, he asked: "What time did Mr Salaman come to see the patient?"

"He came here about ten o'clock this morning, and he was not able to stay more than half an hour as he had an appointment. But he said he would look in again this evening. You can't stay to see him, I suppose?"

"I'm afraid not," Thorndyke replied; "in fact, we must be off now for both Dr Jervis and I have some other matters to attend to."

"Are you going straight back to the chambers, Jervis?" Thorndyke asked, as we walked down the main street towards the station.

"Yes," I replied in some surprise. "Aren't you?"

"No, I have a little expedition in view."

"Oh, have you?" I exclaimed, and as I spoke it began to dawn on me that I had overestimated the importance of my other business.

"Yes," said Thorndyke; "the fact is that – ha! excuse me one moment, Jervis." He had halted abruptly outside a fishing tackle shop and now, after a brief glance in through the window, entered with an air of business. I immediately bolted in after him, and was just in time to hear him demand a fishing rod of a light and inexpensive character. When this had been supplied he asked for a line and one or two hooks; and I was a little surprised – and the vendor was positively scandalised – at his indifference to the quality or character of these appliances. I believe he would have accepted cod-line and a shark-hook if they had been offered.

"And now I want a float," said he.

The shopkeeper produced a tray containing a varied assortment of floats over which Thorndyke ran a critical eye, and finally reduced the shopman to stupefaction by selecting a gigantic, potbellied, scarlet-and-green atrocity that looked like a juvenile telegraph buoy.

I could not let this outrage pass without comment. "You must excuse me, Thorndyke," I said, "if I venture to point out that the Greenland whale no longer frequents the upper reaches of the Thames."

"You mind your own business," he retorted, stolidly pocketing the telegraph buoy when he had paid for his purchases. "I like a float that you can see."

Here the shopman, recovering somewhat from the shock of surprise, remarked deferentially that it was a long time since a really large pike had been caught in the neighbourhood; whereupon Thorndyke finished him off by replying: "Yes, I've no doubt. They don't use the right sort of floats, you know. Now, when the pike see my float, they will just come tumbling over one another to get on the hook." With this he tucked the rod under his arm and strolled out, leaving the shopman breathing hard and staring harder.

"But what on earth," I asked, as we walked down the street (watched by the shopman, who had come out on the pavement to see the last of us), "do you want with such an enormous float? Why it will be visible a quarter of a mile away."

"Exactly," said Thorndyke. "And what more could a fisher of men require?"

This rejoinder gave me pause. Evidently Thorndyke had something in hand of more than common interest; and again it occurred to me that my own business engagements were of no special urgency. I was about to mention this fact when Thorndyke again halted – at an oilshop this time.

"I think I will step in here and get a little burnt umber," said he.

I followed him into the shop, and while the powder-colour was being weighed and made up into a little packet I reflected profoundly. Fishing tackle and burnt umber had no obvious associations. I began to be mystified and correspondingly inquisitive.

"What do you want the burnt umber for?" I asked as soon as we were outside.

"To mix with plaster," he replied readily.

"But why do you want to colour the plaster? And what are you going to do with it?"

"Now, Jervis," he admonished with mock severity, "you are not doing yourself justice. An investigator of your experience shouldn't ask for explanations of the obvious."

"And why," I continued, "did you want to know if I was going straight back to the chambers?"

"Because I may want some assistance later. Probably Polton will be able to do all that I want, but I wished to know that you would both be within reach of a telegram."

"But," I exclaimed, "what nonsense it is to talk of sending a telegram to me when I'm here!"

"But I may not want any assistance, after all."

"Well," I said doggedly, "you are going to have it whether you want it or not. You've got something on and I'm going to be in it."

"I like your enthusiasm, Jervis," he chuckled; "but it is quite possible that I shall merely find a mare's nest."

"Very well," said I. "Then I'll help you to find it. I've had plenty of experience in that line, to say nothing of my natural gifts. So lead on."

He led on, with a resigned smile, to the station, where we were fortunate enough to find a train just ready to start. But our journey was not a long one, for at Chiswick, Thorndyke got out of the train, and on leaving the station struck out eastward with a very evident air of business. As we entered the outskirts of Hammersmith he turned into a by-street which presently brought us out into Bridge Road. Here he turned sharply to the right and, at the same brisk pace, crossed Hammersmith Bridge and made his way to the towing path. As he now slowed down perceptibly, I ventured to inquire whether this was the spot on which he proposed to exhibit his super-float.

"This, I think, will be our fishing-ground," he replied; "but we will look over it carefully and select a suitable pitch."

He continued to advance at an easy pace, and I noticed that, according to his constant habit, he was studying the peculiarities of, the various feet that had trodden the path within the last day or two, keeping, for this purpose, on the right-hand side, where the shade of a few pollard willows overhanging an indistinct dry ditch had kept the ground soft. We had walked on for nearly half a mile when he halted and looked round.

"I think we had better turn back a little way," said he. "We seem to have overshot our mark."

I made no comment on this rather mysterious observation, and we retraced our steps for a couple of hundred yards, Thorndyke still walking on the side farthest from the river and still keeping his eyes fixed on the ground. Presently he again halted, and looking up and down the path, of which we were at the moment the only occupants, placed the canvas case on the ground and unfastened its clasps.

"This, I think, will be our pitch," said he.

"What are you going to do?" I asked.

"I am going to make one or two casts. And meanwhile you had better get the fishing rod fixed together so as to divert the attention of any passers by."

I proceeded to make ready the fishing tackle, but at the same time kept a close watch on my colleague's proceedings. And very curious proceedings they were. First he dipped up a little water from the river in the rubber mixing bowl with which he mixed a bowlful of plaster, and into this he stirred a few pinches of burnt umber, whereby its dazzling white was changed to a muddy buff. Then, having looked up and down the path, he stooped and carefully poured the plaster into a couple of impressions of a walking-stick that were visible at the edge of the path and finished up by filling a deep impression of the same stick, at the margin of the ditch, where it had apparently been stuck in the soft, clayey ground.

As I watched this operation, a sudden suspicion flashed into my mind. Dropping the fishing rod, I walked quickly along the path until I was able to pick up another impression of the stick. A very brief examination of it confirmed my suspicion. At the centre of the little shallow pit was a semicircular impression – clearly that of a half-worn bootstud.

"Why!" I exclaimed, "this is the stick that we saw at Scotland Yard!"

"I should expect it to be and I believe it is," said Thorndyke. "But we shall be better able to judge from the casts. Pick up your rod. There are two men coming down the path."

He closed his "research case" and drawing the fishing line from his pocket, began meditatively to unwind it.

"I could wish," said I, "that our appearance was more in character with the part of the rustic angler; and for the Lord's sake keep that float out of sight, or we shall collect a crowd."

Thorndyke laughed softly. "The float," said he, "was intended for Polton. He would have loved it. And the crowd would have been rather an advantage – as you will appreciate when you come to use it."

The two men – builder's labourers, apparently – now passed us with a glance of faint interest at the fishing tackle; and as they strolled by, I appreciated the value of the burnt umber.

If the casts had been made of the snow-white plaster, they would have stared conspicuously from the ground and these men would almost certainly have stopped to examine them and see what we were doing. But the tinted plaster was practically invisible.

"You are a wonderful man, Thorndyke," I said, as I announced my discovery. "You foresee everything."

He bowed his acknowledgements, and having tenderly felt one of the casts and ascertained that the plaster had set hard, he lifted it with infinite care, exhibiting a perfect facsimile of the end of the stick, on which the worn bootstud was plainly visible, even to the remains of the pattern. Any doubt that might have remained as to the identity of the stick was removed when Thorndyke produced his calliper-gauge.

"Twenty-three thirty-seconds was the diameter, I think," said he as he opened the jaws of the gauge and consulted his notes. He placed the cast between the jaws, and as they were gently slid, into contact, the index marked twenty-three thirty-seconds.

"Good," said Thorndyke, picking up the other two casts and establishing their identity with the one which we had examined. "This completes the first act." Dropping one cast into his case and throwing the other two into the river, he continued: "Now we proceed to the next and hope for a like success. You notice that he stuck his stick into the ground. Why do you suppose he did that?"

"Presumably to leave his hands free."

"Yes. And now let us sit down here and consider why he wanted his hands free. Just look around and tell me what you see."

I gazed rather hopelessly at the very indistinctive surroundings and began a bald catalogue. "I see a shabby-looking pollard willow, an assortment of suburban vegetation, an obsolete tin saucepan – unserviceable – and a bald spot where somebody seems to have pulled up a small patch of turf."

"Yes." said Thorndyke. "You will also notice a certain amount of dry, powdered earth distributed rather evenly over the bottom of the ditch. And your patch of turf was cut round with a large knife before it was pulled up. Why do you suppose it was pulled up?"

I shook my head. "It's of no use making mere guesses."

"Perhaps not," said he, "though the suggestion is fairly obvious when considered with the other appearances. Between the roots of the willow you notice a patch of grass that looks denser than one would expect from its position. I wonder – "

As he spoke, he reached forward with his stick and prised vigorously at the edge of the patch, with the result that the clump of grass lifted bodily; and when I picked it up and tried it on the bald spot, the nicety with which it fitted left no doubt as to its origin.

"Ha!" I exclaimed, looking at the obviously disturbed earth between the roots of the willow, which the little patch of turf had covered; "the plot thickens. Something seems to have been either buried or dug up there; more probably buried."

"I hope and believe that my learned friend is correct," said Thorndyke, opening his case to abstract a large, powerful spatula.

"What do you expect to find there?" I asked.

"I have a faint hope of finding something wrapped in the half of a very dirty towel," was the reply.

"Then you had better find it quickly," said I, "for there is a man coming along the path from the Putney direction."

He looked round at the still distant figure, and driving the spatula into the loose earth stirred it up vigorously.

"I can feel something," he said, digging away with powerful thrusts and scooping the earth out with his hands. Once more he looked round at the approaching stranger – who seemed now to have quickened his pace but was still four or five hundred yards distant. Then, thrusting his hands into the hole, he gave a smart pull. Slowly there came forth a package, about ten inches by six, enveloped in a portion of a peculiarly filthy towel and loosely secured with string. Thorndyke rapidly cast off the string and opened, out the towel, disclosing a handsome morocco case with an engraved gold plate.

I pounced on the case and, pressing the catch, raised the lid; and though I had expected no less, it was with something like a shock of surprise that I looked on the glittering row and the dazzling cluster of steely-blue diamonds.

As I closed the casket and deposited it in the green canvas case, Thorndyke, after a single glance at the treasure and another along the path, crammed the towel into the hole and began to sweep the loose earth in on top of it. The approaching stranger was for the moment hidden from us by a bend of the path and a near clump of bushes, and Thorndyke was evidently working to hide all traces before he should appear. Having filled the hole, he carefully replaced the sod of turf and then, moving over to the little bare patch from whence the turf had been removed, he began swiftly to dig it up.

"There," said he, flinging on the path a worm which he had just disinterred, "that will explain our activities. You had better continue the excavation with your pocket knife, and then proceed to the capture of the leviathans. I must run up to the police station and you must keep possession of this pitch. Don't move away from here on any account until I come back or send somebody to relieve you. I will hand you over the float; you'll want that." With a malicious smile he dropped the gaudy monstrosity on the path and having wiped the spatula and replaced it in the case, picked up the latter and moved away towards Putney.

At this moment the stranger reappeared, walking as if for a wager and I began to peck up the earth with my pocket knife. As the man approached he slowed down by degrees until he came up at something like a saunter. He was followed at a little distance by Thorndyke, who had turned as if he had changed his mind, and now passed me with the remark that "Perhaps Hammersmith would be better." The stranger cast a suspicious glance at him and then turned his attention to me.

"Lookin' for worms?" he inquired, halting and surveying me inquisitively.

I replied by picking one up (with secret distaste) and holding it aloft, and he continued, looking wistfully at Thorndyke's retreating figure:

"Your pal seems to have had enough."

"He hasn't got a rod," said I; "but he'll be back presently."

"Ah!" he said, looking steadily over my shoulder in the direction of the willow. "Well, you won't do any good here. The place where they rises is a quarter of a mile farther down – just round the bend there. That's a prime pitch. You just come along with me and I'll show you."

"I must stay here until my friend comes back," said I. "But I'll tell him what you say."

With this I seated myself stolidly on the bank and, having flung the baited hook into the stream, sat and glared fixedly at the preposterous float. My acquaintance fidgeted about me uneasily, endeavouring from time to time to lure me away to the "prime pitch" round the bend. And so the time dragged on until three-quarters of an hour had passed.

Suddenly I observed two taxicabs crossing the bridge, followed by three cyclists. A minute or two later Thorndyke reappeared, accompanied by two other men, and then the cyclists came into view, approaching at a rapid pace.

"Seems to be a regular procession," my friend remarked, viewing the new arrivals with evident uneasiness. As he spoke, one of the cyclists halted and dismounted to examine his tyre, while the other two approached and shot past us. Then they, too, halted and dismounted, and having deposited their machines in the ditch, they came back towards us. By this time I was able – with a good deal of surprise – to identify Thorndyke's two companions as Inspector Badger and Superintendent Miller. Perhaps my acquaintance also recognised them, or possibly the proceedings of the third cyclist – who had also laid down his machine and was approaching on foot – disturbed him. At any rate he glanced quickly from the one group to the other and, selecting the smaller one, sprang suddenly between the two cyclists and sped away along the path like a hare.

In a moment there was a wild stampede. The three cyclists. remounting their machines, pedalled furiously after the fugitive, followed by Badger and Miller on foot. Then the fugitive, the cyclists, and finally the two officers disappeared round the bend of the path.

"How did you know that he was the man?" I asked, when my colleague and I were left alone.

"I didn't, though I had pretty strong grounds for suspicion. But I merely brought the police to set a watch on the place and arrange an ambush. Their encircling movement was just an experimental bluff; they might have been chary of arresting the fellow if he hadn't taken fright and bolted. We have been fortunate all round, for, by a lucky chance, Badger and Miller were at Chiswick making enquiries and I was able to telephone to them to meet me at the bridge."

At this moment the procession reappeared, advancing briskly; and my late adviser marched at the centre securely handcuffed. As he was conducted past me he glared savagely and made some impolite references to a "blooming nark."

"You can take him in one of the taxis," said Miller, "and put your bicycles on top." Then, as the procession moved on towards the bridge he turned to Thorndyke. "I suppose he's the right man, Doctor, but he hasn't got any of the stuff on him."

"Of course he hasn't," said Thorndyke.

"Well, do you know where it is?"

Thorndyke opened his case and taking out the casket, handed it to the Superintendent. "I shall want a receipt for it," said he.

Miller opened the casket, and at the sight of the glittering jewels both the detectives uttered an exclamation of amazement, and the Superintendent demanded: "Where did you get this, sir?"

"I dug it up at the foot of that willow."

"But how did you know it was there?"

"I didn't," replied Thorndyke; "but I thought I might as well look, you know," and he bestowed a smile of exasperating blandness on the astonished officer.

The two detectives gazed at Thorndyke, then they looked at one another and then they looked at me; and Badger observed, with profound conviction, that it was a "knock-out." "I believe the doctor keeps a tame clairvoyant," he added.

"And may I take it, sir," said Miller, "that you can establish a *prima facie* case against this man, so that we can get a remand until Mr Montague is well enough to identify him?"

"You may," Thorndyke replied. "Let me know when and where he is to be charged and I will attend and give evidence."

On this Miller wrote out a receipt for the jewels and the two officers hurried off to their taxicab, leaving us, as Badger put it, "to our fishing."

As soon as they were out of sight, Thorndyke opened his case and mixed another bowlful of plaster. "We want two more casts," said he; "one of the right foot of the man who buried the jewels and one of the right foot of the prisoner. They are obviously identical, as you can see by the arrangement of the nails and the shape of the new patch on the sole. I shall put the casts in evidence and compare them with the prisoner's right boot."

I understood now why Thorndyke had walked away towards Putney and then returned in rear of the stranger. He had suspected the man and had wanted to get a look at his footprints. But there was a good deal in this case that I did not understand at all.

"There," said Thorndyke, as he deposited the casts, each with its pencilled identification, in his canvas case, "that is the end of the Blue Diamond Mystery."

"I beg your pardon," said I, "but it isn't. I want a full explanation. It is evident that from the house at Brentford you made a bee line to that willow. You knew then pretty exactly where the necklace was hidden. For all I know, you may have had that knowledge when we left Scotland Yard."

"As a matter of fact, I had," he replied. "I went to Brentford principally to verify the ownership of the wallet and the bag."

"But what was it that directed you with such certainty to the Hammersmith towing-path?"

It was then that he made the observation that I have quoted at the beginning of this narrative.

"In this case," he continued, "a curious fact, well known to naturalists, acquired vital evidential importance. It associated a bag, found in one locality, with another apparently unrelated locality. It was the link that joined the two ends of a broken chain. I offered up that fact to Inspector Badger, who, lacking the knowledge wherewith to interpret it, rejected it with scorn."

"I remember that you gave him the name of that little shell that dropped out of the handful of grass."

"Exactly," said Thorndyke. "That was the crucial fact. It told us where the handful of grass had been gathered."

"I can't imagine how," said I. "Surely you find shells all over the country?"

"That is, in general, quite true," he replied, "but *Clausilia biplicata* is one of the rare exceptions. There are four British species of these queer little univalves (which are so named from the little spring door with which the entrance of the shell is furnished); *Clausilia laminata, rolphii, rugosa* and *biplicata*. The first three species have what we may call a normal distribution, whereas the distribution of *biplicata* is abnormal. This seems to be a dying species. It is in process of becoming extinct in this island. But when a species of animal or plant becomes extinct, it does not fade away evenly over the whole of its habitat but it disappears in patches, which gradually extend, leaving, as it were, islands of survival. This is what has happened to *Clausilia biplicata*. It has disappeared from this country with the exception of two localities; one of these is in Wiltshire, and the other is the right bank of the Thames at Hammersmith. And this latter locality is extraordinarily restricted. Walk down a few hundred yards towards Putney, and you have walked out of its domain; walk up a few hundred yards towards the bridge, and again you have walked out of its territory. Yet within that little area it is fairly plentiful. If you know where to look – it lives on the bark or at the roots of willow trees – you can usually find one or two specimens. Thus, you see, the presence of that shell associated the handful of grass with a certain willow tree, and that willow was either in Wiltshire or by the Hammersmith towing-path. But there was nothing otherwise to connect it with Wiltshire, whereas there was something to connect it with Hammersmith. Let us for a moment dismiss the shell and consider the other suggestions offered by the bag and stick."

"The bag, as you saw, contained traces of two very different persons. One was apparently a middle-class man, probably middle-aged or elderly, cleanly, careful as to his appearance and of orderly habits; the other, uncleanly, slovenly and apparently a professional criminal. The bag itself seemed to appertain to the former person. It was an expensive bag and showed signs of years of careful use. This, and the circumstances in which it was found, led us to suspect that it was a stolen bag. Now, we knew that the contents of a bag had been stolen. We knew that an empty bag had been picked up on the line between Barnes and Chiswick, and it was probable that the thief had left the train at the latter station. The empty bag had been assumed to be Mr Montague's, whereas the probabilities – as, for instance, the fact of its having been thrown out on the line – suggested that it was the thief's bag, and that Mr Montague's had been taken away with its contents.

"The point, then, that we had to settle when we left Scotland Yard, was whether this apparently stolen bag had any connection with the train robbery. But as soon as we saw Mr Montague it was evident that he corresponded exactly with the owner of the dressing-wallet; and when we saw the bag that had been found on the line – a shoddy imitation leather bag – it was practically certain that it was not his, while the roughly-stitched leather pockets exactly suited to the dimensions of house-breaking tools, strongly suggested that it was a burglar's bag. But if this were so, then Mr Montague's bag had been stolen, and the robber's effects stuffed into it.

"With this working hypothesis we were now able to take up the case from the other end. The Scotland Yard bag was Montague's bag. It had been taken from Chiswick to the Hammersmith tow-path, where – judging from the clay smears on the bottom – it had been laid on the ground, presumably close to a willow tree. The use of the grass as packing suggested that something had been removed from the bag at this place – something that had wedged the tools together and prevented them from rattling; and there appeared to be half a towel missing. Clearly, the towpath was our next field of exploration.

"But, small as this area was geographically, it would have taken a long time to examine in detail. Here, however, the stick gave us invaluable aid. It had a perfectly distinctive tip, and it showed traces of having been stuck about three inches into earth similar to that on the bag. What we had thus to look for was a hole in the ground about three inches deep, and having at the bottom the impression of a half-worn bootstud. This hole would probably be close to a willow.

"The search turned out even easier than I had hoped. Directly we reached the towpath I picked up the track of the stick, and not one track only, but a double track, showing that our friend had returned to the bridge. All that remained was to follow the track until it came to an end and there we were pretty certain to find the hole in the ground, as, in fact, we did."

"And why," I asked, "do you suppose he buried the stuff?"

"Probably as a precaution, in case he had been seen and described. This morning's papers will have told him that he had not been. Probably, also, he wanted to make arrangements with a fence and didn't want to have the booty about him."

There is little more to tell. When the case was heard on the following morning, Thorndyke's uncannily precise and detailed description of the course of events, coupled with the production of the stolen property, so unnerved the prisoner that he pleaded guilty forthwith.

As to Mr Montague, he recovered completely in a few days, and a handsome pair of Georgian silver candlesticks may even to this day be seen on our mantelpiece testifying to his gratitude and appreciation of Thorndyke's brilliant conduct of the case.

The Stolen Ingots

"In medico-legal practice," Thorndyke remarked, "one must be
constantly on one's guard against the effects of suggestion, whether
intentional or unconscious. When the facts of a case are set forth
by an informant, they are nearly always presented, consciously or
unconsciously, in terms of inference. Certain facts, which appear to
the narrator to be the leading facts, are given with emphasis and in
detail, while other facts, which appear to be subordinate or trivial,
are partially suppressed. But this assessment of evidential value
must never be accepted. The whole case must be considered and
each fact weighed separately, and then it will commonly happen
that the leading fact turns out to be the one that had been passed
over as negligible."

The remark was made apropos of a case, the facts of which had
just been stated to us by Mr Halethorpe, of the Sphinx Assurance
Company. I did not quite perceive its bearing at the time, but
looking back when the case was concluded, I realised that I had
fallen into the very error against which Thorndyke's warning
should have guarded me.

"I trust," said Mr Halethorpe, "that I have not come at an
inconvenient time. You are so tolerant of unusual hours – "

"My practice," interrupted Thorndyke, "is my recreation, and I
welcome you as one who comes to furnish entertainment. Draw
your chair up to the fire, light a cigar and tell us your story."

Mr Halethorpe laughed, but adopted the procedure suggested, and having settled his toes upon the kerb and selected a cigar from the box, he opened the subject of his call.

"I don't quite know what you can do for us," he began, "as it is hardly your business to trace lost property, but I thought I would come and let you know about our difficulty. The fact is that our company looks like dropping some four thousand pounds, which the directors won't like. What has happened is this:

"About two months ago the London House of the Akropong Gold Fields company applied to us to insure a parcel of gold bars that were to be consigned to Minton and Borwell, the big manufacturing jewellers. The bars were to be shipped at Accra and landed at Bellhaven, which is the nearest port to Minton and Borwell's works. Well, we agreed to underwrite the risk – we have done business with the Akropong people before – and the matter was settled. The bars were put on board the *Labadi* at Accra, and in due course were landed at Bellhaven, where they were delivered to Minton's agents. So far, so good. Then came the catastrophe. The case of bars was put on the train at Bellhaven, consigned to Anchester, where Minton's have their factory. But the line doesn't go to Anchester direct. The junction is at Garbridge, a small country station close to the river Crouch, and here the case was put out and locked up in the stationmaster's office to wait for the Anchester train. It seems that the stationmaster was called away and detained longer than he had expected, and when the train was signalled he hurried back in a mighty twitter. However, the case was there all right, and he personally superintended its removal to the guard's van and put it in the guard's charge. All went well for the rest of the journey. A member of the firm was waiting at Anchester station with a closed van. The case was put into it and taken direct to the factory, where it was opened in the private office and found to be full of lead pipe."

"I presume," said Thorndyke, "that it was not the original case."

"No," replied Halethorpe, "but it was a very fair imitation. The label and the marks were correct, but the seals were just plain wax. Evidently the exchange had been made in the stationmaster's office, and it transpires that although the door was securely locked, there was an unfastened window which opened on to the garden, and there were plain marks of feet on the flower-bed outside."

"What time did this happen?" asked Thorndyke.

"The Anchester train came in at a quarter past seven, by which time, of course, it was quite dark."

"And when did it happen?"

"The day before yesterday. We heard of it yesterday morning."

"Are you contesting the claim?"

"We don't want to. Of course, we could plead negligence, but in that case I think we should make a claim on the railway company. But, naturally, we should much rather recover the property. After all, it can't be so very far away."

"I wouldn't say that," said Thorndyke. "This was no impromptu theft. The dummy case was prepared in advance, and evidently by somebody who knew what the real case was like, and how and when it was to be despatched from Bellhaven. We must assume that the disposal of the stolen case has been provided for with similar completeness. How far is Garbridge from the river?"

"Less than half a mile across the marshes. The detective-inspector – Badger, I think you know him – asked the same question."

"Naturally," said Thorndyke. "A heavy object like this case is much more easily and inconspicuously conveyed by water than on land. And then, see what facilities for concealment a navigable river offers. The case could be easily stowed away on a small craft, or even in a boat; or the bars could be taken out and stowed amongst the ballast, or even, at a pinch, dropped overboard at a marked spot and left until the hue and cry was over."

"You are not very encouraging," Halethorpe remarked gloomily. "I take it that you don't much expect that we shall recover those bars."

"We needn't despair," was the reply, "but I want you to understand the difficulties. The thieves have got away with the booty, and that booty is an imperishable material which retains its value even if broken up into unrecognisable fragments. Melted down into small ingots, it would be impossible to identify."

"Well," said Halethorpe, "the police have the matter in hand – Inspector Badger, of the CID, is in charge of the case – but our directors would be more satisfied if you would look into it. Of course we would give you any help we could. What do you say?"

"I am willing to look into the case," said Thorndyke, "though I don't hold out much hope. Could you give me a note to the shipping company and another to the consignees, Minton and Borwell?"

"Of course I will. I'll write them now. I have some of our stationery in my attaché case. But, if you will pardon my saying so, you seem to be starting your inquiry just where there is nothing to be learned. The case was stolen after it left the ship and before it reached the consignees – although their agent had received it from the ship."

"The point is," said Thorndyke, "that this was a preconcerted robbery, and that the thieves possessed special information. That information must have come either from the ship or from the factory. So, while we must try to pick up the track of the case itself, we must seek the beginning of the clue at the two ends – the ship and the factory – from one of which it must have started."

"Yes, that's true," said Halethorpe. "Well, I'll write those two notes and then I must run away; and we'll hope for the best."

He wrote the two letters, asking for facilities from the respective parties, and then took his departure in a somewhat chastened frame of mind.

"Quite an interesting little problem," Thorndyke remarked, as Halethorpe's footsteps died away on the stairs, "but not much in our line. It is really a police case – a case for patient and intelligent inquiry. And that is what we shall have to do – make some careful inquiries on the spot."

"Where do you propose to begin?" I asked.

"At the beginning," he replied. "Bellhaven. I propose that we go down there tomorrow morning and pick up the thread at that end."

"What thread?" I demanded. "We know that the package started from there. What else do you expect to learn?"

"There are several curious possibilities in this case, as you must have noticed," he replied. "The question is, whether any of them are probabilities. That is what I want to settle before we begin a detailed investigation."

"For my part," said I, "I should have supposed that the investigation would start from the scene of the robbery. But I presume that you have seen some possibilities that I have overlooked."

Which eventually turned out to be the case.

"I think," said Thorndyke as we alighted at Bellhaven on the following morning, "we had better go first to the Customs and make quite certain, if we can, that the bars were really in the case when it was delivered to the consignees' agents. It won't do to take it for granted that the substitution took place at Garbridge, although that is by far the most probable theory." Accordingly we made our way to the harbour, where an obliging mariner directed us to our destination.

At the Custom House we were received by a genial officer, who, when Thorndyke had explained his connection with the robbery, entered into the matter with complete sympathy and a quick grasp of the situation.

"I see," said he. "You want clear evidence that the bars were in the case when it left here. Well, I think we can satisfy you on that point. Bullion is not a customable commodity, but it has to be examined and reported. If it is consigned to the Bank of England or the Mint, the case is passed through with the seals unbroken, but as this was a private consignment, the seals will have been broken and the contents of the case examined. Jeffson, show these gentlemen the report on the case of gold bars from the *Labadi*."

"Would it be possible," Thorndyke asked, "for us to have a few words with the officer who opened the case? You know the legal partiality for personal testimony."

"Of course it would. Jeffson, when these gentlemen have seen the report, find the officer who signed it and let them have a talk with him."

We followed Mr Jeffson into an adjoining office where he produced the report and handed it to Thorndyke. The particulars that it gave were in effect those that would be furnished by the ship's manifest and the bill of lading. The case was thirteen inches long by twelve wide and nine inches deep, outside measurement; and its gross weight was one hundred and seventeen pounds three ounces, and it contained four bars of the aggregate weight of one hundred and thirteen pounds two ounces.

"Thank you," said Thorndyke, handing back the report. "And now can we see the officer – Mr Byrne, I think – just to fill in the details?"

"If you will come with me," replied Mr Jeffson, "I'll find him for you. I expect he is on the wharf."

We followed our conductor out on to the quay among a litter of cases, crates and barrels, and eventually, amidst a battalion of Madeira wine casks, found the officer deep in problems of "content and ullage," and other customs mysteries. As Jeffson introduced us, and then discreetly retired. Mr Byrne confronted us with a mahogany face and a truculent blue eye.

"With reference to this bullion," said Thorndyke, "I understand that you weighed the bars separately from the case?"

"Oi did," replied Mr Byrne.

"Did you weigh each bar separately?"

"Oi did not," was the concise reply.

"What was the appearance of the bars – I mean as to shape and size? Were they of the usual type?"

"Oi've not had a great deal to do with bullion," said Mr Byrne. "but Oi should say that they were just ordinary gold bars, about nine inches long by four wide and about two inches deep."

"Was there much packing material in the case?"

"Very little. The bars were wrapped in thick canvas and jammed into the case. There wouldn't be more than about half an inch clearance all round to allow for the canvas. The case was inch and a half stuff strengthened with iron bands."

"Did you seal the case after you had closed it up?"

"Oi did. 'Twas all shipshape when it was passed back to the mate. And Oi saw him hand it over to the consignees' agent; so 'twas all in order when it left the wharf."

"That was what I wanted to make sure of," said Thorndyke; and, having pocketed his notebook and thanked the officer, he turned away among the wilderness of merchandise.

"So much for the Customs," said he. "I am glad we went there first. As you have no doubt observed, we have picked up some useful information."

"We have ascertained," I replied, "that the case was intact when it was handed over to the consignees' agents, so that our investigations at Garbridge will start from a solid basis. And that, I take it, is all you wanted to know."

"Not quite all," he rejoined. "There are one or two little details that I should like to fill in. I think we will look in on the shipping agents and present Halethorpe's note. We may as well learn all we can before we make our start from the scene of the robbery."

"Well," I said. "I don't see what more there is to learn here. But apparently you do. That seems to be the office, past those sheds."

The manager of the shipping agent's office looked us up and down as he sat at his littered desk with Halethorpe's letter in his hand.

"You've come about that bullion that was stolen," he said brusquely. "Well, it wasn't stolen here. Hadn't you better inquire at Garbridge, where it was?"

"Undoubtedly," replied Thorndyke. "But I am making certain preliminary inquiries. Now, first, as to the bill of lading, who has that – the original, I mean?"

"The captain has it at present, but I have a copy."

"Could I see it?" Thorndyke asked.

The manager raised his eyebrows protestingly, but produced the document from a file and handed it to Thorndyke, watching him inquisitively as he copied the particulars of the package into his notebook.

"I suppose," said Thorndyke as he returned the document, "you have a copy of the ship's manifest?"

"Yes," replied the manager, "but the entry in the manifest is merely a copy of the particulars given in the bill of lading."

"I should like to see the manifest, if it is not troubling you too much."

"But," the other protested impatiently, "the manifest contains no information respecting this parcel of bullion excepting the one entry, which, as I have told you, has been copied from the bill of lading."

"I realise that," said Thorndyke, "but I should like to look over it, all the same."

Our friend bounced into an inner office and presently returned with a voluminous document, which he slapped down on a sidetable.

"There, sir," he said. "That is the manifest. This is the entry relating to the bullion that you are inquiring about. The rest of the document is concerned with the cargo, in which I presume you are not interested."

In this, however, he was mistaken; for Thorndyke, having verified the bullion entry, turned the leaves over and began systematically, though rapidly, to run his eye over the long list from the beginning, a proceeding that the manager viewed with frenzied impatience.

"If you are going to read it right through, sir," the latter observed, "I shall ask you to excuse me. Art is long but life short," he added with a sour smile.

Nevertheless he hovered about uneasily, and when Thorndyke proceeded to copy some of the entries into his notebook, he craned over and read them without the least disguise, though not without comment.

"Good God, sir!" he exclaimed. "What possible bearing on this robbery can that parcel of scrivelloes have? And do you realise that they are still in the ship's hold?"

"I inferred that they were, as they are consigned to London," Thorndyke replied, drawing his finger down the "description" column and rapidly scanning the entries in it. The manager watched that finger, and as it stopped successively at a bag of gum copal, a case of quartz specimens, a case of six-inch brass screw-bolts, a bag of beni-seed and a package of kola nuts, he breathed hard and muttered like an angry parrot. But Thorndyke was quite unmoved. With calm deliberation he copied out each entry, conscientiously noting the marks, descriptions of packages and contents, gross and net weight, dimensions, names of consignors and consignees, ports of shipment and discharge, and, in fact, the entire particulars. It was certainly an amazing proceeding, and I could make no more of it than could our impatient friend.

At last Thorndyke closed and pocketed his notebook, and the manager heaved a slightly obtrusive sigh. "Is there nothing more, sir?" he asked. "You don't want to examine the ship, for instance?" The next moment, I think, he regretted his sarcasm, for Thorndyke inquired, with evident interest: "Is she still here?"

"Yes," was the unwilling admission. "She finishes unloading here at midday today and will probably haul into the London Docks tomorrow morning."

"I don't think I need go on board," said Thorndyke, "but you might give me a card in case I find that I want to."

The card was somewhat grudgingly produced, and when Thorndyke had thanked our entertainer for his help, we took our leave and made our way towards the station.

"Well," I said. "You have collected a vast amount of curious information but I am hanged if I can see that any of it has the slightest bearing on our inquiry."

Thorndyke cast on me a look of deep reproach. "Jervis!" he exclaimed, "you astonish me; you do, indeed. Why, my dear fellow, it stares you in the face!"

"When you say 'it'," I said a little irritably, "you mean?"

"I mean the leading fact from which we may deduce the *modus operandi* of this robbery. You shall look over my notes in the train and sort out the data that we have collected. I think you will find them extremely illuminating."

"I doubt it," said I. "But, meanwhile aren't we wasting a good deal of time? Halethorpe wants to get the gold back; he doesn't want to know how the thieves contrived to steal it."

"That is a very just remark," answered Thorndyke. "My learned friend displays his customary robust common sense. Nevertheless, I think that a clear understanding of the mechanism of this robbery will prove very helpful to us, though I agree with you that we have spent enough time on securing our preliminary data. The important thing now is to pick up a trail from Garbridge. But I see our train is signalled. We had better hurry."

As the train rumbled into the station, we looked out for an empty smoking compartment, and having been fortunate enough to secure one, we settled ourselves in opposite corners and lighted our pipes. Then Thorndyke handed me his notebook and as I studied, with wrinkled brows, the apparently disconnected entries, he sat and observed me thoughtfully and with the faintest suspicion of a smile. Again and again I read through those notes with ever-dwindling hopes of extracting the meaning that "stared me in the face." Vainly did I endeavour to connect gum copal, scrivelloes or beni-seed with the methods of the unknown robbers. The entries in the notebook persisted obstinately in remaining totally disconnected and hopelessly irrelevant. At last I shut the book with a savage snap and handed it back to its owner.

"It's no use, Thorndyke," I said. "I can't see the faintest glimmer of light."

"Well," said he, "it isn't of much consequence. The practical part of our task is before us, and it may turn out a pretty difficult part. But we have got to recover those bars if it is humanly possible. And here we are at our jumping-off place. This is Garbridge Station – and I see an old acquaintance of ours on the platform."

I looked out, as the train slowed down, and there, sure enough, was no less a person than Inspector Badger of the Criminal Investigation Department.

"We could have done very well without Badger," I remarked.

"Yes," Thorndyke agreed, "but we shall have to take him into partnership, I expect. After all, we are on his territory and on the same errand. How do you do, Inspector?" he continued, as the officer, having observed our descent from the carriage, hurried forward with unwonted cordiality.

"I rather expected to see you here, sir," said he. "We heard that Mr Halethorpe had consulted you. But this isn't the London train."

"No," said Thorndyke. "We've been to Bellhaven, just to make sure that the bullion was in the case when it started."

"I could have told you that two days ago," said Badger. "We got on to the Customs people at once. That was all plane sailing but the rest of it isn't."

"No clue as to how the case was taken away?"

"Oh, yes; that is pretty clear. It was hoisted out, and the dummy hoisted in, through the window of the stationmaster's office. And the same night, two men were seen carrying a heavy package, about the size of the bullion case, towards the marshes. But there the clue ends. The stuff seems to have vanished into thin air. Of course our people are on the lookout for it in various likely directions, but I am staying here with a couple of plain-clothes men. I've a conviction that it is still somewhere in this neighbourhood, and I mean to stick here in the hope that I may spot somebody trying to move it."

As the inspector was speaking we had been walking slowly from the station towards the village, which was on the opposite side of the river. On the bridge Thorndyke halted and looked down the river and over the wide expanse of marshy country.

"This is an ideal place for a bullion robbery," he remarked. "A tidal river near to the sea and a network of creeks, in any one of which one could hide a boat or sink the booty below tidemarks. Have you heard of any strange craft having put in here?"

"There's a little ramshackle bawley from Leigh – but her crew of two ragamuffins are not Leigh men. And they've made a mess of their visit – got their craft on the mud on the top of the spring tide. There she is, on that spit; and there she'll be till next spring tide. But I've been over her carefully and I'll swear the stuff isn't aboard her. I had all the ballast out and emptied the lazarette and the chain locker."

"And what about the barge?"

"She's a regular trader here. Her crew – the skipper and his son – are quite respectable men and they belong here. There they go in that boat; I expect they are off on this tide. But they seem to be making for the bawley."

As he spoke the inspector produced a pair of glasses, through which he watched the movements of the barge's jolly-boat, and a couple of elderly fishermen, who were crossing the bridge, halted to look on. The barge's boat ran alongside the stranded bawley, and one of the rowers hailed; whereupon two men tumbled up from the cabin and dropped into the boat, which immediately pushed off and headed for the barge.

"Them bawley blokes seems to be taking a passage along of old Bill Somers," one of the fishermen remarked, levelling a small telescope at the barge as the boat drew alongside and the four men climbed on board. "Going to work their passage, too," he added as the two passengers proceeded immediately to man the windlass

152

while the crew let go the brails and hooked the main-sheet block to the traveller.

"Rum go," commented Badger, glaring at the barge through his glasses; "but they haven't taken anything aboard with them. I could see that."

"You have overhauled the barge, I suppose?" said Thorndyke.

"Yes. Went right through her. Nothing there. She's light. There was no place aboard her where you could hide a split pea."

"Did you get her anchor up?"

"No," replied Badger. "I didn't. I suppose I ought to have done so. However, they're getting it up themselves now." As he spoke, the rapid clink of a windlass-pawl was borne across the water, and through my prismatic glasses I could see the two passengers working for all they were worth at the cranks. Presently the clink of the pawl began to slow down somewhat and the two bargemen, having got the sails set, joined the toilers at the windlass, but even then there was no great increase of speed.

"Anchor seems to come up uncommon heavy," one of the fishermen remarked.

"Aye," the other agreed. "Got foul of an old mooring maybe."

"Look out for the anchor, Badger," Thorndyke said in a low voice, gazing steadily through his binocular. "It is out of the ground. The cable is up and down and the barge is drifting off on the tide."

Even as he spoke the ring and stock of the anchor rose slowly out of the water, and now I could see that a second chain was shackled loosely to the cable, down which it had slid until it was stopped by the ring of the anchor. Badger had evidently seen it too, for he ejaculated, "Hallo!" and added a few verbal flourishes which I need not repeat. A few more turns of the windlass brought the flukes of the anchor clear of the water, and dangling against them was an undeniable wooden case, securely slung with lashings of stout chain. Badger cursed volubly, and, turning to the fishermen, exclaimed in a rather offensively peremptory tone:

"I want a boat. Now. This instant."

The elder piscator regarded him doggedly and replied: "All right. I ain't got no objection."

"Where can I get a boat?" the inspector demanded, nearly purple with excitement and anxiety.

"Where do you think?" the mariner responded, evidently nettled by the inspector's masterful tone. "Pastrycook's? Or livery stables?"

"Look here," said Badger. "I'm a police officer and I want to board that barge and I am prepared to pay handsomely. Now where can I get a boat?"

"We'll put you aboard of her," replied the fisherman, "that is, if we can catch her. But I doubt it. She's off, that's what she is. And there's something queer agoing on aboard of her," he added in a somewhat different tone.

There was. I had been observing it. The case had been, with some difficulty, hoisted on board, and then suddenly there had broken out an altercation between the two bargees and their passengers, and this had now developed into what looked like a free fight. It was difficult to see exactly what was happening, for the barge was drifting rapidly down the river, and her sails, blowing out first on one side and then on the other, rather obscured the view. Presently, however, the sails filled and a man appeared at the wheel; then the barge jibed round, and with a strong ebb tide and a fresh breeze, very soon began to grow small in the distance.

Meanwhile the fishermen had bustled off in search of a boat, and the inspector had raced to the bridge-head, where he stood gesticulating frantically and blowing his whistle, while Thorndyke continued placidly to watch the receding barge through his binocular.

"What are we going to do?" I asked, a little surprised at my colleague's inaction.

"What can we do?" he asked in reply.

"Badger will follow the barge. He probably won't overtake her, but he will prevent her from making a landing until they get out into the estuary, and then he may possibly get assistance. The chase is in his hands."

"Are we going with him?"

"I am not. This looks like being an all-night expedition, and I must be at our chambers tomorrow morning. Besides, the chase is not our affair. But if you would like to join Badger there is no reason why you shouldn't. I can look after the practice."

"Well," I said, "I think I should rather like to be in at the death, if it won't inconvenience you. But it is possible that they may get away with the booty."

"Quite," he agreed, "and then it would be useful to know, exactly how and where it disappears. Yes, go with them, by all means, and keep a sharp lookout."

At this moment Badger returned with the two plain-clothes men whom his whistle had called from their posts, and simultaneously a boat was seen approaching the steps by the bridge, rowed by the two fishermen. The inspector looked at us inquiringly. "Are you coming to see the sport?" he asked.

"Doctor Jervis would like to come with you," Thorndyke replied. "I have to get back to London. But you will be a fair boat-load without me."

This appeared to be also the view of the two fishermen, as they brought up at the steps and observed the four passengers; but they made no demur beyond inquiring if there were not any more; and when we had taken our places in the stem sheets, they pushed off and pulled through the bridge and away down stream. Gradually, the village receded and the houses and the bridge grew small and more distant, though they remained visible for a long time over the marshy levels; and still, as I looked back through my glasses, I could see Thorndyke on the bridge, watching the pursuit with his binocular to his eyes.

Meanwhile the fugitive barge, having got some two miles start, seemed to be drawing ahead. But it was only at intervals that we could see her, for the tide was falling fast and we were mostly hemmed in by the high, muddy banks. Only when we entered a straight reach of the river could we see her sails over the land; and every time that she came into view, she appeared perceptibly smaller.

When the river grew wider, the mast was stepped and a good-sized lug-sail hoisted, though one of the fishermen continued to ply his oar on the weather side, while the other took the tiller. This improved our pace appreciably; but still, whenever we caught a glimpse of the barge, it was evident that she was still gaining.

On one of these occasions the man at the tiller, standing up to get a better view, surveyed our quarry intently for nearly a minute and then addressed the inspector.

"She's a-going to give us the go-by, mister," he observed with conviction.

"Still gaining?" asked Badger.

"Aye. She's a-going to slip across the tail of Foulness Sand into the deep channel. And that's the last we shall see of her."

"But can't we get into the channel the same way?" demanded Badger.

"Well, d'ye see," replied the fisherman, " 'tis like this. Tide's a-running out, but there'll be enough for her. It'll just carry her out through the Whitaker Channel and across the spit. Then it'll turn, and up she'll go, London way, on the flood. But we shall catch the flood-tide in the Whitaker Channel, and a rare old job we'll have to get out; and when we do get out, that barge'll be miles away."

The inspector swore long and earnestly. He even alluded to himself as a "blithering idiot." But that helped matters not at all. The fisherman's dismal prophecy was fulfilled in every horrid detail. When we were approaching the Whitaker Channel the barge was just crossing the spit, and the last of the ebb-tide was trickling out. By the time we were fairly in the Channel the tide had turned and was already flowing in with a speed that increased every minute; while over the sand we could see the barge, already out in the open estuary, heading to the west on the flood-tide at a good six knots.

Poor Badger was frantic. With yearning eyes fixed on the dwindling barge, he cursed, entreated, encouraged and made extravagant offers. He even took an oar and pulled with such desperate energy that he caught a crab and turned a neat back somersault into the fisherman's lap. The two mariners pulled until their oars bent like canes; but still the sandy banks crept by, inch by inch, and ever the turbid water seemed to pour up the channel more and yet more swiftly. It was a fearful struggle and seemed to last for hours; and when, at last, the boat crawled out across the spit and the exhausted rowers rested on their oars, the sun was just setting and the barge had disappeared into the west.

I was really sorry for Badger. His oversight in respect of the anchor was a very natural one for a landsman, and he had evidently taken infinite pains over the case and shown excellent judgment in keeping a close watch on the neighbourhood of Garbridge and now, after all his care, it looked as if both the robbers and their booty had slipped through his fingers. It was desperately bad luck.

"Well," said the elder fisherman, "they've give us a run for our money; but they've got clear away. What's to be done now, mister?"

Badger had nothing to suggest excepting that we should pull or sail up the river in the hope of getting some assistance on the way. He was in the lowest depths of despair and dejection. But now, when Fortune seemed to have deserted us utterly, and failure appeared to be an accomplished fact, Providence intervened.

A small steam vessel that had been approaching from the direction of the East Swin suddenly altered her course and bore down as if to speak us. The fisherman who had last spoken looked at her attentively for a few moments and then slapped his thigh. "Saved, by gum!" he exclaimed. "This'll do your trick, master. Here comes a Customs cruiser."

Instantly the two fishermen bent to their oars to meet the oncoming craft, and in a few minutes we were alongside, Badger hailing like a bull of Bashan. A brief explanation to the officer in charge secured a highly sympathetic promise of help. We all scrambled up on deck; the boat was dropped astern at the scope of her painter; the engine-room bell jangled merrily, and the smart, yacht-like vessel began to forge ahead.

"Now then," said the officer, as his craft gathered way, "give us a description of this barge. What is she like?"

"She's a small stumpy," the senior fisherman explained, "flying light; wants paint badly; steers with a wheel; green transom with *Bluebell, Maldon,* cut in and gilded. Seemed to be keeping along the north shore."

With these particulars in his mind, the officer explored the western horizon with a pair of night-glasses, although it was still broad daylight. Presently he reported: "There's a stumpy in a line with the Blacktail Spit buoy. Just take a look at her." He handed his glasses to the fisherman, who, after a careful inspection of the stranger, gave it as his opinion that she was our quarry. "Probably makin' for Southend or Leigh," said he, and added: "I'll bet she's bound for Benfleet Creek. Nice quiet place, that, to land the stuff."

Our recent painful experience was now reversed, for as our swift little vessel devoured the miles of water, the barge, which we were all watching eagerly, loomed up larger every minute. By the time we were abreast of the Mouse Lightship, she was but a few hundred yards ahead, and even through my glasses, the name *Bluebell* was clearly legible. Badger nearly wept with delight; the officer in charge smiled an anticipatory smile; the deckhands girded up their loins for the coming capture and the plain-clothes men each furtively polished a pair of handcuffs.

At length the little cruiser came fairly abreast of the barge – not unobserved by the two men on her deck. Then she sheered in suddenly and swept alongside. One hand neatly hooked a shroud with a grappling iron and made fast while a couple of preventive officers, the plain-clothes men and the inspector jumped down simultaneously on to the barge's deck. For a moment, the two bawley men were inclined to show fight; but the odds were too great. After a perfunctory scuffle they both submitted to be handcuffed and were at once hauled up on board the cruiser and lodged in the fore-peak under guard. Then the chief officer, the two fishermen and I jumped on board the barge and followed Badger down the companion hatch to the cabin.

It was a curious scene that was revealed in that little cupboard-like apartment by the light of Badger's electric torch. On each of the two lockers was stretched a man, securely lashed with lead-line and having drawn over his face a knitted stocking cap, while on the little triangular fixed table rested an iron-bound box which I instantly identified by my recollection of the description of the bullion case in the ship's manifest. It was but the work of a minute to liberate the skipper and his son and send them up, wrathful but substantially uninjured, to refresh on the cruiser; and then the ponderous treasure chest was borne in triumph by two muscular deckhands, up the narrow steps, to be hoisted to the Government vessel.

"Well, well," said the inspector, mopping his face with his handkerchief, "All's well that ends well, but I thought I had lost the men and the stuff that time. What are you going to do? I shall stay on board as this boat is going right up to the Custom House in London; but if you want to get home sooner, I dare say the chief officer will put you ashore at Southend."

I decided to adopt this course, and I was accordingly landed at Southend Pier with a telegram from Badger to his headquarters; and at Southend I was fortunate enough to catch an express train which brought me to Fenchurch Street while the night was still young.

When I reached our chambers, I found Thorndyke seated by the fire, serenely studying a brief. He stood up as I entered and, laying aside the brief, remarked: "You are back sooner than I expected. How sped the chase? Did you catch the barge?"

"Yes. We've got the men and we've got the bullion. But we very nearly lost both;" and here I gave him an account of the pursuit and the capture, to which he listened with the liveliest interest. "That Customs cruiser was a piece of sheer luck," said he, when I had concluded. "I am delighted. This capture simplifies the case for us enormously."

"It seems to me to dispose of the case altogether," said I. "The property is recovered and the thieves are in custody. But I think most of the credit belongs to Badger."

Thorndyke smiled enigmatically. "I should let him have it all, Jervis," he said; and then, after a reflective pause, he continued: "We will go round to Scotland Yard in the morning to verify the capture. If the package agrees with the description in the bill of lading, the case, as you say, is disposed of."

"It is hardly necessary," said I. "The marks were all correct and the Customs seals were unbroken – but still, I know you won't be satisfied until you have verified everything for yourself. And I suppose you are right."

It was past eleven in the following forenoon when we invaded Superintendent Miller's office at Scotland Yard. That genial officer looked up from his desk as we entered and laughed joyously. "I told you so, Badger," he chuckled, turning to the inspector, who had also looked up and was regarding us with a foxy smile. "I knew the doctor wouldn't be satisfied until he had seen it with his own eyes. I suppose that is what you have come for, sir?"

"Yes," was the reply. "It is a mere formality, of course, but, if you don't mind – "

"Not in the least," replied Miller. "Come along, Badger, and show the doctor your prize."

The two officers conducted us to a room, which the superintendent unlocked, and which contained a small table, a measuring standard, a weighing machine, a set of Snellen's test-types, and the now historic case of bullion. The latter Thorndyke inspected closely, checking the marks and dimensions by his notes.

"I see you haven't opened it," he remarked.

"No," replied Miller. "Why should we? The Customs seals are intact."

"I thought you might like to know what was inside," Thorndyke explained.

The two officers looked at him quickly and the inspector exclaimed: "But we do know. It was opened and checked at the Customs."

"What do you suppose is inside?" Thorndyke asked.

"I don't suppose," Badger replied testily. "I know. There are four bars of gold inside."

"Well," said Thorndyke, "as the representative of the Insurance Company, I should like to see the contents of that case."

The two officers stared at him in amazement, as also, I must admit, did I. The implied doubt seemed utterly contrary to reason.

"This is scepticism with a vengeance!" said Miller. "How on earth is it possible – but there, I suppose if you are not satisfied, we should be justified – "

He glanced at his subordinate, who snorted impatiently: "Oh, open it and let him see the bars. And then, I suppose, he will want us to make an assay of the metal."

The superintendent retired with wrinkled brows and presently returned with a screwdriver, a hammer and a case-opener. Very deftly he broke the seals, extracted the screws and prised up the lid of the case, inside which were one or two folds of thick canvas. Lifting these with something of a flourish, he displayed the upper pair of dull, yellow bars.

"Are you satisfied now, sir?" demanded Badger. "Or do you want to see the other two?"

Thorndyke looked reflectively at the two bars, and the two officers looked inquiringly at him (but one might as profitably have watched the expression on the face of a ship's figurehead). Then he took from his pocket a folding foot-rule and quickly measured the three dimensions of one of the bars.

"Is that weighing machine reliable?" he asked.

"It is correct to an ounce," the superintendent replied, gazing at my colleague with a slightly uneasy expression. "Why?"

By way of reply Thorndyke lifted out the bar that he had measured and carrying it across to the machine, laid it on the platform and carefully adjusted the weights.

"Well?" the superintendent queried anxiously, as Thorndyke took the reading from the scale.

"Twenty-nine pounds, three ounces," replied Thorndyke.

"Well?" repeated the superintendent. "What about it?"

Thorndyke looked at him impassively for a moment, and then, in the same quiet tone, answered: "Lead."

"What!" the two officers shrieked in unison, darting across to the scale and glaring at the bar of metal. Then Badger recovered himself and expostulated, not without temper, "Nonsense, sir. Look at it. Can't you see that it is gold?"

"I can see that it is gilded," replied Thorndyke.

"But," protested Miller, "the thing is impossible. What makes you think it is lead?"

"It is just a question of specific gravity," was the reply. "This bar contains seventy-two cubic inches of metal and it weighs twenty-nine pounds three ounces. Therefore it is a bar of lead. But if you are still doubtful, it is quite easy to settle the matter. May I cut a small piece off the bar?"

The superintendent gasped and looked at his subordinate. "I suppose," said he, "under the circumstances – eh, Badger? Yes. Very well, Doctor."

Thorndyke produced a strong pocket knife, and, having lifted the bar to the table, applied the knife to one corner and tapped it smartly with the hammer. The blade passed easily through the soft metal, and as the detached piece fell to the floor, the two officers and I craned forward eagerly. And then all possible doubts were set at rest. There was no mistaking the white, silvery lustre of the freshly-cut surface.

"Snakes!" exclaimed the superintendent. "This is a fair knockout! Why, the blighters have got away with the stuff, after all! Unless," he added, with a quizzical look at Thorndyke, "you know where it is, Doctor. I expect you do."

"I believe I do," said Thorndyke, "and if you care to come down with me to the London Docks, I think I can hand it over to you."

The superintendent's face brightened appreciably. Not so Badger's. That afflicted officer flung down the chip of metal that he had been examining, and, turning to Thorndyke, demanded sourly: "Why didn't you tell us this before, sir? You let me go off chivvying that damn barge, and you knew all the time that the stuff wasn't on board."

"My dear Badger," Thorndyke expostulated, "don't you see that these lead bars are essential to our case? They prove that the gold bars were never landed and that they are consequently still on the ship. Which empowers us to detain any gold that we may find on her."

"There, now, Badger," said the superintendent, "it's no use for you to argue with the doctor. He's like a giraffe. He can see all round him at once. Let us get on to the Docks."

Having locked the room, we all sallied forth, and, taking a train at Charing Cross Station, made our way by Mark Lane and Fenchurch Street to Wapping, where, following Thorndyke, we entered the Docks and proceeded straight to a wharf near the Wapping entrance. Here Thorndyke exchanged a few words with a Customs official, who hurried away and presently returned accompanied by an officer of higher rank. The latter, having saluted Thorndyke and cast a slightly amused glance at our little party, said: "They've landed that package that you spoke about. I've had it put in my office for the present. Will you come and have a look at it?"

We followed him to his office behind a long row of sheds, where, on a table, was a strong wooden case, somewhat larger than the "bullion" case, while, on the desk a large many-leaved document lay open.

"This is your case, I think," said the official; "but you had better check it by the manifest. Here is the entry: 'One case containing seventeen and three-quarter dozen brass six-inch by three-eighths screw-bolts with nuts. Dimensions, sixteen inches by thirteen by nine. Gross weight a hundred and nineteen pounds; net weight a hundred and thirteen pounds.' Consigned to 'Jackson and Walker, 593, Great Alie Street, London, E.' Is that the one?"

"That is the one," Thorndyke replied.

"Then," said our friend, "we'll get it open and have a look at those brass screw-bolts."

With a dexterity surprising in an official of such high degree, he had the screws out in a twinkling, and prising up the lid, displayed a fold of coarse canvas. As he lifted this the two police officers peered eagerly into the case; and suddenly the eager expression on Badger's face changed to one of bitter disappointment.

"You've missed fire this time, sir," he snapped. "This is just a case of brass bolts."

"Gold bolts, Inspector," Thorndyke corrected, placidly. He picked out one and handed it to the astonished detective. "Did you ever feel a brass bolt of that weight?" he asked.

"Well, it certainly is devilish heavy," the inspector admitted, weighing it in his hand and passing it on to Miller.

"Its weight, as stated on the manifest," said Thorndyke, "works out at well over eight and a half ounces, but we may as well check it." He produced from his pocket a little spring balance, to which he slung the bolt. "You see," he said, "it weighs eight ounces and two-thirds. But a brass bolt of the same size would weigh only three ounces and four-fifths. There is not the least doubt that these bolts are gold; and as you see that their aggregate weight is a hundred and thirteen while the weight of the four missing bars is a hundred and thirteen pounds, two ounces, it is a reasonable inference that these bolts represent those bars; and an uncommonly good job they made of the melting to lose only two ounces. Has the consignee's agent turned up yet?"

"He is waiting outside," replied the officer, with a pleased smile, "hopping about like a pea in a frying-pan. I'll call him in."

He did so, and a small, seedy man of strongly Semitic aspect approached the door with nervous caution and a rather pale face. But when his beady eye fell on the open case and the portentous assembly in the office, he turned about and fled along the wharf as if the hosts of the Philistines were at his heels.

"Of course it is all perfectly simple, as you say," I replied to Thorndyke as we strolled back up Nightingale Lane, "but I don't see where you got your start. What made you think that the stolen case was a dummy?"

"At first," Thorndyke replied, "it was just a matter of alternative hypotheses. It was purely speculative. The robbery described by Halethorpe was a very crude affair. It was planned in quite the wrong way. Noting this, I naturally asked myself: What is the right way to steal a case of gold ingots? Now, the outstanding difficulty in such a robbery arises from the ponderous nature of the thing stolen, and the way to overcome that difficulty is to get away with the booty at leisure before the robbery is discovered – the longer the better. It is also obvious that if you can delude someone into stealing your dummy you will have covered up your tracks most completely; for if that someone is caught, the issues are extremely confused, and if he is not caught, all the tracks lead away from you. Of course, he will discover the fraud when he tries to dispose of the swag, but his lips are sealed by the fact that he has, himself, committed a felony. So that is the proper strategical plan; and, though it was wildly improbable, and there was nothing whatever to suggest it, still, the possibility that this crude robbery might cover a more subtle one, had to be borne in mind. It was necessary to make absolutely certain that the gold bars were really in the case when it left Bellhaven. I had practically no doubt that they were. Our visit to the Custom House was little more than a formality, just to give us an undeniable datum from which to make our start. We had to find somebody who had actually seen the case open and verified the contents, and when we found that man – Mr Byrne – it instantly became obvious that the wildly improbable thing had really happened. The gold bars had already disappeared. I had calculated the approximate size of the real bars. They would contain forty-two cubic inches, and would be about seven inches by three by two. The dimensions given by Byrne – evidently correct, as shown by those of the case, which the bars fitted pretty closely – were impossible. If those bars had been gold, they would have weighed two hundred pounds, instead of the hundred and thirteen pounds shown on his report. The astonishing thing is that Byrne did not observe the discrepancy. There are not many Customs officers who would have let it pass."

"Isn't it rather odd," I asked, "that the thieves should have gambled on such a remote chance?"

"It is pretty certain," he replied, " that they were unaware of the risk they were taking. Probably they assumed – as most persons would have done – that a case of bullion would be merely inspected and passed. Few persons realise the rigorous methods of the Customs officers. But to resume: It was obvious that the 'gold' bars that Byrne had examined were dummies. The next question was, where were the real bars? Had they been made away with, or were they still on the ship? To settle this question I decided to go through the manifest and especially through the column of net weights. And there, presently, I came upon a package the net weight of which was within two ounces of the weight of the stolen bars. And that package was a parcel of brass screw-bolts – on a homeward-bound ship! But who on earth sends brass bolts from Africa to London? The anomaly was so striking that I examined the entry more closely, and then I found – by dividing the net weight by the number of bolts – that each of these little bolts weighed over half a pound. But, if this were so, those bolts could be of no other metal than gold or platinum, and were almost certainly gold. Also, their aggregate weight was exactly that of the stolen bars, less two ounces, which probably represented loss in melting."

"And the scrivelloes," said I, "and the gum copal and the kola nuts; what was their bearing on the inquiry? I can't, even now, trace any connection."

Thorndyke cast an astonished glance at me, and then replied with a quiet chuckle: "There wasn't any. Those notes were for the benefit of the shipping gentleman. As he would look over my shoulder, I had to give him something to read and think about. If I had noted only the brass bolts, I should have virtually informed him of the nature of my suspicions."

"Then, really, you had the case complete when we left Bellhaven?"

"Theoretically, yes. But we had to recover the stolen case, for, without those lead ingots we could not prove that the gold bolts were stolen property, any more than one could prove a murder without evidence of the death of the victim."

"And how do you suppose the robbery was carried out? How was the gold got out of the ship's strongroom?"

"I should say it was never there. The robbers, I suspect, are the ship's mate, the chief engineer and possibly the purser. The mate controls the stowage of cargo, and the chief engineer controls the repair shop and has the necessary skill and knowledge to deal with the metal. On receiving the advice of the bullion consignment, I imagine they prepared the dummy case in agreement with the description. When the bullion arrived, the dummy case would be concealed on deck and the exchange made as soon as the bullion was put on board. The dummy would be sent to the strongroom and the real case carried to a prepared hiding place. Then the engineer would cut up the bars, melt them piecemeal and cast them into bolts in an ordinary casting-flask, using an iron bolt as a model, and touching up the screw threads with a die. The mate could enter the case on the manifest when he pleased, and send the bill of lading by post to the nominal consignee. That is what I imagine to have been the procedure."

Thorndyke's solution turned out to be literally correct. The consignee, pursued by Inspector Badger along the quay, was arrested at the dock gates and immediately volunteered King's evidence. Thereupon the mate, the chief engineer and the purser of the steamship *Labadi* were arrested and brought to trial; when they severally entered a plea of guilty and described the method of the robbery almost in Thorndyke's words.

The Funeral Pyre

Thorndyke did not often indulge in an evening paper, and was even disposed to view that modern institution with some disfavour; whence it happened that when I entered our chambers shortly before dinner time with a copy of the *Evening Gazette* in my hand, he fixed upon the folded news-sheet an inquiring and slightly disapproving eye.

" 'Orrible discovery near Dartford," I announced, quoting the juvenile vendor.

The disapproval faded from his face, but the inquiring expression remained.

"What is it?" he asked.

"I don't know," I replied; "but it seems to be something in our line."

"My learned friend does us an injustice," he rejoined, with his eye riveted on the paper. "Still, if you are going to make my flesh creep, I will try to endure it."

Thus invited, I opened the paper and read out as follows: "A shocking tragedy has come to light in a meadow about a mile from Dartford. About two o'clock this morning, a rural constable observed a rick on fire out on the marshes near the creek. By the time he reached it the upper half of the rick was burning fiercely in the strong wind and, as he could do nothing alone, he went to the adjacent farmhouse and gave the alarm. The farmer and two of his sons accompanied the constable to the scene of the conflagration, but the rick was now a blazing mass, roaring in the wind and giving out an intense heat. As it was obviously impossible to save any part of it, and as there were no other ricks near, the farmer decided to abandon it to its fate and went home.

"At eight o'clock he returned to the spot and found the rick still burning, though reduced to a heap of glowing cinders and ashes, and approaching it, he was horrified to perceive a human skull grinning out from the cindery mass. Closer examination showed other bones – all calcined white and chalky – and close to the skull a stumpy clay pipe. The explanation of this dreadful occurrence seems quite simple. The rick was not quite finished, and when the farm hands knocked off work they left the ladder in position. It is assumed that some tramp, in search of a night's lodging, observed the ladder, and climbing up it, made himself comfortable in the loose hay at the top of the rick, where he fell asleep with his lighted pipe in his mouth. This ignited the hay and the man must have been suffocated by the fumes without awakening from his sleep."

"A reasonable explanation," was Thorndyke's comment, "and quite probable; but of course it is pure hypothesis. As a matter of fact, any one of the three conceivable causes of violent death is possible in this case – accident, suicide or homicide."

"I should have supposed," said I, "that could almost exclude suicide. It is difficult to imagine a man electing to roast himself to death."

"I cannot agree with my learned friend," Thorndyke rejoined. "I can imagine a case – and one of great medico-legal interest – that would exactly fit the present circumstances. Let us suppose a man, hopelessly insolvent, desperate and disgusted with life, who decides to provide for his family by investing the few pounds that he has left in insuring his life heavily and then making away with himself. How would he proceed? If he should commit suicide by any of the orthodox methods, he would simply invalidate his policy. But now, suppose he knows of a likely rick; that he provides himself with some rapidly-acting poison, such as potassium cyanide – he could even use prussic acid if he carried it in a rubber or celluloid bottle, which would be consumed in the fire; that he climbs on to the rick; sets fire to it, and as soon as it is fairly alight, takes his dose of poison and falls back dead among the hay. Who is to contest his family's claim? The fire will have destroyed all traces of the poison, even if they should be sought for. But it is practically certain that the question would never be raised. The claim would be paid without demur."

I could not help smiling at this calm exposition of a practicable crime. "It is a mercy, Thorndyke," I remarked, "that you are an honest man. If you were not – "

"I think," he retorted, "that I should find some better means of livelihood than suicide. But with regard to this case: it will be worth watching. The tramp hypothesis is certainly the most probable; but its very probability makes an alternative hypothesis at least possible. No one is likely to suspect fraudulent suicide; but that immunity from suspicion is a factor that increases the probability of fraudulent suicide. And so, to a less extent, with homicide. We must watch the case and see if there are any further developments."

Further developments were not very long in appearing. The report in the morning paper disposed effectually of the tramp theory without offering any other. "The tragedy of the burning rick," it said, "is taking a somewhat mysterious turn. It is now clear that the unknown man, who was assumed to have been a tramp, must have been a person of some social position, for careful examination of the ashes by the police have brought to light various articles which would have been carried only by a man of fair means. The clay pipe was evidently one of a pair – of which the second one has been recovered – probably silver mounted and carried in a case, the steel frame of which has been found. Both pipes are of the 'Burns Cutty' pattern and have neatly scratched on the bowls the initials 'R.R.' The following articles have also been found: Remains of a watch, probably gold, and a rather singular watch-chain, having alternate links of platinum and gold. The gold links have partly disappeared, but numerous beads of gold have been found, derived apparently from the watch and chain. The platinum links are intact and are fashioned of twisted square wire. A bunch of keys, partly fused; a rock crystal seal, apparently from a ring; a little porcelain mascot figure, with a hole for suspension – possibly from the watch-chain – and a number of artificial teeth. In connection with the latter, a puzzling and slightly sinister aspect has been given to the case by the finding of an upper dental plate by a ditch some two hundred yards from the rick. The plate has two gaps and, on comparison with the skull of the unknown man, these have been found by the police surgeon to correspond with two groups of remaining teeth. Moreover, the artificial teeth found in the ashes all seem to belong to a lower plate. The presence of this plate, so far from the scene of the man's death, is extremely difficult to account for."

As Thorndyke finished reading the extract he looked at me as if inviting some comment.

"It is a most remarkable and mysterious affair," said I, "and naturally recalls to my mind the hypothetical case that you suggested yesterday. If that case was possible then, it is actually probable now. It fits these new facts perfectly, not only in respect of the abundant means of identification, but even to this dental plate – if we assume that he took the poison as he was approaching the rick, and that the poison was of an acrid or irritating character which caused him to cough or retch. And I can think of no other plausible explanation."

"There *are* other possibilities," said Thorndyke, "but fraudulent suicide is certainly the most probable theory on the known facts. But we shall see. As you say, the body can hardly fail to be identified at a pretty early date."

As a matter of fact it was identified in the course of that same day. Both Thorndyke and I were busily engaged until evening in the courts and elsewhere and had not had time to give this curious case any consideration. But as we walked home together, we encountered Mr Stalker of the Griffin Life Assurance Company pacing up and down King's Bench Walk near the entry of our chambers.

"Ha!" he exclaimed, striding forward to meet us near the Mitre Court gateway, "you are just the very men I wanted to see. There is a little matter that I want to consult you about. I shan't detain you long."

"It won't matter much if you do," said Thorndyke. "We have finished our routine work for the day and our time is now our own." He led the way up to our chambers, where, having given the fire a stir, he drew up three armchairs.

"Now, Stalker," said he. "Warm your toes and tell us your troubles."

Mr Stalker spread out his hands to the blaze and began reflectively: "It will be enough, I think, if I give you the facts — and most of them you probably know already. You have heard about this man whose remains were found in the ashes of a burnt rick? Well, it turns out that he was a certain Mr Reginald Reed, an outside broker, as I understand; but what is of more interest to us is that he was a client of ours. We have issued a policy on his life for three thousand pounds. I thought I remembered the name when I saw it in the paper this afternoon, so I looked up our books, and there it was, sure enough."

"When was the policy issued?" Thorndyke asked.

"Ah!" exclaimed Stalker. "That's the exasperating feature of the case. The policy was issued less than a year ago. He has only paid a single premium. So we stand to drop practically the whole three thousand. Of course, we have to take the fat with the lean, but we don't like to take it in such precious large lumps."

"Of course you don't," agreed Thorndyke. "But now: you have come to consult me — about what?"

"Well," replied Stalker, "I put it to you: isn't there something obviously fishy about the case? Are the circumstances normal? For instance, how the devil came a respectable city gentleman to be smoking his pipe in a haystack out in a lonely meadow at two o'clock in the morning, or thereabouts?"

"I agree," said Thorndyke, "that the circumstances are highly abnormal. But there is no doubt that the man is dead. Extremely dead, if I may use the expression. What is the point that you wish to raise?"

"I am not raising any point," replied Stalker. "We should like you to attend the inquest and watch the case for us. Of course, in our policies, as you know, suicide is expressly ruled out; and if this should turn out to have been a case of suicide – "

"What is there to suggest that it was?" asked Thorndyke.

"What is there to suggest that it wasn't?" retorted Stalker.

"Nothing," rejoined Thorndyke. "But a negative plea is of no use to you. You will have to furnish positive proof of suicide, or else pay the claim."

"Yes, I realise that," said Stalker, "and I am not suggesting – but there, it is of no use discussing the matter while we know so little. I leave the case in your hands. Can you attend the inquest?"

"I shall make it my business to do so," replied Thorndyke.

"Very well," said Stalker, rising and putting on his gloves, "then we will leave it at that and we couldn't leave it in better case."

When our visitor had gone I remarked to Thorndyke: "Stalker seems to have conceived the same idea as my learned senior – fraudulent suicide."

"It is not surprising," he replied. "Stalker is a shrewd man and he perceives that when an abnormal thing has happened we may look for an abnormal explanation. Fraudulent suicide was a speculative possibility yesterday: today, in the light of these new facts, it is the most probable theory. But mere probabilities won't help Stalker. If there is no direct evidence of suicide – and there is not likely to be any – the verdict will be Death by Misadventure, and the Griffin Company will have to pay."

"I suppose you won't do anything until you have heard what transpires at the inquest?"

"Yes," he replied. "I think we should do well to go down and just go over the ground. At present we have the facts at third hand, and we don't know what may have been overlooked. As tomorrow is fairly free I propose that we make an early start and see the place ourselves."

"Is there any particular point that you want to clear up?"

"No; I have nothing definite in view. The circumstances are compatible with either accident, suicide or homicide, with an undoubted leaning towards suicide. But, at present, I have a completely open mind. I am, in fact, going down to Dartford in the hope of getting a lead in some definite direction."

When we alighted at Dartford Station on the following morning, Thorndyke looked enquiringly up and down the platform until he espied an inspector, when he approached the official and asked for a direction to the site of the burnt rick.

The official glanced at Thorndyke's canvas-covered research case and at my binocular and camera as he replied with a smile: "You are not the first, by a long way, that has asked that question. There has been a regular procession of Press gentlemen that way this morning. The place is about a mile from here. You take the footpath to Joyce Green and turn off towards the creek opposite Temple Farm. This is about where the rick stood," he added, as Thorndyke produced his one-inch ordnance map and a pencil, "a few yards from that dyke."

With this direction and the open map we set forth from the station, and taking our way along the unfrequented path soon left the town behind. As we crossed the second stile, where the path rejoined the road, Thorndyke paused to survey the prospect. "Stalker's question," he remarked, "was not unreasonable. This road leads nowhere but to the river, and one does rather wonder what a city man can have been doing out on these marshes in the small hours of the morning. I think that will be our objective, where you see those men at work by the shepherd's hut, or whatever it is."

We struck off across the level meadows, out of which arose the red sails of a couple of barges, creeping down the invisible creek; and as we approached our objective the shepherd's hut resolved itself into a contractor's office van, and the men were seen to be working with shovels and sieves on the ashes of the rick. A police inspector was superintending the operations, and when we drew near he accosted us with a civil inquiry as to our business.

Thorndyke presented his card and explained that he was watching the case in the interests of the Griffin Insurance Company. "I suppose," he added, "I shall be given the necessary facilities?"

"Certainly," replied the officer, glancing at my colleague with an odd mixture of respect and suspicion; "and if you can spot anything that we've overlooked, you are very welcome. It's all for the public good. Is there anything in particular that you want to see?"

"I should like to see everything that has been recovered so far. The remains of the body have been removed, I suppose?"

"Yes, sir. To the mortuary. But I have got all the effects here."

He led the way to the office – a wooden hut on low wheels – and unlocking the door, invited us to enter. "Here are the things that we have salved," he said, indicating a table covered with white paper on which the various articles were neatly set out, "and I think it's about the lot. We haven't come on anything fresh for the last hour or so."

Thorndyke looked over the collection thoughtfully; picked up and examined successively the two clay pipes each with the initials "R.R.", neatly incised on the bowl – the absurd little mascot figure, so incongruous with its grim surroundings and the tragic circumstances, the distorted keys, the platinum chain-links to several of which shapeless blobs of gold adhered, and the crystal seal; and then, collecting the artificial teeth, arranged them in what appeared to be their correct order, and compared them with the dental plate.

"I think," said he, holding the latter in his fingers, "that as the body is not here, I should like to secure the means of comparison of these teeth with the skull. There will be no objection to that, I presume?"

"What did you wish to do?" the inspector asked.

"I should like to take a cast of the plate and a wax impression of the loose teeth. No damage will be done to the originals, of course."

The inspector hesitated, his natural, official tendency to refuse permission apparently contending with a desire to see with his own eyes how the famous expert carried out his mysterious methods of research. In the end the latter prevailed and the official sanction was given subject to a proviso, "You won't mind my looking on while you do it?"

"Of course not," replied Thorndyke. "Why should I?"

"I thought that perhaps your methods were a sort of trade secret."

Thorndyke laughed softly as he opened the research case. "My dear Inspector," said he, "the people who have trade secrets are those who make a profound mystery of simple processes that any schoolboy could carry out with once showing. That is the necessity for the secrecy."

As he was speaking he half-filled a tiny aluminium saucepan with water, and having dropped into it a couple of cakes of dentist's moulding composition, put it to heat over a spirit-lamp. While it was heating he greased the dental plate and the loose teeth, and prepared the little rubber basin and the other appliances for mixing the plaster.

The inspector was deeply interested. With almost ravenous attention he followed these proceedings, and eagerly watched Thorndyke roll the softened composition into the semblance of a small sausage and press it firmly on the teeth of the plate; peered into the plaster tin and when the liquid plaster was mixed and applied, first to the top and then to the lower surface of the plate, not only observed the process closely but put a number of very pertinent questions.

While the plaster and composition were setting Thorndyke renewed his inspection of the salvage from the rick, picking out a number of iron boot protectors which he placed apart in a little heap.

Then he proceeded to roll out two flat strips of softened composition, into one of which he pressed the loose teeth in what appeared to be their proper order, and into the other the boot protectors – eight in number – after first dusting the surface with powdered French chalk. By this time the plaster had set hard enough to allow of the mould being opened and the dental plate taken out. Then Thorndyke, having painted the surfaces of the plaster pieces with knotting, put the mould together again and tied it firmly with string, mixed a fresh bowl of plaster and poured it into the mould.

While this was setting Thorndyke made a careful inventory, with my assistance, of the articles found in the ashes and put a few discreet questions to the inspector. But the latter knew very little about the case. His duty was merely to examine and report on the rick for the information of the coroner. The investigation of the case was evidently being conducted from headquarters. There being no information to be gleaned from the officer we went out and inspected the site of the rick. But here, also, there was nothing to be learned; the surface of the ground was now laid bare and the men who were working with the sieves reported no further discoveries. We accordingly returned to the hut, and as the plaster had now set hard Thorndyke proceeded with infinite care to open the mould. The operation was a complete success, and as my colleague extracted the cast – a perfect replica, in plaster, of the dental plate – the inspector's admiration was unbounded. "Why," he exclaimed, "excepting for the colour you couldn't tell one from the other; but all the same, I don't quite see what you want it for."

"I want it to compare with the skull," replied Thorndyke, "if I have time to call at the mortuary. As I can't take the original plate with me, I shall need this copy to make the comparison. Obviously, it is most important to make sure that this is Reed's plate and not that of some other person. By the way, can you show us the spot where the plate was picked up?"

"Yes," replied the inspector. "You can see the place from here. It was just by that gate at the crossing of the ditch."

"Thank you, Inspector," said Thorndyke. "I think we will walk down and have a look at the place." He wrapped the new cast in a soft cloth, and having repacked his research case, shook hands with the officer and prepared to depart.

"You will notice, Jervis," he remarked as we walked towards the gate, "that this denture was picked up at a spot beyond the rick – farther from the town, I mean. Consequently, if the plate is Reed's, he must have dropped it while he was approaching the rick from the direction of the river. It will be worthwhile to see if we can find out whence he came."

"Yes," I agreed. "But the dropping of the plate is a rather mysterious affair. It must have happened when he took the poison – assuming that he really did poison himself; but one would have expected that he would wait until he got to the rick to take his dose."

"We had better not make too many assumptions while we have so few facts," said Thorndyke. He put down his case beside the gate, which guarded a bridge across a broad ditch, or drainage dyke, and opened his map.

"The question is," said he, "did he come through this gate or was he only passing it? This dyke, you see, opens into the creek about three-quarters of a mile farther down. The probability is, therefore, that if he came up from the river across the marshes he would be on this side of the ditch and would pass the gate. But we had better try both sides. Let us leave our things by the gate and explore the ground for a few hundred yards, one on either side of the ditch. Which side will you take?"

I elected to take the side nearer the creek and, having put my camera down by the research case, climbed over the padlocked gate and began to walk slowly along by the side of the ditch, scanning the ground for footprints showing the impression of boot-protectors. At first the surface was far from favourable for imprints of any kind, being, like that immediately around the gate, covered with thick turf. About a hundred and fifty yards down, however, I came upon a heap of wormcasts on which was plainly visible the print of a heel with a clear impression of a kidney-shaped protector such as I had seen in the hut. Thereupon I hailed Thorndyke and, having stuck my stick in the ground beside the heelprint, went back to meet him at the gate.

"This is rather interesting, Jervis," he remarked, when I had described my find. "The inference seems to be that he came from the creek – unless there is another gate farther down. We had better have our compo impressions handy for comparison." He opened his case and taking from it the strip of composition – now as hard as bone – on which were the impressions of the boot-protectors, slipped it into his outer pocket. We then took up the case and the camera and proceeded to the spot marked by my stick.

"Well," said Thorndyke, "it is not very conclusive, seeing that so many people use boot-protectors, but it is probably Reed's footprint. Let us hope that we shall find something more distinctive farther on."

We resumed our march, keeping a few yards apart and examining the ground closely as we went. For a full quarter of a mile we went on without detecting any trace of a footprint on the thick turf. Suddenly we perceived ahead of us a stretch of yellow mud occupying a slight hollow, across which the creek had apparently overflowed at the last spring tide. When we reached it we found that the mud was nearly dry, but still soft enough to take an impression; and the surface was covered with a maze of footprints.

We halted at the edge of the patch and surveyed the complicated pattern; and then it became evident that the whole group of prints had been produced by two pairs of feet, with the addition of a row of sheep-tracks.

"This seems to raise an entirely new issue," I remarked.

"It does," Thorndyke agreed. "I think we now begin to see a definite light on the case. But we must go cautiously. Here are two sets of footprints, of which one is apparently Reed's – to judge by the boot-protectors – while the other prints have been made by a man, whom we will call X, who wore boots or shoes with rubber soles and heels. We had better begin by verifying Reed's." He produced the composition strip from his pocket, and, stooping over one pair of footprints, continued: "I think we may assume that these are Reed's feet. We have on the compo strip impressions of eight protectors from the rick, and on each footprint there are four protectors. Moreover, the individual protectors are the same on the compo and on the footprints. Thus the compo shows two pairs of half-protectors, two single edge-pieces, and two kidney-shaped protectors; while each footprint shows a pair of half-protectors on the outside of the sole, a single one on the inside and a kidney-shaped piece on the heel. Furthermore, in both cases the protectors are nearly new and show no appreciable signs of wear. The agreement is complete."

"Don't you think," said I, "that we ought to take plaster records of them?"

"I do," he replied, "seeing that a heavy shower or a high tide would obliterate them. If you will make the casts, I will, meanwhile, make a careful drawing of the whole group to show the order of imposition."

We fell to work forthwith upon our respective tasks, and by the time I had filled four of the clearest of the footprints with plaster, Thorndyke had completed his drawing with the aid of a set of coloured pencils from the research case. While the plaster was setting he exhibited and explained the drawing.

"You see, Jervis, that there are four lines of prints and a set of sheep-tracks. The first in order of time are these prints of X, drawn in blue. Then come the sheep, which trod on X's footprints. Next comes Reed, alone and after some interval, for he has trodden both on the sheep-tracks and on the tracks of X. Both men were going towards the river. Then we have the tracks of the two men coming back. This time they were together, for their tracks are parallel and neither treads into the prints of the other. Both tracks are rather sinuous as if the men were walking unsteadily, and both have trodden on the sheep-tracks and on the preceding tracks. Next, we have the tracks of X going alone towards the river and treading on all the others excepting number four, which is the tracks of X coming from the river and turning off towards that gate, which opens on to the road. The sequence of events is therefore pretty clear.

"First, X came along here alone to some destination which we have yet to discover. Later – how much later we cannot judge – came Reed, alone. The two men seem to have met, and later returned together, apparently the worse for drink. That is the last we see of Reed. Next comes X, walking back – quite steadily, you notice – towards the river. Later, he returns; but this time, for some reason – perhaps to avoid the neighbourhood of the rick – he crosses the ditch at that gate, apparently to get on the road, though you see by the map that the road is much the longer route to the town. And now we had better get on and see if we can discover the rendezvous to and from which these two men went and came."

As the plaster had now set quite hard I picked up the casts, and when I had carefully packed them in the case we resumed our progress riverwards. I had already noticed, some distance ahead, the mast of what looked like a small cutter yacht standing up above the marshes, and I now drew Thorndyke's attention to it. But he had already observed it and, like me, had marked it as the probable rendezvous of the two men. In a few minutes the probability became a certainty, for a bend in the creek showed us the little vessel – with the name *Moonbeam* newly painted on the bow – made fast alongside a small wooden staging; and when we reached this the bare earth opposite the gangway was seen to be covered with the footprints of both men.

"I wonder," said I, "which of them was the owner of the yacht."

"It is pretty obvious, I think," said Thorndyke, "that X was the owner if either of them was. He came to the yacht alone, and he wore rubber-soled shoes such as yachtsmen favour; whereas Reed came when the other man was there, and he wore iron boot-protectors, which no yacht owner would do if he had any respect for his deck-planks. But they may have had a joint interest; appearances suggest that they were painting the woodwork when they were here together, as some of the paint is fresh and some of it old and shabby." He gazed at the yacht reflectively for some time and then remarked: "It would be interesting – and perhaps instructive – to have a look at the inside."

"It would be a flagrant trespass, to put it mildly," said I.

"It would be more than trespass if that padlock is locked," he rejoined. "But we need not take a pedantic view of the legal position. My learned friend has a serviceable pair of glasses and commands an unobstructed view of a mile or so; and if he maintains an observant attitude while I make an inspection of the premises any trifling irregularity will be of no consequence." As he spoke he felt in his pocket and produced an instrument which our laboratory assistant, Polton, had made from a few pieces of stiff steel wire, and which was euphemistically known as a smoker's companion. With this appliance in his hand he dropped down on to the yacht's deck and after a quick look round, tried the padlock. Finding it locked he proceeded to operate on it with the smoker's companion, and in a few moments it fell open, when he pushed back the sliding hatch and stepped down into the little cabin.

His exploration did not take long. In a few minutes he reappeared and climbed the short ladder to the staging. "There isn't much to see," he reported, "but what there is is highly suggestive. If you slip down and have a look round, I think you will have no difficulty in forming a plausible reconstruction of the recent events. You had better take the camera. There is light enough for a time exposure."

I handed him the glasses, and dropping on to the deck, stepped down through the open hatch into the cabin. It was an absurd little cave, barely four feet high from the floor to the coach-roof, open to the forepeak and lighted by a little skylight and two portholes. Of the two sleeping berths, one had evidently been used as a seat, while the other appeared to have been slept in, to judge by the

182

indented pillow and the tumbled blankets, left just as the occupant had crawled out of them. But the whole interior was in a state of squalid disorder. Paint pots and unwashed brushes lay about the floor, in company with a couple of whisky bottles – one empty and one half-full – two tumblers, a pair of empty siphons and a litter of playing cards scattered broadcast and evidently derived from two packs. It was, as Thorndyke had said, easy to reconstruct the scene of sordid debauchery that the light of the two candles – each in its congealed pool of grease – must have displayed on that night of horror whose dreadful secret had been disclosed by the ashes of the rick. But I could see nothing that would enable me to give a name to the dead man's mysterious companion.

When I had completed my inspection and taken a photograph of the interior, I rejoined Thorndyke, who then descended and replaced the padlock on the closed hatch, relocking it with the invaluable smoker's companion.

"Well, Jervis," said he, as we turned our faces towards the town, "it seems as if we had accomplished our task, so far as Stalker is concerned. It is still possible that this was a case of suicide, but it is no longer probable. All the appearances point to homicide. I think my learned friend will agree with me in that."

"Undoubtedly," I replied. "And to me there is a strong suggestion of premeditation. I take it that X, the owner of the yacht, enticed Reed out here, possibly to prepare for a cruise; that the two men worked at the repainting while the daylight lasted and then spent the evening drinking and gambling. The fact that they used several packs of cards suggests that they played for pretty heavy stakes. Then, I think, Reed became drunk and X offered to see him safely off the marshes. It is evident that X was not drunk, because, although both tracks appear unsteady when the men were walking together, the tracks of X returning to the yacht are quite steady and straight. I should say that the actual murder took place just after they had got over the gate; that Reed's false teeth fell out while his body was being dragged to the rick, and that this was unnoticed by X owing to the darkness. Then X dragged the body up the ladder and laid it in the middle of the rick at the top, set fire to the rick – probably on the lee side – and at once made off back to the yacht. There he passed the night, and in the morning he returned to the town along the road, giving the neighbourhood of the rick a wide berth. That is my reading of the evidence."

"Yes," said Thorndyke, "that seems to be the interpretation of the facts. And now all that remains is to give a name to the mysterious X, and I should think that will present no difficulties."

"Are you proposing to inspect the remains at the mortuary?" I asked.

"No," he replied. "It would be interesting, but it is not necessary. We have all the available data for identification, and our concern is now not with Reed but with X. We had better get back to London."

On our arrival at the station, we found the bookstall keeper in the act of sticking up a placard of the evening paper on which was the legend: *"Rick tragedy; Sensational development."*

We immediately provided ourselves each with a copy of the paper, and sitting down on a seat, proceeded to read the heavily-leaded report.

"A new and startling aspect has been given to the rick tragedy by some further inquiries that the police have made. It seems that the dead man, Reed, was a member of the firm of Reed and Jarman, outside brokers, and it now transpires that his partner, Walter Jarman, is also missing. There has been no one at the office this week, but the caretaker states that on Monday evening at about eight o'clock, he saw Mr Jarman let himself into the office with his key (the rick was first seen to be on fire at two o'clock on Monday morning). It appears that three cheques, payable to the firm and endorsed by Jarman, were paid into the bank – Patmore's – by the first post on Tuesday morning, and that, also on Tuesday morning, Jarman purchased a parcel of diamonds of just over a thousand pounds in value from a diamond merchant in Hatton Garden, who accepted a cheque in payment after telephoning to the bank. It further appears that on the previous Saturday morning, Reed and Jarman visited the bank together and drew out in cash practically their whole balance, leaving only thirty-two pounds. The diamond merchant's cheque was met by the cheques that had just been paid in. It is premature to make any comments, but we may expect some strange disclosures at the inquest, which will be held at Dartford the day after tomorrow."

"I assume," said I, "that the identity of X is no longer a mystery. It looks as if these two men had agreed to realise their assets and abscond, and had then spent the night gambling for the swag, and oddly enough, Reed appears to have been the winner, for otherwise there would have been no need to murder him."

"That is so," Thorndyke agreed, "assuming that X is Jarman, which is probable, though not certain. But we mustn't go beyond our facts, and we mustn't construct theories from newspaper reports. I think we had better call at Scotland Yard on our way home and verify those particulars."

The report and our own observations occupied us during the journey to London, though our discussion produced no further conclusions. As soon as we arrived at Charing Cross, Thorndyke sprang out of the train, and emerging from the station, walked swiftly towards Whitehall.

Our visit was fortunately timed, for as we approached the entrance to the headquarters, our old friend, Superintendent Miller, came out. He smiled as he saw us and halted to utter the laconic query: "Rick Case?"

"Yes," replied Thorndyke. "We have come to verify the particulars given in the evening paper. Have you seen the report?"

"Yes; and you may take it as correct. Anything else?"

"I should have liked to look over a series of the cheques drawn by the firm. The last two, I suppose, are inaccessible?"

"Yes. They will be at the bank, and we couldn't inspect them without an order of the Court. But, as to the others, if they are at the office, I think you could see them. I'll come along with you now if you like, and have a look round myself. Our people are in possession."

Dr Thorndyke's Casebook

We at once closed with the superintendent's offer and proceeded with him by the Underground Railway to the Mansion House, from whence we made our way to Queen Victoria Street, where Reed and Jarman had their offices. A sergeant was in charge at the moment, and to him the superintendent addressed himself.

"Have you found any returned cheques?"

"Yes, sir," replied the sergeant; "lots of 'em. We've been through them all."

As he spoke he produced several bundles of cheques and laid them on a desk, the drawers of which all stood open.

"Well," said Miller, "there they are, doctor. I don't know what you want to find out, but I expect you do." He placed a chair by the desk, and as Thorndyke sat down and proceeded to turn the cheques over, he watched him with politely-suppressed curiosity.

"It appears," said Thorndyke, "as if these two men had mixed up their private affairs with the business account. Here, for instance, is a cheque drawn by Reed for the Picardy Wine Company. But that company could hardly have been a client. And this one of Jarman's for the Secretary of the St John's Nursing Home must be a private cheque, and so I should say are these two for F Waller, Esq., FRCS, and for Andrew Darton, Esq., LDS. They are drawn for professional men and both are – like the Nursing Home cheque – stated in even amounts of guineas, whereas the business cheques are in uneven amounts of pounds, shillings and pence."

"I think you are right, sir," said Miller. "The business seems to have been conducted in a very casual manner. And just look at those signatures! Never twice alike. The banks hate that sort of thing, naturally. When a customer signs in the signature book he has given a specimen for reference and he ought to keep to it strictly. A man who varies his signature is asking for trouble."

"He is," Thorndyke agreed, as he rapidly entered a few particulars of the cheques in his notebook; "particularly in the case of a firm with a staff of clerks."

He stood up, and having pocketed his notebook, held out his hand.

186

"I am very much obliged to you, superintendent," he said.

"Seen all that you wanted to see?" Miller asked.

"Thank you, yes," Thorndyke replied.

"I should very much like to know what you *have* seen," Miller rejoined; to which my colleague replied by waving his hand towards the cheques, as he turned to go.

"I don't quite see the bearing of those cheques on our inquiry," I said, as we took our way homeward along Cheapside.

"It is not very direct," Thorndyke replied; "but the cheques help us to understand the characters of these two men and their relations with one another; which may be very necessary when we come to the inquest."

During the following day I saw very little of Thorndyke, for our excursion to Dartford had put our work somewhat in arrear and we had to secure a free day for the inquest on the morrow. We met at dinner after the day's work, but, beyond settling the programme for the next day, nothing of importance passed with reference to the "Rick Case."

The opening phases of the inquest, though of thrilling interest to the numerous spectators and Press men, did not particularly concern us. The evidence of the rural constable, the farmer and the police inspector – with whom Thorndyke had a little confidential talk and apparently surprised the officer considerably – merely amplified what we knew already. Of more interest was that of a local dentist who testified to having examined the dental plate and to having compared it with the skull of the dead man. "The plate and the jaw of deceased," he said, "agree completely. The jaw contains five natural teeth in two groups, and the plate has two spaces which exactly correspond to those two groups of teeth. I have tried the plate on the jaw and have no doubt whatever that it belonged to deceased."

"That is a very important fact," Thorndyke remarked to me as the witness retired. "It is the indispensable link in the chain."

"But surely it was obvious?" said I.

187

"No doubt," he replied. "But now it is proved and in evidence."

I was somewhat puzzled by Thorndyke's remark, but the appearance of a new witness forbade discussion. Mr Arthur Gerrard was an alert-looking, rather tall man, with bushy, Mephistophelian eyebrows and a small, dark moustache, who wore a pair of large bifocal spectacles, and to whom a small mole at the corner of the mouth imparted the effect of a permanent one-sided smile.

"It was on your information," said the coroner, "that the identity of the deceased was established."

"Yes," replied the witness, who spoke with a slight, but perceptible, Irish accent. "I saw the description in the papers of the things that had been found in the rick and at once recognised them as Reed's. I knew deceased intimately and had often noticed his peculiar watch-chain and the little china mascot and seen him smoking the clay pipe with his initials scratched on it; and I knew that he wore false teeth."

"Did you meet him frequently?"

"Oh, yes. For more than a year he was my partner in business, and we remained friends after I had dissolved the partnership."

"Why did you dissolve the partnership?"

"I had to. Reed was impossible in a business sense. He gambled incessantly in stocks and I had to pay his losses. I lent him, for this purpose, at one time and another, over two thousand pounds. He gave me bills for the loans, but he was never able to meet them, and in the end, when we dissolved, I got him to insure his life for three thousand pounds and to draw up a document making his debt to me the first charge on his estate in the event of his death."

"Had you ever any reason to suppose that he contemplated suicide?"

"None whatever. After he left me, he entered into partnership with a Mr Walter Jarman, and whenever I met him, he seemed to be quite happy and contented, though I gathered that he was still gambling a good deal. I saw him a week ago today and he then told me that he proposed to take a short yachting holiday with his partner, who owned a small cutter. That was the last time that I saw him alive."

As the witness was about to retire, Thorndyke rose, and having obtained the coroner's permission to cross-examine, asked:

"You have spoken of a yacht. Do you know what her name is and where she has been kept lately?"

"Her name is the *Moonbeam,* and I believe Jarman kept her somewhere in the Thames, but I don't know where."

"And as to Jarman himself: what do you know about him, as to his character, for instance?"

"I knew him very slightly. He appeared to be rather a dissipated man. Drank a good deal, I should say, and I think he was a bit of a gambler."

"Do you know if he was a heavy smoker?"

"He didn't smoke at all, but he was an inveterate snuff-taker."

At this point the foreman of the jury interposed with the audible remark that "he didn't see what this had to do with the inquiry," and the coroner looked dubiously at Thorndyke; but as my colleague sat down, the objection was not pursued.

The next witness was the caretaker of the building in which Reed and Jarman's office was situated. His evidence was to the effect that on the previous Monday evening at about eight o'clock, he saw Mr Jarman let himself into the office with his key. "I don't know how long he stayed there," he continued, in reply to the coroner's question. "I had finished my work and was going up to my rooms at the top of the building. I didn't see him again."

"Did you notice anything unusual in his appearance?" asked Thorndyke, rising to cross-examine. "Was his face at all flushed, for instance?"

"I couldn't say. I was going up the stairs and I just looked back over my shoulder when I heard him. His face was turned away from me."

"But you had no difficulty in recognising him?"

"No: I should have known him a mile off. He had his overcoat on, and it is a very peculiar overcoat – light brown with a sort of greenish check. You couldn't possibly mistake it."

"What should you say was Mr Jarman's height?"

"About five feet nine or ten, I should say."

Here the foreman of the jury again interposed. "Aren't we wasting time, sir?" he inquired impatiently. "These details about Jarman may be very important to the police, but they don't concern us. We are inquiring into the death of Mr Reginald Reed."

The coroner looked deprecatingly at Thorndyke and remarked: "There is some truth in what the foreman says."

"I submit, sir," replied Thorndyke, "that there is no truth in it at all. We are not inquiring into the death of Reginald Reed, but into that of a man whose remains were found in a burned rick."

"But the body has been identified as that of Reginald Reed."

"Then," said Thorndyke, "I submit that it has been wrongly identified. I suggest that the body is that of Walter Jarman and I am prepared to produce witnesses who will prove that it is."

"But," exclaimed the coroner, "we have just heard the evidence of a witness who states that he saw Jarman alive eighteen hours after the rick was fired."

"I beg your pardon, sir," said Thorndyke. "We have heard the witness say that he saw Jarman's overcoat. He expressly stated that he did not see the man's face."

The coroner hastily conferred with the jury – who openly scoffed at Thorndyke's suggestion – and then said: "I find what you say perfectly incredible and so do the jury. It is utterly irreconcilable with the facts. You had better call your witnesses and let us dispose of this extraordinary suggestion."

Thorndyke bowed to the coroner and called Mr Andrew Darton; whereupon a middle-aged man of markedly professional aspect came forward and, having been sworn, gave evidence as follows:

"I am a dental surgeon. A little over two years ago, Mr Walter Jarman was under my care. I extracted some loose teeth from both jaws and made him two plates – an upper and a lower."

"Could you identify those plates?"

"Yes. I have with me the plaster model on which those plates were made." He opened a bag and produced a plaster cast of a pair of jaws fitted with a brass hinge so that the jaws could be opened and shut. On the upper jaw were two groups of teeth separated by a space of bare gums, while the lower jaw bore a single group of four front teeth.

"This model," the witness explained, "is an exact replica of the patient's jaws, and the two plates were actually moulded on it." He picked the dental plate from the table, and amidst a hush of breathless expectancy, opened the mouth of the model and applied the plate to the upper jaw. At a glance, it was obvious that it fitted perfectly. The two groups of the plaster teeth slipped exactly into the spaces on the plate, making a complete row of teeth. Then the witness covered the lower gums with strips of plastic wax and taking the loose teeth from the table, attached them to the wax; and again the correspondence was evident. The teeth thus applied exactly filled the vacant spaces.

"Can you now identify that plate?" Thorndyke asked.

"Yes," was the reply. "I am quite certain that this is the plate I made for Mr Jarman and that those loose teeth are from his lower plate."

Thorndyke looked at the coroner, who nodded emphatically. "This evidence seems perfectly conclusive," he admitted. "What do you say, gentleman?" he added, turning to the jury.

There was no doubt as to their sentiments. With one voice they declared their complete conviction. Had they not seen the demonstration with their own eyes?

"And now, sir," said the coroner, "as you appear to know more than anyone else about this case, and as it is perfectly incomprehensible to me, and probably also to the jury, I suggest that you give us an explanation. And you had better make it a sworn statement, so that it can go into the depositions."

"Yes," Thorndyke agreed, "especially as I have some evidence to give." He was accordingly sworn and then proceeded to make the following statement:

"The first thing that struck me on reading the report of this case, was the very remarkable character of the objects found in the ashes of the rick. They included objects composed of platinum, of pipe-clay, of iron and of porcelain – all substances practically indestructible by fire. And these imperishable objects were all highly distinctive, and easily identifiable, and two of them actually bore the initials of their owner. There was almost a suggestion of the body having been prepared for identification after burning. This mere suggestion, however, gave place to definite suspicion when I saw the dental plate. That plate presented a most striking discrepancy. Here it is, sir, and you see that it is a clean polished plate of red vulcanite, with not a trace of stain or discoloration. But associated with that plate, were two clay pipes. Now the man who smokes a clay pipe is not only – as a rule – a heavy smoker, but he smokes strong and dark coloured tobacco. And if he wears a dental plate, that plate becomes encrusted with a black deposit which is very difficult to remove. There is, as you see, no trace of any such deposit or of any tobacco stain in the interstices of the teeth. It appeared to be almost certainly the plate of a non-smoker. But if that were so, it could not be Reed's. But it had been ascertained by the police surgeon that it fitted the jaw of the skull and undoubtedly belonged to the burned body. Consequently if the plate was not Reed's plate, the skull was not Reed's skull, and the body was not Reed's body. But the watch-chain was Reed's, the pipes were his and the mascot was his. That is to say that the very identifiable and fireproof property of Reed was associated with the burned body of some other person; that, in other words, the body of some unknown person had been deliberately prepared to counterfeit the body of Reed. This offered a further suggestion and raised a question. The suggestion was that the unknown person had been murdered – presumably somewhere near the spot where the dental plate was found. The question was – What was the object of causing the body to counterfeit that of Reed?

"Now, I knew, from the insurance company, that Reed had insured his life for three thousand pounds. Therefore, somebody stood to gain three thousand pounds by his death. The question was – Who was that somebody? I proceeded to make certain investigations on the spot;" and here Thorndyke gave a summary of our discoveries on the marsh and on the yacht. "It thus appeared," he continued, "that there were two men on the marshes that night, going towards the rick. One of them was the person whose body was found in the ashes; the other, who went back alone to the yacht, was presumably the person who stood to gain three thousand pounds by Reed's death."

"Have you formed any opinion as to who that person was?" the coroner asked.

"Yes," replied Thorndyke. "I have very little doubt that he was Reginald Reed."

"But," exclaimed the coroner, "we have heard in evidence that it was Mr Arthur Gerrard who stood to gain the three thousand pounds!"

"Precisely," said Thorndyke; and for a while he and the coroner looked at one another without speaking.

Suddenly the latter cast a searching look around the court. "Where is Mr Gerrard?" he demanded.

"He left the court about ten minutes ago," said Thorndyke; "and the police inspector left immediately afterwards. I had advised him not to lose sight of Mr Gerrard."

"Then I take it that you suspect Gerrard of being in collusion with Reed?"

"I suspect that Arthur Gerrard and Reginald Reed are one and the same person."

As Thorndyke made this statement, a murmur of astonishment arose from the jurymen and the spectators. The coroner, after a few moments' puzzled reflection, remarked: "You are not forgetting that Reed's caretaker was present while Gerrard was giving his evidence?" Then, turning to the caretaker, he asked: "What do you say? Was that Mr Reed who gave evidence under the name of Gerrard?"

The caretaker, who had evidently been thinking furiously, was by no means confident. "I should say not," he replied, "unless he was made up a good deal. He was certainly about the same height and build and colour; but he had a moustache, whereas Mr Reed was cleanshaved; he had a mole on his face, which Mr Reed hadn't; he had bushy eyebrows, whereas Mr Reed had hardly any eyebrows to speak of; and he wore spectacles, which Mr Reed didn't, and he spoke like an Irishman, whereas Mr Reed was English. Still it is possible – "

Before he could finish, the door rattled to a heavy concussion. Then it flew open, and Mr Gerrard staggered into the room, thrust forward by the police inspector. His appearance was marvellously changed, for he had lost his spectacles, and one of his eyebrows had disappeared, as had also the mole and a portion of the built-up moustache. The caretaker started up with an exclamation, but at this moment Gerrard, with a violent effort, wrenched himself free. The inspector sprang forward to recapture him. But he was too late. The prisoners hand flew upwards, there was a ringing report; and Arthur Gerrard – or Reginald Reed – fell back across a bench with a trickle of blood on his temple and a pistol still clutched in his hand.

"And so," said Stalker, when he called on us the next day for details, "it was a suicide after all. Very lucky, too, seeing that there was no provision in the policy for death by judicial hanging."

R Austin Freeman

The D'Arblay Mystery
A Dr Thorndyke Mystery

When a man is found floating beneath the skin of a green-skimmed pond one morning, Dr Thorndyke becomes embroiled in an astonishing case. This wickedly entertaining detective fiction reveals that the victim was murdered through a lethal injection and someone out there is trying a cover-up.

Dr Thorndyke Intervenes
A Dr Thorndyke Mystery

What would you do if you opened a package to find a man's head? What would you do if the headless corpse had been swapped for a case of bullion? What would you do if you knew a brutal murderer was out there, somewhere, and waiting for you? Some people would run. Dr Thorndyke intervenes.

R Austin Freeman

Felo De Se
A Dr Thorndyke Mystery

John Gillam was a gambler. John Gillam faced financial ruin and was the victim of a sinister blackmail attempt. John Gillam is now dead. In this exceptional mystery, Dr Thorndyke is brought in to untangle the secrecy surrounding the death of John Gillam, a man not known for insanity and thoughts of suicide.

Flighty Phyllis

Chronicling the adventures and misadventures of Phyllis Dudley, Richard Austin Freeman brings to life a charming character always getting into scrapes. From impersonating a man to discovering mysterious trapdoors, *Flighty Phyllis* is an entertaining glimpse at the times and trials of a wayward woman.

R Austin Freeman

Helen Vardon's Confession
A Dr Thorndyke Mystery

Through the open door of a library, Helen Vardon hears an argument that changes her life forever. Helen's father and a man called Otway argue over missing funds in a trust one night. Otway proposes a marriage between him and Helen in exchange for his co-operation and silence. What transpires is a captivating tale of blackmail, fraud and death. Dr Thorndyke is left to piece together the clues in this enticing mystery.

Mr Pottermack's Oversight

Mr Pottermack is a law-abiding, settled homebody who has nothing to hide until the appearance of the shadowy Lewison, a gambler and blackmailer with an incredible story. It appears that Pottermack is in fact a runaway prisoner, convicted of fraud, and Lewison is about to spill the beans unless he receives a large bribe in return for his silence. But Pottermack protests his innocence, and resolves to shut Lewison up once and for all. Will he do it? And if he does, will he get away with it?

OTHER TITLES BY R AUSTIN FREEMAN AVAILABLE DIRECT
FROM HOUSE OF STRATUS

Quantity		£	$(US)	$(CAN)	€
	THE ADVENTURES OF ROMNEY PRINGLE	6.99	12.95	19.95	13.50
	AS A THIEF IN THE NIGHT	6.99	12.95	19.95	13.50
	THE CAT'S EYE	6.99	12.95	19.95	13.50
	A CERTAIN DR THORNDYKE	6.99	12.95	19.95	13.50
	THE D'ARBLAY MYSTERY	6.99	12.95	19.95	13.50
	DR THORNDYKE INTERVENES	6.99	12.95	19.95	13.50
	DR THORNDYKE'S CRIME FILE	6.99	12.95	19.95	13.50
	THE EXPLOITS OF DANBY CROKER	6.99	12.95	19.95	13.50
	THE EYE OF OSIRIS	6.99	12.95	19.95	13.50
	FELO DE SE	6.99	12.95	19.95	13.50
	FLIGHTY PHYLLIS	6.99	12.95	19.95	13.50
	FOR THE DEFENCE: DR THORNDYKE	6.99	12.95	19.95	13.50
	FROM A SURGEON'S DIARY	6.99	12.95	19.95	13.50
	THE FURTHER ADVENTURES OF ROMNEY PRINGLE	6.99	12.95	19.95	13.50
	THE GOLDEN POOL: A STORY OF A FORGOTTEN MINE	6.99	12.95	19.95	13.50
	THE GREAT PORTRAIT MYSTERY	6.99	12.95	19.95	13.50
	HELEN VARDON'S CONFESSION	6.99	12.95	19.95	13.50

ALL HOUSE OF STRATUS BOOKS ARE AVAILABLE FROM GOOD BOOKSHOPS
OR DIRECT FROM THE PUBLISHER:

Internet: www.houseofstratus.com including synopses and features.

Email: sales@houseofstratus.com
info@houseofstratus.com
(please quote author, title and credit card details.)

OTHER TITLES BY R AUSTIN FREEMAN AVAILABLE DIRECT FROM HOUSE OF STRATUS

Quantity		£	$(US)	$(CAN)	€
☐	THE JACOB STREET MYSTERY	6.99	12.95	19.95	13.50
☐	JOHN THORNDYKE'S CASES	6.99	12.95	19.95	13.50
☐	THE MAGIC CASKET	6.99	12.95	19.95	13.50
☐	MR POLTON EXPLAINS	6.99	12.95	19.95	13.50
☐	MR POTTERMACK'S OVERSIGHT	6.99	12.95	19.95	13.50
☐	THE MYSTERY OF 31 NEW INN	6.99	12.95	19.95	13.50
☐	THE MYSTERY OF ANGELINA FROOD	6.99	12.95	19.95	13.50
☐	THE PENROSE MYSTERY	6.99	12.95	19.95	13.50
☐	PONTIFEX, SON AND THORNDYKE	6.99	12.95	19.95	13.50
☐	THE PUZZLE LOCK	6.99	12.95	19.95	13.50
☐	THE RED THUMB MARK	6.99	12.95	19.95	13.50
☐	A SAVANT'S VENDETTA	6.99	12.95	19.95	13.50
☐	THE SHADOW OF THE WOLF	6.99	12.95	19.95	13.50
☐	A SILENT WITNESS	6.99	12.95	19.95	13.50
☐	THE SINGING BONE	6.99	12.95	19.95	13.50
☐	THE STONEWARE MONKEY	6.99	12.95	19.95	13.50
☐	THE SURPRISING EXPERIENCES OF MR SHUTTLEBURY COBB	6.99	12.95	19.95	13.50
☐	THE UNWILLING ADVENTURER	6.99	12.95	19.95	13.50
☐	WHEN ROGUES FALL OUT	6.99	12.95	19.95	13.50

ALL HOUSE OF STRATUS BOOKS ARE AVAILABLE FROM GOOD BOOKSHOPS
OR DIRECT FROM THE PUBLISHER:

Tel: Order Line
            0800 169 1780 (UK)
            International
            +44 (0) 1845 527700 (UK)

Fax: +44 (0) 1845 527711 (UK)
            (please quote author, title and credit card details.)

Send to: House of Stratus Sales Department
            Thirsk Industrial Park
            York Road, Thirsk
            North Yorkshire, YO7 3BX
            UK

PAYMENT

Please tick currency you wish to use:

☐ £ (Sterling)   ☐ $ (US)   ☐ $ (CAN)   ☐ € (Euros)

Allow for shipping costs charged per order plus an amount per book as set out in the tables below:

CURRENCY/DESTINATION

	£(Sterling)	$(US)	$(CAN)	€ (Euros)
Cost per order				
UK	1.50	2.25	3.50	2.50
Europe	3.00	4.50	6.75	5.00
North America	3.00	3.50	5.25	5.00
Rest of World	3.00	4.50	6.75	5.00
Additional cost per book				
UK	0.50	0.75	1.15	0.85
Europe	1.00	1.50	2.25	1.70
North America	1.00	1.00	1.50	1.70
Rest of World	1.50	2.25	3.50	3.00

PLEASE SEND CHEQUE OR INTERNATIONAL MONEY ORDER
payable to: HOUSE OF STRATUS LTD or card payment as indicated

STERLING EXAMPLE

Cost of book(s):..................... Example: 3 x books at £6.99 each: £20.97

Cost of order:...................... Example: £1.50 (Delivery to UK address)

Additional cost per book:.............. Example: 3 x £0.50: £1.50

Order total including shipping:.......... Example: £23.97

VISA, MASTERCARD, SWITCH, AMEX:

☐☐☐☐☐☐☐☐☐☐☐☐☐☐☐☐☐☐☐☐☐☐

Issue number (Switch only):

☐☐☐

Start Date: **Expiry Date:**

☐☐/☐☐   ☐☐/☐☐

Signature: _____

NAME: _____

ADDRESS: _____

COUNTRY: _____

ZIP/POSTCODE: _____

Please allow 28 days for delivery. Despatch normally within 48 hours.

Prices subject to change without notice.
Please tick box if you do not wish to receive any additional information. ☐

House of Stratus publishes many other titles in this genre; please check our website (**www.houseofstratus.com**) for more details.